KT-142-868

LOVE AND MARRIAGE

A Selection of Recent Titles by Margaret Thornton

ABOVE THE BRIGHT BLUE SKY
DOWN AN ENGLISH LANE
A TRUE LOVE OF MINE
REMEMBER ME
UNTIL WE MEET AGAIN
TIME GOES BY
CAST THE FIRST STONE★
FAMILIES AND FRIENDSHIPS★
OLD FRIENDS, NEW FRIENDS★
FIRST IMPRESSIONS★
ONE WEEK IN AUGUST★
LOVE AND MARRIAGE★

★ *available from Severn House*

LOVE AND MARRIAGE

Margaret Thornton

This first world edition published 2016
in Great Britain and the USA by
SEVERN HOUSE PUBLISHERS LTD of
19 Cedar Road, Sutton, Surrey, England, SM2 5DA.
Trade paperback edition first published
in Great Britain and the USA 2017 by
SEVERN HOUSE PUBLISHERS LTD

Copyright © 2016 by Margaret Thornton.

British Library Cataloguing in Publication Data
A CIP catalogue record for this title is available from the British Library.

ISBN-13: 978-0-7278-8661-3 (cased)
ISBN-13: 978-1-84751-763-0 (trade paper)
ISBN-13: 978-1-78010-829-2 (e-book)

All Severn House titles are printed on acid-free paper.

Severn House Publishers support the Forest Stewardship Council™ [FSC™],
the leading international forest certification organisation.
All our titles that are printed on FSC certified paper carry the FSC logo.

Typeset by Palimpsest Book Production Ltd.,
Falkirk, Stirlingshire, Scotland.
Printed and bound in Great Britain by
TJ International, Padstow, Cornwall.

One

'You look real bonny, the pair of you!' Sally Horrocks smiled fondly at her daughter, Valerie, and her best friend, Cissie, as they showed off the dresses they would be wearing the following day for the wedding of Valerie and Samuel Walker.

'I'll be that proud of you when you walk down the aisle on your dad's arm, and as for your dad, he'll be like a dog with two tails.'

'I should think so,' said Cissie with a sly grin. 'It isn't every day that you watch your daughter marrying the boss's son!'

Sally laughed. 'That's true enough, I suppose. But, do you know, Cissie? We never think of Sam like that now. He's just like one of the family. I know Val will be Mrs Samuel Walker, a member of their important family, but she'll still be our daughter and I know she'll not forget to come and see her mum and dad.' A tear glistened in the corner of Sally's eye.

Val was quick to notice it and respond. 'Now don't be silly, Mum,' she said. 'Of course I'll come to see you, and so will Sam. And we're not a million miles away, are we? Only just up the road really, at the top of the hill.'

'In a posher part of Halifax, though,' said Cissie. 'Don't forget that. It's real swanky up at Queensbury.'

Val frowned at her friend. 'I'm not likely to forget, am I? Not with you harping on about me moving up in the world, as you call it. Give over, Cissie!'

Val loved her friend dearly, but Cissie seemed unable to ignore the fact that Val's status would change, in Cissie's eyes at least, once she was married to Samuel Walker. Val was determined that it would make no difference – certainly not to their close friendship – but Cissie was still conscious of the differences between the two of them.

They had been friends ever since they were five years old. They lived in the same street and attended the same schools. They had both left school at fifteen and started work at Walker's woolen mill in the West Riding town of Halifax, but not in the same capacity. Val was the cleverer of the two girls, although it had never made any difference to their friendship. Val worked harder and was of a more serious frame of mind than her somewhat scatter-brained friend.

Val had started work as an office junior at the mill but had soon worked up to a position as accounts clerk. She had gone to night school to learn the skills of shorthand and typing. Cissie, on the other hand, had started work in the weaving shed, progressing later to the 'burling and mending' room where the women put right the mistakes that had been made in the weaving of the cloth.

Cissie had never really got used to the idea of her friend getting friendly with Samuel Walker, the son of Joshua Walker, who was the owner of the mill. Their friendship had started in Blackpool in the August of 1955, when the two girls were on holiday at the resort. On the first night they had gone dancing at the Winter Gardens ballroom. Sam Walker had been there as well with two friends and, not knowing who she was at the time, had asked Val to dance with him.

She had told him, rather diffidently, that she worked in the office at his father's mill, where both Sam and his brother, Jonathan, held senior positions. She had assumed that it would be a holiday friendship, coming to an end when they returned home. But Sam had other ideas, much to Val's surprise and delight. The couple were mutually attracted to one another. An engagement followed, then plans for the wedding which was to take place on Saturday, 4 May, 1957, less than two years after their first meeting.

'I'll leave you two to take off your finery,' said Val's mother, 'but I'm glad I've had a preview. Your dad'll have to wait till tomorrow to see the beautiful bride, and bridesmaid, of course. I'm going to make a cup of tea for Bert and me. Shall I make some for you? Put those dresses away first, though; we don't want any spillages.'

'Yes, please, Mum,' said Val.

'That'd be lovely, Mrs Horrocks,' said Cissie. 'Then I'd best be getting back. I've left Walter minding our Paul, not that he'll be any trouble once he's settled.'

'Let's see; your little lad's nearly one year old now, isn't he, Cissie?' said Mrs Horrocks. 'How time flies!'

'Yes,' replied Cissie. 'He'll be one on the first of June.' She was unable to stop a smile spreading over her face. 'An' I'll tell you summat else,' she said. 'I'm expecting another one! I've just been telling Val but not many folks know yet. We've only just found out.'

'Well, fancy that!' said Mrs Horrocks. 'And you're pleased, are you, you and Walter?'

'Yes, we're thrilled to bits. It's not till the end of the year, though. Round about Christmas time.'

'And you're feeling all right, are you, love?'

'Yes, I've been much better this time; not much sickness an' feeling tired. Walter's hoping we have a little girl but I've told him not to make his mind up about that. You just don't know, do you? An' it'll be loved whatever it is, like our Paul is.'

As her mother went to make the tea Val reflected how Cissie's love for her little boy had grown over the past year. She had been swept along into a necessarily hasty marriage to Walter Clarkson. Although they had been going out together for a couple of years she had been uncertain about her feelings for him. When the baby boy was born some six months after their marriage Cissie had, at first, resented the child and the loss of her freedom. Val knew now, though, how much she loved her little son, and her husband, too. She was still a happy-go-lucky sort of girl, but there was no doubt that she had turned out to be a natural mother and was delighted at the prospect of another child.

When Mrs Horrocks had left them alone, Cissie mentioned her own wedding.

'At least you don't have to wear a coloured wedding dress like I had to, do you?' Cissie's mother, Hannah Foster, had been horrified when she was told of her daughter's pregnancy. Nevertheless, she would not hear of a registry office wedding. No, it had to be a proper 'do' in church, but on no account could Cissie wear white when she was not entitled to do so. So she had been married in pale blue, and her only bridesmaid, Val, had worn pink.

'No,' agreed Val with a quiet smile. 'But I didn't choose pure white, did I?'

'No, you decided on cream,' said Cissie, grinning at her. 'Why was that, I wonder?'

'I thought the white dresses looked insipid,' she replied, 'with my colouring. You remember – you were there when I tried them on. They made my complexion look sallow, or so I thought. But this deep cream lace is lovely. I knew straight away that it was the one I wanted. And it goes so well with your buttercup yellow dress. Real springtime colours.'

'I believe you but thousands wouldn't,' said Cissie with a laugh. 'At least you're not three months' pregnant like I was.'

'Shush . . .' said Val, glancing at the door in case her mother reappeared. 'Yes, I must admit that Sam and I . . . well, we know quite a lot about each other, but it wasn't till after we were engaged,' she whispered. 'We're hoping we might start a family quite soon, though. There doesn't seem to be any point in waiting, and it's what we both want.'

'Yes, and you can afford it, can't you?' said Cissie,

'Don't start all that again!' said Val jokingly. 'You're not doing too badly yourselves, are you? Walter's been promoted, hasn't he?'

Walter Clarkson also worked at Walker's mill. He was now one of the chief overseers, in charge of a large section of looms.

'Yes, we're doing OK,' admitted Cissie. 'We've managed to get most of the furniture we need now and we can afford a holiday this year. Scarborough, we thought. It's not too far to drive with Paul; he gets restless in the car.'

'That's where we're going for our honeymoon,' said Val. 'Sam suggested we might go to Paris or the south of France but I persuaded him to stay near home. There's nowhere nicer than England in the springtime; all the flowers and the blossom on the trees. Anyway, we want to get settled in our new home so we're only having a few days away. We might go abroad later in the year; it would be the first time for me, of course . . .'

Val knew she'd better not talk any more about foreign holidays. Cissie, also, had never been abroad. But her friend made no comment about her remark.

'Tonight will be the last night that you sleep here,' Cissie commented, looking round at Val's bedroom: the pretty flowered curtains that matched the blue of the carpet and the bedspread; the teddy bear and the old china doll, Peggy, that she and Val had played with when they were small. They sat on a shelf with Val's favourite books and ornaments.

'Yes, it's rather sad, isn't it?' replied Val. 'In some ways. I know Mum and Dad will feel it with me being the only one at home now.'

Her twin brothers, a few years older than herself, had never settled at home after doing their National Service. Peter had enjoyed army life and had decided to make it his career, while Patrick and his young wife had emigrated to Canada. It had been a wrench for Bert and Sally Horrocks and Val had become even more precious to them.

'But like I was saying to Mum, we won't be living far away and we'll come and see them whenever we can. Peter and his wife and baby girl are coming to the wedding and staying for a few days. They're down in Colchester so we don't see them very often. Little Amy's two years old now so that'll give Mum and Dad something else to take their minds off me leaving.'

'I'm dying to see your new house – the inside of it, I mean,' said Cissie. 'It looks very grand from the outside.'

'It's only a semi,' replied Val, 'and it was rather run down and neglected inside when we got it,' she added, conscious that it was quite a lot larger than the house that Walter and Cissie had bought, one very similar to the houses in the street where the two friends had grown up.

'But we've had the decorators in – every room needed doing – and we've got a new bathroom suite. Our parents have bought us some furniture, like yours did when you and Walter got married, and we'll add the rest of it bit by bit, same as you've done.'

Val knew, though, that their new house was in a rather salubrious part of Queensbury, a few miles from Halifax, and not far from the large detached house that was the Walker family home.

'You'll be the first people invited round once it's all ship-shape,' she told her friend, 'apart from the family, of course,' she added. 'Sam's mother can't wait to cast her eagle eye on it!'

'You're getting along OK with her now, though, aren't you?'

'Yes, she seems to have got used to the idea of her son marrying one of their employees! She wasn't able to keep up her "Queen Mother" act when a few skeletons were unleashed from the cupboard.'

Val's mother reappeared at that moment with a tray holding mugs of tea and a plate of chocolate biscuits.

'We're just talking about Beatrice Walker, Mum,' said Val. 'I'm saying she's had to climb down from her high horse, to a certain extent, although she still likes to play the grand lady of the manor sometimes.'

Mrs Horrocks laughed as she put the tray down on the bedside cupboard. 'I'll say she does! But I remember her from way back when she was Beattie Halliwell. They lived in the next street to us and we're about the same age. We were never friends but I knew her well enough. Just an ordinary working family like the rest of us round there. Then she married Joshua Walker, the mill owner's son, and she'd no time any more for the likes of us.'

'So you'll have met up with her again then, Mrs Horrocks,' said Cissie, 'about the wedding arrangements an' all that?'

'Oh, yes,' agreed Sally, handing round the mugs of tea and chocolate digestives. 'She remembered me all right, though she pretended not to at first. But Mr Walker – Joshua – he's been real friendly in spite of him being our boss at work. I used to work there, you know, until a few years back. And Bert's still there, of course, in the packing department. Supervisor, he is now, and Mr Walker relies on him a lot . . .

'They've been very good about this wedding, I must admit. It's usually the bride's parents that pay for everything but Mr Joshua insisted on footing the bill.'

'I should think so,' said Cissie, 'seeing that they wanted such a big posh do!'

'It was Beatrice that wanted that, you might know,' said Val, 'but she didn't get it all her own way, did she, Mum?'

'No, not entirely,' Sally agreed, 'but Bert and me, we've had to go along with a lot of it. Morning suits and top hats and all that malarkey! Just imagine my Bert in a morning suit! We've hired them, of course.'

'And Dad looks real distinguished in it, doesn't he, Mum?' said Val.

'Aye, I must admit he looks quite handsome. Mind you, we insisted on paying for some of it, Bert and me. The bridesmaids' dresses and the flowers.'

'If Sam's mother had had her way I'd have had a whole retinue of bridesmaids and page boys and goodness knows what!' said Val. 'But I was determined to have my way there. I told them that you were going to be my bridesmaid and I had to ask Thelma because she's Jonathan's wife and he's the best man.'

'Strictly speaking, they're not bridesmaids, are they?' said Sally. 'Matrons of honour; isn't that what they're called when they're married?'

Jonathan and Thelma had been married at around the same time as Walter and Cissie, and their little girl, Rosemary, had been born at roughly the same time as the Clarksons' little boy.

'Yes, matrons of honour,' agreed Val. 'Just you and Thelma. Thelma's OK. She and I get along very well. She's been a great help to me with regards to getting to know the family. She's told me I mustn't kowtow to Sam's mother. Jonathan was very disdainful when I first starting going out with Sam. He just knew me as an office girl – he used to dictate letters to me – but we got over that hurdle quite nicely thanks to Thelma.'

'She's the one that'll hold your flowers after you've walked down the aisle, isn't she?' asked Cissie. 'The chief bridesmaid?'

'Yes, but she's not the chief one,' said Val. 'You're both equal. It's just that she's Jonathan's wife so I had to ask her. And at the end of the service they'll walk back down the aisle together. You'll be partnered by Jeff or Colin; I'm not sure which of them. They're both acting as groomsmen or ushers, or whatever they call them. I thought you'd be OK with that, seeing as you've met both of them.'

'Two years ago,' said Cissie. 'Yes, I remember them. So Sam's still friendly with them?'

'Yes, and neither of them are married yet.'

The two young men had been on holiday with Sam when they had all met in the tower ballroom following Sam's first encounter with Val in the Winter Gardens. Cissie had danced with both Jeff and Colin; they had told her that they had been good friends of Sam Walker since their schooldays. The three of them had been in Blackpool on a golfing holiday, as well as enjoying the other attractions that the resort had to offer.

'And you'll be meeting up with that other friend of yours as well,' said Val's mother. 'That nice girl you met at the hotel in Blackpool.'

'Yes . . . Janice,' said Val, 'and Phil. They're both coming to the wedding.'

'So that's another friendship that has lasted,' remarked Cissie. 'Just another pick-up, you might say, in the Winter Gardens, and they're still together, same as you and Sam.'

Val objected, rather, to the term 'pick-up', but she didn't say so. Neither her own Sam nor Phil Grundy were the sort of young men to treat girls in a cavalier manner.

'Are those two engaged yet?' asked Cissie.

'Not as far as I know,' replied Val. 'We'll be able to catch up with all the news tomorrow, won't we?'

'Well, I'd best be off now,' said Cissie. 'I must get an early night ready for the big day, and you'll want to do the same, won't you, Val?'

'Yes; the hairdresser's coming at nine o'clock. It was nice of her, wasn't it, to say she'd come to the house instead of me going there. Then the flowers will be arriving, and Thelma's coming here at about ten o'clock. You can manage that, can you? It should give us plenty of time to get ready.'

The wedding was arranged for twelve o'clock – noon – at the parish church in Halifax, followed by a reception at a country inn a few miles from the town.

'Yes, I'll be here bright and early,' said Cissie. 'I'm getting real excited, and a few colly-wobbles as well. I don't want to let you down.'

'You'd never do that,' Val assured her as the two friends embraced.

'See you tomorrow, then. Thanks for the tea and choccie

biccies, Mrs Horrocks. I'm looking forward to seeing you in your posh outfit an' all.'

Val's mother laughed as she went downstairs with Cissie, leaving Val staring dreamily at her wedding dress, covered in polythene and hanging on the back of the door.

'We'll do our best an' all, me and Bert, to keep up with the Joneses!' Sally said. 'But she's marrying a grand lad and I know he'll take care of her. Thanks for being such a good friend to our Valerie.' She put her arms round Cissie and kissed her cheek. 'Good friends are worth their weight in gold. See you tomorrow, love.'

Two

'It's good to be back in Yorkshire,' said Janice Butler, looking out of the car window at the familiar scene of limestone hills, a scene she had grown to love while on her visits to Phil's home every few months or so. He had met her from the train at Leeds station and they were now on their way to his home near the town of Ilkley. She was to stay for the weekend at the Coach and Horses, the country inn where Phil worked along with his parents who owned the old residence. It had once been a coaching inn.

The following day, Saturday, they would be attending the wedding of Valerie Horrocks and Samuel Walker, whom they had first met in Blackpool in the August of 1955.

'How nice of Val to invite us both to the wedding,' said Phil. 'I don't know her very well but you've stayed friendly with her, haven't you, with both her and Cissie?'

'That's true. They're good friends, although we don't meet very often. We got on well together as soon as we met. That happens sometimes, doesn't it? You form an immediate attachment with some folks and not with others? And now they're both married . . . or from tomorrow they will be . . .'

Janice stopped speaking rather abruptly for fear that Phil should think she was dropping a hint. She hadn't meant to do so. They had started as good friends but were rather more than that now, but there had not been any definite talk about their future together. They met rather infrequently as they were both working hard, Janice at her course on hotel management in Blackpool and Phil as a chef in the family business.

They had first met at the Winter Gardens ballroom where Janice had gone on the Saturday evening, along with Val and Cissie. The two girls from Halifax had come on a week's holiday to Blackpool and were staying at the Florabunda Hotel in North Shore, which was owned and managed by Janice's mother, Lilian. Janice had been helping out as a waitress during the busy season, just a temporary job as she would be starting as a student at Leeds University that September.

The girls had invited her to go dancing with them and she had met Philip Grundy, who had asked her to dance, and they had spent the rest of the evening together. They had discovered that they had a lot in common. Phil, at that time, was in the RAF on National Service. He was stationed at Weeton Camp, a few miles from Blackpool, but he had almost completed his two years and would be going home in a few weeks' time, back to Ilkley in Yorkshire. He had explained that he worked with his father in a country inn owned by the family. The National Service had broken into his training as a chef but he intended to carry this on and become more proficient.

Janice had been brought up in a similar environment – a Blackpool boarding house, now known as a private hotel. The business had been started just after the First World War by Janice's grandmother, Florence, and had then been taken over by her mother, Lilian.

Phil was pleased to hear that Janice would be starting a degree course at Leeds University in September. Leeds was not far from Ilkley, so they made plans to meet up again.

Fate stepped in, however, and all changed when Lilian was taken ill suddenly towards the end of September. She was rushed into hospital for an emergency operation to remove a brain tumour. Janice decided immediately that she must stay in Blackpool and do her best to keep the hotel running in her mother's absence. She gave up her university place and set to work with a will hoping, along with the other members of staff, to keep the business going. Her father, Alec, was most concerned at her decision – both he and Lilian had been keen for her to continue her studies – but Janice was adamant.

When Phil heard of the dilemma he had gone to help out at the hotel until the end of the holiday season in October, and then again when they opened the following year. Lilian had never fully recovered from the operation and was unable to take any part in the running of the business. She died in the early summer of 1956 following a second operation, leaving behind a heartbroken husband, daughter and son.

But they had to carry on despite the deep sadness of life without Lilian. Janice had decided, as she had been feeling for quite a while, that her future lay in the hotel business; she had always been unsure about going to university. They were forced to sell the hotel, however, and Janice then enrolled on a catering course at a college in Blackpool – a day course so she could go home each evening to see to the needs of her father and brother.

The three of them, Alec Butler, Janice, and fourteen-year-old Ian now lived in a bungalow close to Stanley Park on the outskirts of the town. It was conveniently situated, not too far from Ian's grammar school, Janice's college and Alec's place of work as a maintenance engineer with an electrical firm.

Phil made no comment to Janice's remark about her two friends now being married. 'How are your father and Ian going on?' he asked. 'Have they settled down in the bungalow? And you as well, of course?'

'Yes, we're getting used to living there,' replied Janice. 'It seemed strange at first, living in such a small space after the hotel. And it's so quiet and peaceful near the park. Not that it was a rowdy area where we lived before, like the centre of Blackpool can be sometimes, but there was always a lot of activity with the holidaymakers during the summer and always somebody different to talk to. We don't see much of the neighbours; retired couples live on either side of us. But Dad seemed really taken with the bungalow so I went along with the idea. I was pleased he'd found somewhere he liked, at last. It took ages, of course, to sell the hotel. There were so many on the market at the same time and we had to stick out for a good price.'

'Yes, it was well maintained, wasn't it? And there's what they call the goodwill of the business. Your mum had put her heart and soul into that hotel, hadn't she?'

'Yes. I hope some of the same visitors return, for the sake of the new owners. They're a fairly young, go-ahead sort of couple who have bought it. And the husband will be part of it as well. Dad was never involved, as you know, with the running of the hotel.'

'But he did the odd jobs, didn't he, and carried the luggage upstairs?'

'He did, and he enjoyed the company of the visitors, too. He was never the sort of man to go off to the pub every night. I thought he might be lonely – he and Mum were all in all to each other – but he's gradually coming to terms with it . . . although we still miss her like mad. A fellow he works with persuaded him to go along to the club that he's a member of. He took some convincing at first but he goes a couple of times a week now. He's learnt to play darts and he's a reserve for the team. They play bowls in the summer – something else he'd never done before.'

'Good for him! He's too young to sit around and mope, though I know he'll still miss your mother very much. And what about Ian? Has he any friends nearby?'

'Not all that near, not like when we lived in North Shore. But he's growing up fast and he gets around on his bike or on the bus. So long as he and his mates have somewhere to play football, that's all he's bothered about – outside of school, I mean. He works hard while he's there but he enjoys his leisure time as well. They used to go down to the sands to play football but now he goes to Stanley Park, which is better. He sends his best wishes, by the way, and so does Dad. They want to know when are you coming to see us?'

'Quite soon, I hope. I'll see when Dad can spare me for the weekend, although he's managed without me before, hasn't he? He'll have to manage without me permanently when I start up on my own . . .'

Phil didn't elaborate on that remark and Janice didn't enquire any further. Ever since she met him Phil had been saying that one day he would set up on his own or find a position elsewhere, away from his parents' place. He got on very well with them but Janice knew that his two years in the RAF had given him a taste of freedom. He had enjoyed the companionship of his fellow servicemen, so maybe, now, he was finding it difficult to settle at home again.

Did he have something definite in mind? she wondered. And did his plans for the future involve her as well? She decided to leave well alone for the moment. No doubt he would tell her more over the weekend, if there was anything to tell.

Phil was quiet for a while and Janice looked out of the window at the passing scenery. Their journey led through Wharfedale, one of the picturesque dales only a short distance from the industrial towns of the West Riding but a vista far removed from the streets of terraced houses and the smoking mill chimneys. Ilkley was situated near to the River Wharfe and Phil's home was a mile or so outside the town on the road which led to Skipton.

'So here we are again,' Phil said as they reached the long, low, white-painted building which opened right on to the road. There was a view from the front of the inn across to the famous Ilkley Moor. Phil drove the car round to the back where there was a garden area, garage and car park, and the entrance to the family quarters.

Janice felt that the place was a home from home to her. Phil's parents always made her feel very welcome. She felt it even more so this time, after losing her own mother so suddenly. She followed Phil up the stairs to where his mother, Patience, greeted her with a warm hug and a kiss.

'How lovely to see you again, Janice, love. Ralph's down in the bar but he'll be up presently, then we'll have a meal. You're in the usual room, love; just make yourself at home . . . Phil, take Janice's case up to her room, then you can go and tell your dad that you're back again.'

'OK, Mum,' he replied with just a slight air of impatience. He was the only son and therefore had been doted upon all the more, especially by his mother. She was probably unaware that she sometimes treated him as her little boy rather than a grown man. 'You don't think I'd let Janice carry her own case, do you?' He smiled at her, but with a touch of annoyance.

'No, of course not, dear,' said Patience. 'I was only trying to make her welcome.'

'Thank you, Mrs Grundy,' said Janice. 'You always make me welcome, and it's great to be here again.'

Phil heaved her case up on to the bed and grinned at her, back to his usual cheerful self. 'Sort yourself out,' he said, 'and I'll see you in a little while.' He kissed her cheek. 'I'll go and drag Dad away from the bar.'

The room felt rather more familiar to Janice than her room in the new bungalow. It was a pretty, feminine room with a pink theme in the carpet, curtains, bedspread and the towels by the washbasin. There was a magnificent view across to Ilkley Moor with the spring sunshine highlighting the varied browns, greys and greens of the landscape.

It was a peaceful scene and Janice was already feeling the benefit of a change of environment. And it was lovely to see Phil again, of course. Theirs was not a passionate relationship – more a friendship of two young people who were compatible and enjoyed one another's company. Their relationship, inevitably, had progressed as time had gone on, as there was also a strong physical attraction between them. She knew, though, that Phil would never want to make love to her in the fullest sense until he was sure that they had a future together.

She pondered on the remark he had made earlier about starting up on his own. It was not the first time he had mentioned it but she felt now that he might have something definite in mind. He had been quiet and reflective afterwards and she had not wanted to press him further until he was ready. He played his cards very close to his chest at times and, like a true Yorkshireman, was not given to flowery words or expansive gestures.

Janice unpacked her case, carefully hanging up her outfit she had bought for the wedding the following day. She had chosen it with care, feeling that she must make a special effort to look her very best. She guessed it would be a 'posh do', as Val was marrying the boss's son. Last year she and Phil had attended Cissie's wedding to Walter, which had also taken place in Halifax. That had been an informal occasion, with more of a tea party in the church hall following the service. It had been very enjoyable, though, and now Cissie had her little boy, almost one year old. Janice was looking forward to seeing her two friends again. It was amazing the way the three girls had taken to one another when they had met at the hotel in the summer of 1955, and more surprising that the friendship had continued.

Her new outfit, purchased from Sally Mae's in Blackpool – a shop she only visited for a special occasion – was a slim-fitting silky rayon dress in hyacinth blue and a short bolero styled jacket with elbow-length sleeves. Her hat – which she felt was obligatory, though she rarely wore one – was a navy pill-box with a pink rose at the side. High-heeled navy shoes and a matching small clutch bag completed her ensemble.

The assistant had enthused – but then they always did – that the outfit suited her slim figure and her fair hair and complexion. Janice had never concerned herself overmuch about her appearance but she had no complaints about her medium height and slender form, her shoulder-length hair with a natural wave framing a face with regular features. She usually wore casual clothes but it was good to dress up once in a while.

She had a quick wash and tidied her hair, then joined the Grundy family in the large living-cum-dining room. Mr Grundy – Ralph – had returned from the bar and he greeted her warmly as his wife had done.

'Great to see you again, Janice. And you're off to a posh wedding, I believe? Jolly good! I hope the sun shines on the bride. It looks as though this good weather might be with us for a while . . . Sit yerself down, love, and tell us your news. You're still on with your catering course, are you?'

'Yes; it's just for a year – it ends in July. I've learnt a lot that I was unsure about before. Accounts and book-keeping and management, although I must admit they're not my strong point. And I'm more proficient at cooking and baking now; even Dad's remarked on the difference, though he never complained about my previous meals. What I enjoy most is baking – all sorts of fancy cakes and pastries and gateaux – and finishing them off in a professional way. My efforts were very amateurish before but I feel I'm really getting somewhere now.'

'Sounds good to me,' remarked Ralph. 'A good pastry cook can always find a job. Have you anything in mind for when you finish your course?'

'No . . . not yet. I'm keeping my eyes and ears open; there should be something in Blackpool with all its hotels and restaurants. Or I may look further afield – I'm not sure yet. I'll have to consider my dad now he's on his own. Well, he's got Ian, I know, but it's taken him a while to adjust to Mum not being there.'

'Yes, I should imagine so,' said Ralph. 'I won't say I know how it feels because I don't. No one can know till it happens to them . . . but I can guess how it would be if I lost Patience, God forbid. Don't know what I'd do without her.' He cast a loving glance at his wife.

Patience laughed, making light of his remark. 'No one would think so at times, the hours he spends in that bar, chatting to everyone who comes in. I can't tell you the number of times I have to call down to tell him his meal's on the table. We've plenty of bar staff to cope with it all.'

'I'm just being a good host, love,' said Ralph. 'Aye, I know I've a lot of Yorkshire traits. I'm not right good with fancy speeches an' all that. But Patience and me, we're a real Darby and Joan, aren't we, love? Like your mum and dad were, Janice, from what you say.'

'I don't think we're quite at that stage yet,' said Patience with a wry grin. 'We're nowhere near retiring age and I can't see Ralph ever wanting to give up, he enjoys it so much.'

'Oh, I don't know; I dare say the time will come, but you have to make the most of it while you can. You never know what might be round the corner.'

'It's just as well that you don't,' said Janice, looking pensive for a moment. 'But Dad's getting out and about more now, and he assures me he'll be OK if I want to get a job away from home – spread my wings, as he puts it. But I still feel a certain responsibility towards him. And as for Ian, I'm sure he thinks I'll always be there to see to everything. I've taken the place of Mum, in a way. Losing her has hit him a lot harder than he lets on to us. Anyway, we'll have to see how things turn out.'

Patience smiled at her understandingly. 'Well now, I'd best get cracking with our meal. It's ready in the oven. I've made a meat and potato pie, so I'll dish it out in the kitchen, then you can put on your own pickles or whatever you like. Janice, perhaps you can come and show me how much you want. I can guess that my two men will be as hungry as hunters as usual.'

The 'hot pot', as it was usually called, smelled delicious as Janice served out a good portion for herself with a wedge of the shortcrust pastry top. It tasted delicious, too, with the addition of pickled onions, red cabbage and a small amount of brown sauce. The onions and cabbage were in glass dishes on the table; the HP sauce was in its bottle.

'We usually have jars on the table not fancy dishes,' remarked Ralph, winking at Janice, 'but we're being all posh tonight 'cause we've got company.'

Patience laughed. 'Take no notice of him, Janice. I do know what's right and proper. I've even remembered the serviettes . . . or should I say napkins?'

'It's all lovely, Mrs Grundy,' said Janice. She knew that they were quite informal when they dined on their own, but in the restaurant downstairs everything was just as it ought to be with vegetables served in separate dishes. There was also an area near the bar where sandwiches and snacks were served more informally.

'Now then, are you going to tell Janice your news?' said Ralph to his son when the first course had been cleared away and they were enjoying an apple crumble with custard. 'Unless you've already told her, but I don't think you have?'

Janice looked enquiringly at Phil. She had thought earlier in the day that there was something he was not telling her.

'I've had a stroke of good luck,' he said. 'Well, in a way it was sad, I suppose,' he added. 'My aunt Bertha died; she was Mum's sister – much older than Mum, though. She had never married so she had no family.'

'Yes, you mentioned in one of your letters a while ago that she had died,' said Janice.

'Well, what I didn't know at the time was that she had left me practically all that she owned.'

'She was always very fond of our Phil,' said Patience, 'and, like he says, she had no children of her own and we've only got the one son. We're quite comfortably off, Ralph and me, and Bertha knew that, so she left us just a small share and anything we wanted as keepsakes from the house. The rest goes to Phil.'

'And it's no more than he deserves,' said his father. 'He was very good to his aunty and she regarded him as the son she'd never had. So it's up to him to make good use of it. I know he's had itchy feet for a while so now he can do summat about it.'

'Yes, I fully intend to,' added Phil.

'Jolly good,' said Janice faintly, wondering where she fitted into these plans, if at all.

'I'm looking around,' said Phil. 'I don't want to go too far away – certainly not far from Yorkshire. On the other hand, I don't intend to set up in competition to Dad near here. It'll have to be something rather different. Anyway, we'll talk about it later?' He looked at Janice questioningly.

She was feeling rather bewildered and realized it must show on her face. It was odd that this was the first time he had mentioned his windfall. He had not said a word about it on their journey here.

'I thought you had something up your sleeve,' she said, 'so now I know.'

'I was waiting for the right time to tell you. It'll be a big undertaking, whatever I decide to do.'

She noticed he had said 'I' and not 'we'. 'I'm dying to know what you've got in mind,' she said with a slight touch of irony.

'Don't worry; all will be revealed,' he said.

Patience, as if aware of the constraint on Janice's part, changed the subject, asking her about the outfit she would be wearing for the wedding the following day. 'It'll be a posh do, will it, with Sam being the mill owner's son?'

'I should think so,' said Janice, 'but if I know Val, she'll try to keep it within limits.'

'Well, I hope you have a really good day.'

'I'm sure we will,' said Janice.

Patience made coffee to finish off the meal, then refused Janice's offer to help clear away and wash up. 'No, I wouldn't dream of it. Anyway, it's not much trouble. I've got a dishwasher up here now as well as the one downstairs for the restaurant. Ralph said we didn't need one but I managed to convince him.'

'Yes, they're a great help,' agreed Janice. 'Mum bought one for the hotel just before she was taken ill and we couldn't imagine how we'd managed without it. But we haven't got one now at the bungalow. Dad says we don't need one and I suppose he's right.' She laughed. 'He actually does the washing-up now, though he never used to.'

'Some do, some don't,' said Patience, looking pointedly at Ralph, who pretended he hadn't heard. 'Now, off you go, you and Phil, and have some time on your own. It should be nice and quiet now, down in the bar.'

'Yes, let's go and have an after-dinner drink,' said Phil, 'before it starts getting busy.'

They went downstairs to the bar area, a cosy room despite the stone-flagged floor. There was a huge fireplace with a log fire burning, giving a warm and cheerful ambience to the place. During the summer months – provided there was a decent summer – Patience made an arrangement of leaves and fir cones to fill the hearth, but there was still a nip in the air now when the sun went down.

They sat in wheel-backed chairs near to one of the small, round tables which wobbled a little on the uneven floor. Chintz cushions on the chairs and matching curtains at the mullioned windows added to the homely, countrified feel of the place.

'What are you drinking?' asked Phil. 'I shall have a pint of the special Black Sheep ale. Something more ladylike for you, eh?'

'Yes, I'm not really into quaffing pints,' said Janice, 'though I know some girls do nowadays. I'll have a sweet martini, please, with a dash of lemonade.'

It was only recently, since she had got to know Phil, that she had drunk any alcohol at all. The hotel in Blackpool had not had a licence to serve wine and spirits; very few smaller hotels had one. She and her friends would never have dreamed of going into a public house on their own. Now, though, it seemed that young women were no longer frowned upon for doing so.

There was a well-stocked bar at the end of the room nearest to the restaurant. Phil returned a few moments later with a tankard brimming over with frothy-topped ale and a smaller glass with Janice's drink, served with a cherry on a cocktail stick and a slice of lemon.

'Cheers,' he said, raising his glass, and she did the same.

'It's great to have you here,' he told her, and the warmth in his smile showed her he meant what he said.

'Yes, it's good to be back,' she replied, though not over-effusively.

Phil looked at her steadily. 'I think you want to hear about my ideas for the future, don't you?' he said.

'Yes, I think that might be a good idea . . .'

'Well, I've been thinking,' he went on, 'after you were talking about your course and how you'd got interested in making fancy cakes and pastries. That's never been my forte; I'm more for the main courses and interesting starters, and planning interesting menus. So . . . I was thinking that maybe we could run a tea shop – you know, where they serve morning coffee, then light lunches and afternoon teas. And maybe special evening meals that have to be booked in advance, for birthdays and anniversaries and that sort of thing . . .'

'Hold on a minute,' interrupted Janice. 'You are including me in this venture, are you?'

'Of course I am!' He stared at her in surprise. 'I thought you would realize that. I wouldn't dream of making plans that didn't include you as well. Surely you weren't thinking . . .?'

'I didn't know what to think,' replied Janice. 'We've never really talked much about the future, have we? We've been seeing each other for almost two years and we've worked together, so I did wonder . . . But a girl likes to be put in the picture, Phil.'

'Oh, Janice, I'm sorry . . .' He leaned forward and took hold of both of her hands in his own. He looked into her hazel-brown eyes, his own grey ones full of concern. 'You must know how much I care about you, and I think that you feel the same way about me?'

Janice nodded slowly, looking keenly at him.

'I suppose I've taken it for granted,' he went on, 'that we would carry on seeing each other. I suppose I'm like my father – you know, what he was saying earlier – he's not good at putting his feelings into words. Maybe I'm the same, but I do know what I want.'

A slow smile spread over Janice's face. 'What are you trying to say, Phil?' she asked quietly.

'I'm asking you to marry me, Janice,' he said. 'Not the most romantic of proposals, I know, but I do love you. So . . . you will say yes, won't you?'

Janice laughed out loud. 'Of course I will!'

Phil leaned closer and kissed her on the lips. There was no one else in the room; Janice guessed he would not have done so if there had been.

'I haven't got a ring,' he said, 'but of course you must have one. I'd like you to choose your own 'cause I wouldn't know what to buy. I know I've been acting a bit strange, like, but I wasn't sure what I wanted to do with Aunt Bertha's legacy. Then it came to me when you were talking about cake-making an' all that. I think we'll make a good team, don't you?'

'I'm sure we will, Phil . . . but we can't rush into anything, can we? As I said before, there's my dad to consider, and I'm still not "of age", as they say. I was twenty in January; I don't come of age for another eight months.'

'But your dad isn't likely to say no, is he?'

'I shouldn't think so. He already thinks of you as one of the family and Ian regards you as a brother. All the same, it might come as a surprise to Dad to think of me getting married and moving away from Blackpool.'

'I'll have to ask him then, won't I?' said Phil. 'In the old-fashioned way, you know; I'm asking for your daughter's hand in marriage sort of thing. I could come over to Blackpool next weekend, maybe? What do you think? Then we could go and choose a ring?'

'Gosh! It's all happening so quickly,' said Janice. 'I feel quite light-headed and dizzy with it all.'

'That's the drink that's gone to your head. You knocked it back quite quickly. You're supposed to sip it.'

Janice giggled. 'It was to help me get over the shock, I suppose.'

'Are you ready for another drink?'

She shook her head. 'Perhaps just a pineapple juice. I'd better get my thoughts in order. I'm all over the place at the moment . . . Are we going to tell your parents?'

'I think that might be a good idea. We'll have another drink then we'll go up and tell them. Ah . . . I see Dad's down in the bar already. I'll ask him if he can spare a few minutes because we've got something to tell him and Mum.'

Janice sat in a contented haze as Phil went to the bar again. Just one drink tended to make her feel light-headed so she was never tempted to let herself get to the stage where she lost control.

When Phil returned they sat in a companionable silence for a few moments, Janice with her Britvic juice and Phil with his half pint of ale.

'You're quiet, love,' he said. 'Penny for them?'

She smiled happily. 'I was just thinking how lovely it is here. Not just here . . .' She gestured round the room. 'I mean here in Yorkshire; so beautiful and peaceful. I've really taken to your home county.'

'That's just as well, seeing as you're going to be living here,' said Phil. 'Come on; let's go and break the news to my parents.'

Phil beckoned to his father at the bar and Ralph followed them upstairs.

'It seems that these two have some news for us,' Ralph said to his wife when they were all seated. 'I wonder whatever that can be?' There was a twinkle in his eye.

Phil took hold of Janice's hand as they sat on the settee. 'Janice and I . . . well, we've decided we're going to get engaged,' he said.

His parents looked at one another and smiled. 'That's wonderful news,' said Patience. She went over to Janice and hugged her, then kissed her cheek. Then she kissed her son. 'We're very pleased, aren't we, Ralph? But not surprised.'

'It's all to be kept secret at the moment,' said Phil, 'until we've told Janice's dad next weekend. And then . . . well, we've not got any further than that, have we, Janice, love?'

'No, not yet,' said Janice simply. 'One step at a time . . .'

'This certainly calls for a celebration,' said Ralph. 'Get the glasses, Patience, and I'll fetch some champagne from the bar.'

'Oh, isn't this exciting?' said Patience, laughing happily as she brought four champagne flutes from the sideboard.

Ralph returned a few moments later with a bottle of pink champagne. 'Stand back, everyone,' he said as he drew out the cork and the frothy liquid sprayed across the room. 'This always happens no matter how many times I do it. But we've not lost much; it always looks worse than it is.'

He handed round the full glasses then raised his own. 'Here's to Phil and Janice. You're a grand couple and we wish you good luck and happiness as you plan your future together.'

Janice sipped gingerly at the champagne. She had tasted it only a couple of times before and knew the bubbles would go up her nose. She managed a few sips without it making her splutter, but her eyes started to water with the sharp, tangy taste.

'This is what we've been waiting for,' said Patience. 'Well, waiting and wondering . . .' You're not the only one! thought Janice to herself. 'And we're really delighted, aren't we, Ralph?'

'Indeed we are,' he agreed. 'I know you're still very young, the pair of you. But I know our Phil pretty well and I reckon he's made up his mind.'

'Yes, I'm only twenty,' said Janice.

'And our Phil's only twenty-two,' said his father, 'but I reckon he's got his head screwed on the right way.'

'What Janice means is that she doesn't come of age, as they say, until January,' explained Phil, 'so I shall have to do the correct thing and go and ask her father before we go any further with our plans.'

'He'll not say no, not if he's any sense,' said Ralph, 'but I see what you mean . . . I'd best get back to the bar,' he said after a few moments. 'It'll get busy when the diners finish their meals and we get quite a few regulars in on a Friday night . . . Great news, you two, but I'll keep it to myself for now, like you said.'

Phil and Janice strolled along the road back to the town, hand in hand. They walked by the side of the river as the sun was setting. It was a quiet and peaceful scene with few people around, but during the day Ilkley was a busy, bustling market town.

'I shall start looking around, here and a bit further afield,' said Phil. 'You're happy to come and live over here, aren't you, darling?'

'Very happy,' replied Janice, 'once we've sorted things out at home. My course finishes in July so I suppose I'll have to get a job in Blackpool for the time being – hotel or restaurant work. It'll all be good experience.'

'For when we have our own place,' said Phil. He stopped to kiss her as they made their way back. 'I love you, Janice. You've made me so very happy . . .'

Three

Phil and Janice set off mid-morning to drive to Halifax for the wedding of Val and Sam. The mill town in the West Riding was only a short distance from Ilkley. They took the road to Bingley then drove through the outskirts of Bradford, finally dropping down to Halifax at the bottom of the valley.

As it was Saturday and some of the mills worked a five-day week the air was not as polluted as it might have been with the smoke from the factory chimneys. Away from the shopping centre with its busy market and the famous Piece Hall – where local merchants used to gather to display their various cloths – the town consisted of streets of terraced houses rising up from the valley floor.

Phil parked the car in a side street while they had a cup of coffee at Woolies and availed themselves of the amenities to make sure they were neat and tidy, ready for the wedding. Janice combed her hair, renewed her pink lipstick and made sure her pill-box hat was at the right angle before they drove to the church. Val had given clear instructions, and they found the imposing-looking steepled church on an incline just outside the town. The greystone building was soot-grained from the smoke of more than a century but the small garden area was well tended and the bright and cheerful noticeboard indicated that it was a thriving and well-attended place of worship.

There was room to park in an adjacent street, then they followed other guests up the path and through the oaken door. They were greeted by an usher in a morning suit, probably one of Sam's friends, handed an order of service and asked whether they were 'for the bride or the groom'.

'The bride,' whispered Janice, and they followed the young man who led them to a pew a few rows from the front. Janice bowed her head to say a little silent prayer then glanced at the impressive-looking order of service. An ivory-coloured card with a gold silken tassel and gold writing proclaimed the marriage of Samuel James Walker to Valerie Anne Horrocks, surrounded by a border of flowers and leaves and golden hearts.

Janice didn't expect to recognize anyone apart from Sam, whom she had met a few times. She guessed that it was him sitting in a front pew with another young man, and when he turned his head to look round she recognized his pleasant, open face. He saw her and gave a smile and a slight wave. The young man beside him must be his elder brother, Jonathan, who was his best man. When he also turned his head she could see the family likeness, but Jonathan's features were sharper and he did not have the same friendly look as his brother. Or maybe she was just imagining that because of what she had heard of him.

He had been quite scathing about his younger brother's relationship with one of their office workers. But Jonathan had needed Sam's support when his fiancée, Thelma, was pregnant and he had to break the unwelcome news to their mother, Beatrice. Since then the brothers had become closer, and Val had been accepted as Sam's young lady, the girl he was determined to marry.

Janice looked with interest at the couple who were now walking down the aisle. The grey-haired man in a morning suit seemed a pleasant sort of chap, smiling and nodding at the guests as he passed by them. But it was the woman holding his arm – a well-corseted figure in a pale blue chiffon suit with a large, matching feather hat – that Janice recognized as Beatrice Walker, although she had never seen her before. But it couldn't be anyone else. She smiled graciously, inclining her head in the manner of the Queen Mother as she made her way to the front pew.

When a demure-looking woman in a simple lilac suit with a small matching hat walked, far more self-consciously, down the aisle a few moments later, Janice made a guess that this was the mother of the bride. Her husband, of course, would be accompanying his daughter. The young man with her – presumably Val's brother as there was a family resemblance – led her to the front pew then sat down beside her with his wife and small daughter. Janice guessed that Mrs Horrocks was not used to splendid occasions such as this but would make a valiant effort for the sake of her daughter.

There was certainly a good crowd of guests assembled in the church. It was half full of people, all 'dressed to kill', as Janice's mother might have said, and others at the back of the church – probably friends and colleagues from Walker's mill – who had come to watch the ceremony.

It was a Victorian church with high-backed pews, a stone floor and stained-glass windows through which the sunlight filtered, though not over brightly. Flowers, in shades of yellow, with leaves and ferns, decorated the window ledges and a large display graced the altar.

The organ was playing softly; Janice recognized Bach's 'Air on the G String' then Mozart's 'Ave Verum' before there was a sudden change of mood – an air of expectancy in the building. When the organist played the first bars of the 'Bridal Chorus' everyone stood, waiting for their first glimpse of the bride.

Janice realized as she watched Valerie holding her father's arm and the two bridesmaids walk down the aisle that Val must have insisted on a certain amount of simplicity to counteract the showiness expected by some members of the bridegroom's family.

Val was a beautiful and radiant bride. Her slim-fitting dress of heavy, cream-coloured lace was a simple design with long sleeves, a high neckline and a gently flaring skirt. Her short veil was held in place with a coronet of orange blossom, highlighting her dark hair and a complexion that was more sallow than pink and white.

Cissie, her best friend and bridesmaid, could not be more different in looks, as she was in personality. Cissie was now a little plumper than when Janice had first met her in Blackpool. Her dress, and that of the other bridesmaid, was buttercup yellow, simply styled in heavy silken material. A coronet of artificial yellow flowers sat on top of Cissie's fair, fluffy hair. She was what might be termed a 'dizzy blonde', with a rosy complexion and big blue eyes. She noticed Janice as she passed by and grinned broadly.

The other bridesmaid, who Janice knew was Thelma, Jonathan's wife, was blonde as well, but her elegantly groomed pageboy style was a sharp contrast to Cissie's mop of unruly hair. Thelma's classic features and regal bearing, with her delicate colouring, made one think of a snow princess in a fairy tale.

When they reached the steps leading to the altar Val handed her bouquet of golden and white flowers – a mixture of late spring and early summer blooms – to Thelma. Janice noticed the look of love that passed between Val and her bridegroom. She stole a sideways look at Phil; he was looking at her and smiling, too. She hoped it might not be very long before they also stood at the altar to make their own marriage vows.

A small choir, mostly of boy choristers with a few older men and women, had filed into the choir stalls and led the singing of the hymns. The first one was traditional: 'Praise my soul the King of Heaven', chosen by so many couples throughout the last hundred years. The service that followed was simple and meaningful. Sam gave his promises in a clear and confident voice. Val responded in a quieter voice but one that was just as sincere.

The psalm that was included in the service, 'I will lift up my eyes unto the hills', was sung by the choir with the congregation following as best they could. A tribute to the hills and valleys of Yorkshire, thought Janice, where both Val and Sam lived, and Phil as well. And she, too, would soon be starting a new life there. The countryside of the Fylde, where Janice lived, was flat and somewhat featureless by contrast, but it had been home to her for twenty years. There would surely be some pulling at the heartstrings when she left, from her father and brother and herself as well.

She collected her rambling thoughts as the vicar spoke the final prayers and the choir and congregation stood to sing another traditional hymn: 'Now thank we all our God'.

The bridal party adjourned to the vestry and the guests settled back to chat quietly and to half listen to the choir as they sang 'Sheep may safely graze' followed by 'O, for the wings of a dove'.

It was several moments before the organist struck up with the opening bars of Mendelssohn's 'Wedding March' and the bridal party reappeared. Val and Sam led the way down the aisle, both of them nodding and smiling happily as they passed their friends and family members. They were followed by Thelma and Jonathan. He smiled acknowledgement at everyone but in a more restrained way than his brother. The two were alike, Jonathan maybe a little taller and slimmer than Sam, with features that were sharper and bore a trace of superiority.

Cissie was grinning broadly, clearly enjoying the importance of her role as she held the arm of a pleasant-looking young man. Janice thought she recognized him as one of Sam's friends who had been with him on the holiday to Blackpool when they had all met.

As was traditional, the bride's mother, Mrs Horrocks, was paired with the bridegroom's father. Janice knew he was the boss of the mill and that Val's father worked there, as Mrs Horrocks had done at one time. She guessed that Val's mother might still be a little in awe of him, but he looked friendly and cheerful, chatting with her as though to put her at her ease.

Beatrice Walker held the arm of Mr Horrocks. They, in contrast, both looked somewhat ill at ease. He was smiling nervously while she inclined her head with scarcely the glimmer of a smile, paying no attention to the man at her side. Janice pondered that she wouldn't like to have Mrs Walker as a mother-in-law! What a contrast to Patience Grundy, who already treated her like a beloved daughter.

The guests and onlookers surged through the door then stood around in small groups on the path and the lawn, a dazzling kaleidoscope of colour as the sun shone on the bright summer clothes of the women and girls. They watched as a myriad of photographs was taken of the bridal couple by themselves, then with the bridesmaids, best man and groomsmen, family group shots, then one with all the guests crowded together. Janice stood at the back with Phil at the end of a row. The photographer adjusted his lens, trying to fit everyone in. There must be between sixty or seventy guests, Janice thought at a glance. It was doubtful if they would all be seen, hidden behind large hats and tall men.

Gradually, those who were not invited guests drifted away and the guests went to find their own cars. But not before Sam and Val had been showered with confetti – another photo opportunity – as they entered the bridal car to be driven to the venue for the reception.

This was a large country hotel a few miles outside of Halifax. It stood in its own grounds, with a well-tended lawn and flower beds and a wooded area to each side. When Janice and Phil arrived – having been given clear instructions on how to find the place – more photographs were being taken in a setting that was far prettier than that of the church grounds.

They all trooped into the spacious reception area, their feet sinking into a deep pile carpet of a rich red and gold design, and from there into the bar area adjoining the large dining room. The bar was open and a few folk were already enjoying a pre-luncheon drink. Janice and Phil stood to one side, not knowing anyone and waiting to see what would happen next. Janice paid a quick visit to the ladies' room, another luxurious room with pink porcelain bowls and washbasins, pink fluffy towels and rose-scented soap.

In a little while the bride and groom appeared with their parents, the six of them standing in a line while the guests filed past them, shaking hands and saying words of congratu-lation – a formal tradition which meant little to many of the guests who had not met the parents before. Val, standing next to her mother, greeted Janice warmly, hugging her and kissing her cheek.

'Mum, this is Janice,' she said. 'You know, my friend from Blackpool – and this is her friend, Phil.'

'Oh, how lovely to meet you at last!' said Mrs Horrocks. 'I've heard such a lot about you. I'm so pleased you could come, and you as well, Phil.'

What a nice, genuine person, thought Janice, recognizing another Yorkshire accent that was becoming so familiar to her.

'See you later; we must have a chat and keep up with what's happening,' said Val hurriedly as she turned to the next person in line.

'Good to see you again, Janice, and you, too, Phil,' said Sam. 'We both did well for ourselves in Blackpool, didn't we?' he added with a grin. 'See you both later . . .'

They all found their seats at the tables, name cards having been placed by each setting. Janice and Phil were seated at a table with three more young couples, their own age or maybe a little older. They discovered as the meal progressed and they began to chat together more freely that the three young women, Susan, Jill and Pauline were friends of Val who worked with her in the office at Walker's mill. None of the men worked at the mill; one couple was married and the other two were engaged.

Wine flowed freely – there was a choice of red or white – throughout the three-course meal. A starter of prawn cocktail was followed by breast of chicken with bread sauce, stuffing, roast potatoes and a selection of vegetables. The dessert was strawberry pavlovas with both ice cream and whipped cream. They were small works of art and the most delicious that Janice had ever tasted.

They heard various tit-bits of news from the conversation that went on during the meal. Mr Joshua Walker was a good boss, not that they saw him very much, but he was always friendly and approachable. They didn't see much of 'that wife of his' but rumour had it that she was a real old harridan.

'I don't envy Val her mother-in-law!' said Susan.

'Nor her brother-in-law,' added Jill. 'Samuel's ever so friendly, just like his father, but Jonathan's a real stuck-up so-and-so. Mind you, he seems to have changed a bit lately.'

'Val's a lovely girl,' said Pauline, 'and we all hope she'll be very happy with Sam. That's what we call him, now, though we never used to.'

There had been a certain amount of surprise and gossip when it'd been revealed that Val had become friendly with the boss's son. No one thought it would last.

'But he obviously thinks the world of her,' said Susan, 'and she's crazy about him. She doesn't say much but you can tell. She says she's going to carry on working for a little while, though we know she doesn't need to.'

'She's in charge of the office now,' added Jill. 'Not because she was engaged to the boss's son; it's because she's very good at her job.'

'But we don't think she'll stay very long,' said Pauline. 'From what she's hinted we think they'll want to start a family quite soon. She thinks the world of her godson, Cissie's little boy.'

The girls were interested to find out that Janice was from Blackpool and was the girl whom Val had met when she was on holiday there.

'We all went dancing at the Winter Gardens,' Janice told them. 'That was when Val met Sam . . . and I met Phil as well that night.' She smiled at him. 'He was in the RAF, stationed near Blackpool. He asked me to dance and we got talking . . .'

Phil grinned. 'We've never looked back, Janice and me. We're getting engaged soon – next weekend, when I go over to Blackpool to see Janice's father.'

'Mum died last year,' explained Janice, 'so we sold the hotel and Dad will be on his own when I leave. Well, there's my younger brother, but it'll be rather a wrench for Dad.'

'We thought you were a Yorkshire lad, same as us,' said one of the young men to Phil. 'Are you from round here?'

'Not far away. I help to run a country inn near Ilkley with my parents. But Janice and I want to start up in a place of our own . . .'

Conversation came to a halt when the best man stood up and tapped his glass to indicate that he wanted their attention. The waiters were going round filling the glasses with champagne. It was time for the speeches and toasts. There were the customary speeches; the best man thanked the bridesmaids, then Sam replied on their behalf, making the usual remark about 'my wife and I', and how they were very pleased to see everyone there to share in their happiness.

The speech from the bride's father was short and to the point: Mr Horrocks was clearly a little overawed by the occasion. Jonathan wished the newly married couple every happiness as they started their life together, saying that his younger brother was a true friend and a brother in a million, sentiments that some knew he had not always held.

In a slight break from tradition, Joshua Walker made a short speech saying how pleased he was to welcome Valerie into their family and how she had charmed them all with her grace and friendliness. His wife smiled and nodded her agreement. She could do no other but at least some of the guests hoped that she was sincere.

The three-tiered wedding cake was decorated with yellow flowers and a silver vase holding yellow roses stood on the top tier. The cutting of the bottom tier by the bride and groom was a chance for another photograph. The proceedings were then at an end and the guests began to leave their places to circulate and speak with others that they knew.

Val and Sam spoke with their family members first but it wasn't long before they came over to Janice and Phil with Cissie, Walter following close behind. Walter had been seated at a table with some of the other employees from the mill. Only a privileged few of the workforce had been invited but all were pleased to hear of Samuel's marriage to Valerie Horrocks; they were both very popular with the workers. Cissie and Walter's little son, Paul, had been left in the care of his parents for the day.

The three girls were delighted to meet again. 'It's been a lovely wedding,' said Janice, 'and you look beautiful. Both of you,' she added, smiling at Cissie.

'Oh . . . for a moment I thought you meant me!' said Sam.

'You as well, Sam,' said Janice, laughing. He was, indeed, a nice-looking young man with pleasing rather than handsome features. His warm brown eyes were almost the same colour as his mid-brown hair. It was his candid, honest face that one noticed and which put folk at their ease.

Walter, Cissie's husband, was the only one who had not been in Blackpool during that memorable week in the August of 1955. Janice had met him only once before, at his marriage to Cissie. He was dark and thin-featured with a slightly aquiline nose, and he could look quite stern and unapproachable. But it seemed that his marriage to Cissie had brought about a more friendly and easy manner.

Janice had formed the impression, when she had first met Cissie, that the girl's feelings about Walter were lukewarm. They had been going out together for a couple of years but she had seemed glad to be away from him for a week. Cissie, too, had met someone that week; a lad called Jack, Janice seemed to remember, from somewhere in Yorkshire. But that, apparently, had not come to anything. Janice did not know the full story but the next news was that Cissie and Walter were engaged, then the marriage followed very swiftly.

'How is your little boy?' asked Janice. 'He's called Paul, isn't he?'

'Yes, that's right. He's a little treasure, isn't he, Walter?' she replied. 'He's nearly one year old, and . . . guess what? We're expecting another one, aren't we, Walter?'

'Oh, that's lovely,' said Janice, thinking that they weren't wasting much time.

'It's not for ages yet,' said Walter. 'We were supposed to be keeping it to ourselves for a while but Cissie can't resist telling everyone.' He was smiling, though, and seemed quite resigned to his wife's impetuous ways.

'I haven't had the pleasure of seeing Paul yet,' said Janice, 'but I hope it won't be too long before I do. We have some news as well.' She looked at Phil, smiling a little coyly. 'We're getting engaged . . . next weekend!'

'Oh, that's great news,' said Cissie, flinging her arms round Janice. Then Val, also, added her congratulations, kissing her cheek and shaking hands with Phil.

'So I shall be coming to live in Yorkshire,' added Janice. 'We want to find somewhere of our own; a restaurant or something of the sort for Phil to run . . . with my help, of course. Not too far from Ilkley, we hope.'

'So we'll all be within spitting distance of one another,' said Cissie. 'Isn't that great, Walter?'

'Yes, very commendable,' he replied soberly. 'I hope you'll be very happy.'

'We'd better move on, Sam,' said Val, a trifle regretfully. 'We've lots more people to talk to. We mustn't leave anyone out. And thank you for the lovely wedding present. It was a complete surprise and so very appropriate. It will take pride of place in our lounge, won't it, Sam?'

'Indeed it will,' said Sam. 'We'll never forget that week that brought us together, although I feel it would have been bound to happen, one way or another.' He smiled lovingly at his new wife.

Janice and Phil's gift was a limited edition print of a typical Blackpool scene: the promenade viewed from North Pier with the outgoing tide and a stretch of sand, the famous tower and the cream and green tramcars.

'We thought you'd have enough toast racks and towels and tea services,' said Janice. 'It will bring back memories for you.'

'We're off to another seaside resort in a little while,' said Sam. 'We're going to Scarborough, just for a few days because we want to get our new house ship-shape, don't we, darling?'

'Yes, so we do,' said Val happily. 'We'll look forward to seeing you there before too long. Bye for now; we'll keep in touch . . .' The friends hugged again before the bridal pair moved away. Cissie and Walter stayed a while talking to Phil and Janice. Janice was surprised at how domesticated Cissie had become. She had not known her in her home environment but she had gained the impression that she would not be a natural housewife or mother. Her talk, though, was all of little Paul; how he was already walking, had cut several teeth and was trying to talk. Then she went on to talk about their little home and the improvements they were making.

'Our parents have forgiven us now for having to get married all in a rush,' she said with a laugh. 'That was when the baby was born but they don't know about the next one yet. I never got on all that well with my mam but it's been better since Paul was born. Dad was always OK, though. You must miss your mam, Janice,' she went on. 'She was a smashing lady and I know you got on well with her.'

'Yes, my memories are happy ones and I'm glad about that.

I'm sorry, though, that she won't see me married or have the pleasure of her grandchildren. She was taken from us too soon. But we have to look to the future, don't we?'

Cissie didn't appear to miss the companionship of the girls at work and was only too happy to stay at home. 'Val and me are still good friends, though,' she said. 'She babysits for us now and again. She's among the posh folk up in Queensbury.' Janice sensed a faint hint of envy in the last remark and she remembered that Cissie had been quite worried when her friend had got friendly with Samuel Walker, the boss's son. She had warned her that she was heading for trouble and that it could never work.

'Sam's OK, though,' she said now. 'I'm glad they're happy together. I hope it won't be too long before we're both pushing our babies out in prams. Not that she is . . .' she added hurriedly. 'I didn't mean that, but she's hinted that they'd like to start a family quite soon.'

In a little while Val and Sam reappeared, ready to depart for their honeymoon. Val wore a smart but casual summer dress of bright pink with a white collar and a little white jacket. Sam, too, was casual in grey flannels and a sport's jacket, just right for a seaside holiday.

Val threw her bouquet to the crowd and it was caught by Susan, one of the engaged girls from Janice and Phil's table. She blushed prettily as she smiled at her fiancé.

The happy couple departed in another shower of confetti, driving off in Sam's almost new Ford Anglia car.

'So that's that,' said Phil, putting an arm round Janice. Everything had fallen a little flat after Sam and Val's departure. 'Never mind, love. It'll be our turn next . . .'

Four

Their hotel in Scarborough was quite small compared to such places as the Crown or the Grand Hotel. It was situated on the South Cliff, near to the spa and the valley gardens.

After their evening meal Val and Sam strolled along the promenade northwards to the Spa Bridge which crossed the busy roads in the valley below. They paused on the bridge, gazing out towards the vast expanse of sea. It was not yet dark, although dusk was falling, and the lights around the South Bay were shining out, a twinkling necklace of bright colours in the fading light.

The great bulk of the Grand Hotel loomed large against the darkening blue of the sky, and in the distance they could make out the outline of the castle at the top of the hill and St Mary's Church on the horizon with the roofs of the fishermen's cottages on the lower slopes.

'I can't imagine a lovelier scene than this,' observed Sam. 'I always think so when I come here and now it's even lovelier with you at my side.' He put an arm round Val, kissing her gently. 'Happy, my darling?'

'I've never been happier,' she replied.

'And I hope you will always feel that way,' he whispered.

'I really think . . . well, I don't like to say it . . . but Blackpool has nothing to compare with a view like this, has it?' said Val. 'Even though that's where we found one another, and it'll always have a special meaning for us.'

'It has very little natural beauty but Blackpool is unique. I know the folk in Lancashire think so,' said Sam. 'It was thoughtful of Janice and Phil to give us that picture. It's so colourful and cheerful and it'll bring back so many happy memories.' Sam kissed her again. 'We'll have lots more happy memories of our time here, won't we, darling? Come along . . . Let's head back, shall we?'

She noted the gleam of anticipation and longing in his eyes and she nodded in agreement. They walked back to the hotel hand in hand.

Their lovemaking, now, was free and unrestrained. It was not the first time they had expressed their love for one another in that way. But Val had never been able to do so without a slight feeling of guilt at the thought of what her mother might think if she knew. Sam had always taken care that nothing should go wrong but there had always been that niggling fear at the back of her mind. Now their marriage and the vows they had made had given them the freedom that they needed to give themselves to each other in perfect love and understanding.

'Goodnight, my darling,' said Sam eventually. She knew that he had fallen asleep almost at once but Val lay awake, listening to the soft sounds of the night: the distant murmur of the sea and the faint cry of a seagull. It felt strange – but nice, though – to share her bed after all her years of solitude. The thought thrilled her, making her feel warm and safe and soon she, too, fell asleep.

They spent an idyllic few days in Scarborough, a time they would look back on in years to come, remembering the perfect start to their marriage. They were blessed with almost ideal weather, apart from the odd rain showers when they were least expecting them, but such were the vagaries of an English springtime.

They visited the fishing port of Whitby, some twenty miles away across a wild stretch of moorland. They climbed the steep hill to where the statue of Captain Cook and the whalebone arch overlooked the harbour. Then, fortified by a delicious meal of freshly caught haddock and chips, they climbed the hundreds of steps at the other side of the town up to the ruined abbey and the church and graveyard at the top of the hill.

Another day they journeyed across the Yorkshire Wolds to Flamborough Head, then on to the cathedral town of Beverley. In Scarborough they enjoyed the pleasures of Peasholm Park and the elegant shops on Westborough. They watched the fishing boats unloading their catch in the harbour, heard the cries of the seagulls as they wheeled overhead and smelled the aroma of the salty air from the fish stalls along the quay where crabs and lobsters, cockles and mussels and potted shrimps were on sale.

'We'll maybe venture further afield later in the year,' said Sam. 'We were thinking of Paris in August, weren't we, when the mill closes for a week?'

'I've been more than contented here,' replied Val happily. 'Yes, it would be nice. I've never been abroad, you know. But we'll wait and see how we feel, shall we?'

Val was eager to get back to their new home, to arrange their furniture, put up the curtains and fill the cupboards with their many and varied wedding gifts. They travelled back on the Thursday to give themselves a long weekend in which to settle down before they both returned to work on Monday. Val was hoping she might not be working for very long, even though she loved her job. She was wondering if she might already have conceived a child. There had been plenty of opportunity for her to do so!

Sam carried her over the threshold of their new home, hugging and kissing her as he put her down in the short passageway. 'So here we are – just you and me in our own little palace. I'll go and unload the car then we'll have a cuppa, shall we?'

'Yes; I'll go and put the kettle on,' said Val. 'First things first.'

They had made sure that one of the two electric kettles they had received as wedding gifts was installed and ready for use. They had bought some fresh milk on the way back and there was a tun containing tea in a kitchen cupboard.

Most of their belongings were still in packing cases in the middle of the dining-room floor. They looked at them in some perplexity as they drank their tea.

'We'll make a good start at it all tomorrow,' said Sam. 'There's a heck of a lot to do . . . but we're very fortunate, aren't we, darling? Far luckier than a lot of folk.'

Val knew that Sam did not take his good fortune for granted. He was aware that he was far more 'well off' than many young people of his age, and this was mainly due to his father and his grandfather before him. He had had a job at the mill ready and waiting for him when he left school. His father, however, had insisted that he should start on the bottom rung of the ladder and have experience in all the departments of the mill before becoming one of the managers. Neither had he been excused National Service. His time in the army had given him a greater insight into the lives of his contemporaries and he had made friends with lads from all walks of life.

Walker's mill, right from the start, in Jacob's time, had been a good place to work. The working conditions and the needs of the employees had always been of primary importance.

Consideration had been given to sons and daughters seeking employment at the mill. Val's parents had both been employed there, and this applied to several of the girls with whom she worked.

Val knew that Sam's mother, Beatrice, had been a mill worker herself, not at Walker's but in the office of another mill in a different part of the town. She had chosen to forget about her humble beginnings, though, when she had met and then married Joshua Walker. Her superior manner had influenced her eldest son, and the workers were quick to notice the difference in the attitude of the two brothers. Samuel was more 'one of them' but they respected him as their boss far more than they respected his brother.

'Yes, we're lucky in all sorts of ways,' Val answered. 'You've worked hard, though, Sam. It wasn't all handed to you on a plate so don't think that you don't deserve it. One of the most important things is that your family have got used to me now.' By 'family', Sam would know that she meant his mother and his brother. 'And I've got over the feeling that it wasn't quite right – you and me, I mean – getting friendly. As you said, I think we might have discovered one another eventually. It all seems so right, doesn't it?'

'It'll be even more right when we've got this lot sorted out,' said Sam, looking at the packing cases and tea chests that covered the floor and the boxes of wedding presents on the table. 'Shall we treat ourselves to fish and chips tonight? I'll go and get them; there's a nice place not far away. We can start cooking our own meals tomorrow when we've sorted out the pots and pans.'

Val thought that was an excellent idea. They had bought some fresh bread and a pack of butter on the way home so they could at least have toast for breakfast. She buttered the bread, but as the plates were cold they ate the fish and chips from the paper just like the holidaymakers in Blackpool. They did no work that evening but were ready to start in earnest the next morning.

By Monday, when they returned to work, the house was more or less ship-shape although the garden was in need of tending. The house had been built in the thirties and, being pre-war, had several attractive features. There was a stained-glass window in the front door depicting a sunset, and coloured glass motifs in the upper window panes, a highly polished dark oak banister, spindles and a newel post, and deep skirting boards and cornices to all the rooms.

It had now been decorated, however, in a modern style in bright contemporary colours, and they had chosen bold designs of geometrical shapes for the curtains and cushions. Their furniture was from the latest G-Plan and Ercol ranges, and the kitchen was fitted with cupboards and a working top in pale blue Formica. The kitchen was rather small, in keeping with most semi-detached houses built around that era, but there was room for two tall stools so they could eat their breakfast there in the mornings. Val was thrilled to bits with her new home and couldn't wait to start being a real housewife.

She had already cooked a few meals using their new pans and Pyrex dishes and utensils, and their modern Wedgwood dinner service which was a present from Jonathan and Thelma. It was pale blue and beige pottery and did not need to be handled with too much care, unlike the Crown Derby tea service of delicate china, in the Imari design of red, blue and gold, given to them by Sam's grandparents. It had pride of place in the top drawer of the glass-fronted sideboard, and Val felt that she would never dare to use it.

'You never know, the Queen might decide to come to tea one day,' joked Sam.

'Or your mother!' added Val with a wry grin. 'Joking apart, though, we'd better invite them to come to tea very soon, hadn't we?'

'Yes, perhaps we must. Next Sunday, maybe – just the two of them. We'll have Jonathan and Thelma and little Rosemary another time. And Cissie will be waiting for an invitation, of course, with Walter and little Paul. You mustn't forget Cissie. And your parents . . . Goodness me! We're going to be busy, aren't we?'

Val couldn't wait to have what her mother called 'company' in their new home. She was looking forward to being the hostess, but above all she wanted to be a good wife to Sam. It was Sunday evening and they were to start work again the next day. Val would soon be a working wife as were some of her friends; it was becoming more usual, now, for married women to work outside of the home.

'We could have a house-warming party,' Sam suggested now. 'We have so many friends, one way and another, both yours and mine. It might be a nice idea to have them all round together. What do you think, darling?'

'You mean . . . invite everybody, all at the same time?' queried Val. She was thinking that it might be an awkward mix: Sam's parents, her parents, and what about grandparents and aunts and uncles? Would they be included? And friends . . . there were so many of them. 'I'm not sure,' she replied. 'We've already had the wedding reception and everybody came to that. But they didn't all mix together, did they? Not as well as we might have hoped. They were obliged to be at the wedding, though. This would be a much more informal occasion. I'm not sure, Sam, that it would be a good idea.'

Sam looked at her anxious face and realized that she might have got the wrong idea. He laughed. 'When I said everybody I didn't mean absolutely everyone. Not the older generation, parents and grandparents. Goodness me, no! I just meant our age group, our own friends.'

'Oh, I see,' said Val. 'Yes, that would be a lovely idea.'

'Your parents and mine must be the first to be invited here, then Jonathan and Thelma, and Cissie and Walter . . . not together, of course! I was thinking we could have a get-together of our friends later in the year; late June or July, maybe. We could invite the girls from your office and their boyfriends – or husbands, and my pals, Jeff and Colin – they've both got girlfriends now. I can think of at least twenty already. The house should be just as we want it by then.'

'And the garden,' said Val, rapidly warming to the idea. 'If it was a nice evening we could eat in the garden. Or have supper in the house then go into the garden to chat together afterwards.'

'Not the way the garden is at the moment!' Sam gave a painful grimace. 'It does have potential but it's been badly neglected. It's like a wilderness out there; the grass has run riot and the bushes are overgrown. There are some decent rose bushes, though; those seem hardy enough . . . Yes, it's a brilliant idea. We'll have a garden party; well, a party in the garden, I mean – not a summer fete like they have at church! It'll give me an incentive to get it sorted. I'm not much of a gardener but I'm sure I could find somebody to sort it all out for us. And to heck with the expense! We've done most of the work in the house ourselves, haven't we? I'll get cracking with the garden idea right away.'

Val was still thinking about the people they would invite. 'There's Janice as well,' she said, 'and Phil. It would probably be on a Saturday, wouldn't it? She sometimes comes to Ilkley for the weekend . . . That reminds me, Phil was going to Blackpool this weekend and they were planning to get engaged. I wonder if it's official now? I must find out before we send them a Congratulations card . . .'

Five

'Phil's coming to stay next weekend, Dad,' Janice told her father when she returned from the wedding. 'He'll come on Friday and stay till Sunday . . . if that's OK with you?'

'You know it is, don't you, lass?' said Alec Butler. 'Phil's always welcome here. You're only just seen him, though, haven't you?'

'Well . . . yes, but it's rather important Dad, actually. He wants to have a chat with you.'

'Oh, I see.' Alec's warm brown eyes lit up with interest and he smiled knowingly at his daughter. 'Say no more, eh? Is he going to ask me an important question?'

Janice laughed. 'You've just told me to say no more and I don't intend to. Shush . . . Ian's coming in now. I'll tell him that Phil's coming, of course.'

Fourteen-year-old Ian dashed into the living room in his usual boisterous way. There had been a football practice after school so it was now six o'clock on the Monday evening.

'Good lad; you've taken your muddy boots off,' said his father. 'Was it a good practice?'

'Yeah, it was OK. I've been chosen for the second team on Saturday. We're playing a school from Fleetwood. But you know I like football best; I wish they played it at school instead of rugby.' Ian was a devoted fan of Blackpool Football Club, who were living in past glory, having won the FA Cup in 1953.

'Never mind; you've done really well to get in the team,' Janice told him. 'I'll put the tea out now you're here. We've waited for you. It's your favourite – one of them, anyway – sausage and mash.'

'Goody!' said Ian as they sat down at the table. He was a pleasant-looking boy, brown-eyed and dark-haired, a younger version of his father. He was almost as tall as Alec now with a cheerful smile – most of the time – like his father. None of them had smiled much, though, following the death of their beloved wife and mother the previous year. They were all trying to adjust now to life without Lilian; she had left a tremendous void for all of them.

'I was just telling Dad that Phil's coming to stay next weekend,' Janice told her brother.

'Goody!' said Ian again. 'D'you think he'd like to come and watch me play on Saturday morning?'

'I'm not sure,' replied Janice cagily. 'We might have something else to do.' Phil had suggested that they should go and choose a ring after he had spoken to her father.

'You could come as well,' Ian added, 'though you're not right keen on rugby, are you?'

'Not really,' agreed Janice. 'It's so rough and I'm always afraid somebody's going to get hurt.'

'They do sometimes,' said Ian. 'Phil will be sleeping in my room, won't he, same as he did before?'

'Yes, of course.' Janice smiled to herself. There was absolutely no question of Phil sharing a room with her, either at her home or at his. It was never even hinted at. Their parents would be horrified at the idea. 'That sort of thing' was strictly for after you were married. That was what Janice and all of her friends had been brought up to believe. Nevertheless, there were some who had to get married in a hurry.

Even when they were left alone in Janice's home, or in Phil's, they kept a limit on their behaviour. Janice doubted that she would have any real experience of 'that' until after their marriage.

The bungalow that Alec had chosen was not large but there were three bedrooms – quite smallish ones. Two were on ground level, occupied by Alec and by Janice, and there was a dormer room which Ian had been pleased to claim as his own. It had a sloping ceiling and a triangular window that jutted out above the front door, and he liked being up in the roof away from everyone.

Phil arrived on Friday in time for the meal that Janice had made when she returned from her day at college. She had prepared a chicken casserole the previous night which only needed heating up in the oven. She had wondered while she was making it how her dad would manage when she married Phil and went to live in Yorkshire. Her dad came to lend a hand in the kitchen now, especially with the washing up, as if to get ready for a time when she would not be there. When her mother had been alive, Alec, like most men of his generation, had hardly ever entered the kitchen. It was believed that this was the woman's province. But things were gradually changing as more women worked outside the home.

Phil complimented Janice on the casserole but she admitted that the apple pie had been bought from a bakery that prided itself on homemade produce.

'And why not?' said Phil. 'Mum buys fruit pies from a shop in Ilkley to serve in the restaurant. It's impossible to do everything yourself. We concentrate on the starters and the main courses.'

'So you're still working for your father, are you?' asked Alec.

Janice guessed that her dad was fishing as he already knew the answer to that.

'Yes, for the time being,' replied Phil, 'but Dad knows that I won't stay there for ever. I'm looking around . . . There's plenty of scope in Yorkshire; new places opening up all the time. But Dad knows I would never set up in opposition to him.' He cast a quick glance at Janice and they smiled at one another, a look that didn't pass unnoticed by Alec.

When the meal ended Janice cleared the plates away quickly

and started the washing up. 'I'll help,' said Phil, grabbing a pot towel, but Janice shook her head.

'Now's a good time for you to go and talk to Dad,' she said. 'He'll be expecting you anyway. I've not said very much but I've dropped a hint. I thought I'd make it easier for you, although you've nothing to worry about. And Ian's going out.'

Her brother was already shouting 'Cheerio' as he went out of the door. He was going round to a pal's house to play a game of chess. They had recently joined a chess club at school and this was the latest craze when they were not playing or watching football.

'See you later,' called Ian. 'I won't be late, Dad . . .'

'OK then. I'll brave the lion in his lair!' said Phil, giving Janice a quick kiss.

'Oh, come on, now! Dad's an old softie. I'll give you twenty minutes or so then I'll come in with some coffee.'

'Come in, lad, and sit down,' said Alec as Phil reappeared in the living room. This was the room at the back of the house where they dined and then took their leisure in the evening. There was also a small 'front room', as it was always called, which was kept for best, for high days and holidays, such as Christmas or family celebrations. Janice didn't see the point of it really and was trying to persuade her father to have central heating installed, then they could use all the rooms in the house all the year round.

Phil sat down in the armchair opposite to Alec, one on either side of the fireplace. Alec noticed the slightly anxious look on the young man's face and felt a little sorry for him. He remembered the time, back in the early thirties, when he had plucked up courage to ask Florrie Cartwright if he might marry her daughter, Lilian.

Florrie had been a formidable woman, a seaside landlady of the old school, although well-liked by her visitors. Fortunately she had taken to Alec and the two of them had always got along well together. Alec had known, though, right from the start, that if he wanted to marry the girl he loved he would have to give up his job at the mill in Burnley, despite his chance of promotion, and live at the boarding house in Blackpool. That was where he had met Lilian when he was on holiday there. Lilian could not possibly be spared to go and live in Burnley. Her work was there in Blackpool and Florrie's word was law. Alec had known that his sacrifice would be worthwhile. After a spell of casual work he had found employment as a maintenance engineer for an electrical company.

He understood now how Phil must be feeling. He had liked the young man ever since Janice had brought him home two years ago, when he was doing his National Service in the RAF. Lilian had liked him as well, and they had been pleased when the friendship had progressed. Phil had been most helpful while Lilian was ill and after she had died. He had worked along with Janice and the rest of the staff when they needed help with the catering and had proved to be a very able chef. Alec was prepared for the inevitable outcome; he knew that when the two of them were married they would live in Yorkshire and work together in their own business.

'So I think you've something you want to tell me, haven't you, Phil?' Alec leaned forward, smiling at the young man in an encouraging way.

'To ask you, really, rather than tell you,' said Phil. 'I love Janice very much – I think you know that – and I believe she loves me. And . . . we would like to be married but we want to know, first, if it's all right with you? You see . . . it will mean Janice leaving here and living in Yorkshire. I'm looking – that is to say, Janice and I will be looking – for a business somewhere in the county. My aunt left me quite a substantial sum when she died, not long ago. So I do have the where-withall, and I want to spend my life with Janice.'

Alec nodded. 'Of course it's all right with me, lad. You surely didn't think I would raise any objections, did you? I'm only too pleased that she's met you and that she's so happy, because I can see that she is. Lilian would have been pleased as well. I've been trying to prepare myself for the time when Janice leaves home. I knew it would happen one day. I shall manage, don't you worry about that . . . And you won't be a million miles away, will you?'

'No, just across the Pennines. And you'll be able to come and stay with us, you and Ian. But that's in the future – the not-too-distant future, I hope. We haven't thought about a wedding date yet or bought a ring. We're hoping to do that tomorrow.'

'We must have a celebration,' said Alec. 'It isn't every day that my only daughter gets engaged to be married.' He beamed at Phil, his smile becoming even broader when Janice, rather tentatively, entered the room carrying a tray laden with cups and saucers and a coffee pot.

'I'm really pleased, love; very happy for both of you.' Alec took the tray from Janice and put it on the table. Then he put his arms round her and kissed her cheek. 'Wonderful news! I was just saying to Phil that we must have a celebration. What about a nice meal out, somewhere posh, tomorrow night? Just the four of us; that's if Ian would like to join us, and I don't see why he wouldn't.'

'So . . . I take it you said yes to Phil?' Janice's eyes twinkled as she handed her father a cup of coffee.

'Of course I did. I know you're underage, not twenty-one till next January. But I'm sure you're old enough to know your own mind, and I know that Phil will take care of you. He's been telling me about his windfall, so that makes things easier, doesn't it? Have you anything in mind about the sort of business that you're looking for?'

'We wondered about a tea shop – a rather exclusive one, I mean, not a "greasy spoon" cafe,' said Phil. 'Serving morning coffee, afternoon tea and light lunches, and maybe catering for larger parties in the evening. Then Janice can use her talents as a confectioner. That's one idea; we'll just have to see what turns up.'

'It's early days yet, Dad,' said Janice. 'We're not officially engaged yet. We'll tell Ian tomorrow once we've got the ring. I'm sure he'll be pleased that Phil's going to be his brother-in-law! Where were you thinking of for tomorrow night? You usually go to your club on Saturday night, don't you? And I know you enjoy it. Isn't there a darts match?'

'No, not tomorrow. And I can miss the club for once; this is more important.'

It was true, though, as Janice said, that he enjoyed the club, far more than he had thought he would. He had made a few new friends there. It was really a working men's club but ladies were invited along as well. Alec had never been interested in that sort of thing before, spending evenings in the pub with a crowd of fellers. He had preferred to be with Lilian in the comfort of their home. During the summer, when the hotel was busy, there had been little time for leisure but they had sometimes gone out for a quiet drink or a visit to the cinema when the hotel closed after the illuminations ended.

Alec had gone quiet, thinking of someone he had met at the club quite recently. For the first time since Lilian had died he had felt a faint stirring of . . . something. But it was far too soon, he told himself.

'What's up, Dad?' said Janice. 'You're miles away.'

'Am I?' said Alec, shaking his head and trying to rearrange his thoughts. 'Sorry . . . I was thinking about where to go tomorrow night. But you'll have a better idea about the places than I have, Janice.'

'There are a few good places in town,' she replied. 'What about the Lobster Pot? They do a nice meal; mainly fish dishes, of course. Scampi and lobster and crab, as well as the usual plaice and haddock. It makes a change from steak and chips, which seems to be the standard fare in most places. What do you think, Dad?'

'Yes, it sounds fine to me.'

'We'll book then, shall we, when we go to town in the morning? For the four of us.'

Janice was doubtful, though, that Ian would want to go, especially to somewhere where he would have to get 'all dressed up'.

'You two go out now if you want to,' said Alec. 'Don't worry about me. I'll watch the telly and wait for Ian coming back. He's a good lad; if he says he'll be back by half past nine I know he will be.'

Janice and Phil strolled along to Stanley Park, a short distance away. They had time to wander near the lake and the Italian Garden, but dusk was falling and the few people who were there, mainly courting couples like themselves, were making their way to the gates before the park closed.

Alec was dozing and came round with a start as they

entered the room. 'Just an old gangster film,' he said, nodding towards the screen where the sound was blaring away at top blast. 'James Cagney, but I'm blessed if I know what the heck they're doing.' He got up and turned it off. 'I wonder if they'll ever get round to colour on TV, like they have at the cinema? That'd be great, wouldn't it? Won't happen in my lifetime, though.'

'Don't say that, Alec!' said Phil. 'They've got it in America and I bet there'll be colour telly here, maybe in ten years or so. You're going to live longer than that, aren't you?'

'I damn well hope so! I'm only just turned fifty, but then . . . you never know, do you?' He was pensive for a moment and it was clear that he was thinking about Lilian. 'It's a good job that you don't know what's round the corner . . .' He stopped speaking as Ian burst in.

'Aren't you watching the telly, Dad?'

'No, it was a load of rubbish. What about you? Did you win your game?'

'Nah . . . Gary beat me again. He's a whizz at chess. But I'll get my own back next time, you'll see!'

Janice wondered if he might have other plans for the following night but she decided not to mention the proposed meal in town. She would wait until she was wearing her ring.

'I'm off to bed now,' said Ian. 'I'm knackered!'

Janice smiled at him. 'Shall I bring you a drink of hot chocolate?'

'No, s'all right, thanks . . . I had some supper at Gary's. G'night. See you in the morning.'

'What about, you, Dad?' asked Janice. 'A cup of tea? Or chocolate?'

'Tea will be fine, love.'

'Then we'll all have tea,' said Phil. 'It'll make it easier. You stay there and I'll see to it.'

'No, you're the guest,' said Janice. 'It's my job, for now.'

'But I'll soon be one of the family . . .'

'I'll make sure you do it then,' said Janice with a smile. 'Never fear!'

Alec turned in, as he put it, when he had drunk his tea, leaving them on their own.

'Alone at last!' said Phil, throwing his arms round her and kissing her in the way he had wanted to do all day. They indulged in gentle lovemaking for a while, but Phil knew when it was time to put a stop to it. This was getting increasingly hard to do, but he knew how Janice felt about it while she was in her family home, and the same applied when they were at his home in Ilkley.

Eventually he left her with a fond kiss at her bedroom door and climbed the stairs up to the dormer room. He crept in and undressed in the dark as Ian was fast asleep in the camp bed, having left his more comfortable single bed for Phil.

Next morning Phil drove into town. He managed to find a parking spot but not without difficulty as it was Saturday. The town was busy with weekend shoppers and there were quite a few visitors, although the summer season had not yet started in earnest.

Beaverbrooks jewellers was the place to go and Janice could not restrain her smile of joy as they entered the shop.

'Engagement rings, please,' said Phil to the young lady assistant. She smiled at them both.

'Certainly, sir. Have you anything in mind? And, of course . . . the price range?'

Phil had a quiet word with her and Janice stood to one side. She had insisted that he mustn't spend too much as they would need their savings, plus Phil's inheritance, to obtain the business they wanted. Phil wanted Janice to have a nice, decent-sized ring of her choice but, like a true Yorkshireman, he told himself that he wasn't made of money.

After trying several she finally decided on an emerald surrounded by small diamonds. Some people might think that green was unlucky but she was not overly superstitious and it was the one she liked best. Fortunately it fitted perfectly and didn't need altering.

'Congratulations,' said the assistant. 'I hope you'll be very happy.'

'I know we will,' answered Phil, smiling broadly. 'Keep it on,' he said to Janice. 'We're really engaged now.' He did not kiss her, though, not wanting to behave in a demonstrative way in public.

He handed her the little velvet box and she put it away in her shoulder bag. As they walked along the street hand in hand she could not stop smiling and she kept glancing down, almost unbelievingly, at her left hand.

'Now, where's this Lobster Pot place?' said Phil. 'Let's go and book for tonight.'

It was very close to the jeweller's and they booked a table for four for seven o'clock. Janice knew that her father did not like to eat late at night. She was still doubtful that it would be Ian's 'cup of tea'.

Alec became quite emotional when Janice showed him her ring. There were tears in his eyes as he kissed her then shook hands with Phil. 'I'm a silly old fool, aren't I? I'm really pleased for you both and I know you'll be happy together. But it's the thought of Janice leaving . . .'

'You won't be losing me, Dad. You'll be gaining a son – isn't that what they say? – not losing a daughter.'

'And we'll see you as often as we can,' added Phil.

'Anyway, it may not be for ages yet,' said Janice. 'I'll find a temporary job in Blackpool when my course ends and we have to find somewhere that we both really want. It might take a long time.'

She hoped, though, that it might not be too long. She and Phil wanted to be together now, and had talked, tentatively, about a wedding towards the end of the year. She could live with Phil at his family home in Ilkley if they had not found a suitable place by then. But she would not say that to her father; better to take one step at a time.

Janice, with Phil's help, prepared a quick lunch of soup and sandwiches as they would be dining out later. When Ian arrived back at one o'clock he was full of beans because their team had won and he had scored a try. Janice decided to tell him their news after lunch. He ate as though he was starving and did not notice the ring sparkling on her finger. But why should he? Why would any lad of his age?

'We've got some news for you,' Janice told him when the pots were cleared away and they were having an after-lunch cup of tea. She knew that he might be dashing out somewhere again before long.

'Go on then, what is it?'

She held out her hand. 'Look! Phil and I have got engaged.'

'Gosh, that's great!' he said, his brown eyes opening wide. 'You mean . . . you're getting married?'

'Yes . . . in a little while,' said Janice.

'So I shall be your brother-in-law,' said Phil.

'That's wizard,' said Ian. 'I've always wanted a brother. She's all right, though . . .' He gestured towards Janice. 'But she's only a sister. A brother's different. So you'll be coming to live here all the time, won't you?'

'Er . . . no,' said Janice. 'We'll be living in Yorkshire after we're married. But it won't be just yet,' she added, noting that the look of pleasure on Ian's face had been replaced by one of puzzlement.

'Why can't you live here?' he said rather belligerently. 'I mean, p'raps not here in this house, but in Blackpool? I thought you'd want to have a hotel like we did before. You came and worked there, didn't you, Phil, when Mum was ill, and after . . . afterwards? There are lots of hotels in Blackpool.'

'But we want to do something different,' said Janice. 'Phil's always lived in Yorkshire and we want to find somewhere there; a cafe with a shop, or a restaurant, we're not sure yet . . .'

'That's not fair!' said Ian, revealing a petulance that was most unlike his usual sunny nature. 'I don't see why Phil can't come and live here instead of you going there.'

'You're being very unreasonable and very childish, Ian,' said his father.

'No, I'm not!' he retorted. 'Janice lives here and she looks after us. She has done ever since . . . ever since Mum died. She cooks our meals and . . . everything.'

He looked like a little boy lost and Janice's heart went out to him. She knew he was being selfish, looking at things from his own point of view, but who could blame him? He had lost his mother and now this had brought it home to him in a different way. She knew that her departure would leave a gap in his life; he had assumed – foolishly, maybe – that she would always be there. She hoped Dad wouldn't be too hard on him.

Fortunately Alec tried to cajole rather than to scold him.

'Well, we'll have to start looking after ourselves, won't we, son?' he said. 'I know I left the cooking and all that to your mum, and then to Janice. But I'm not too old to learn and you're old enough to help me.'

'But I can't cook and I don't want to learn,' Ian argued. 'I'm a boy and boys don't cook. Nobody can cook like my mum used to.' He was very close to tears.

'Come on, now,' said Alec. 'We all miss Mum but we've been managing all right, you and me. And we'll manage when Janice goes away. Anyway, what about Phil? He's a wonderful cook; he's a chef, and he started learning when he was a lad like you.'

'But it's his job and he likes doing it.'

'Well, we all have to do things we don't like sometimes,' said Alec, beginning to lose patience. 'Snap out of it, Ian, there's a good lad. Janice won't be going anywhere for a while yet and you'll get used to the idea.'

Phil had kept quiet so far, not knowing what to say. Quite possibly the lad was blaming him. 'You'll be able to come and stay with us,' he said now. 'There are some great football teams in Yorkshire, like Leeds United and Sheffield Wednesday. We could go and watch them on a Saturday, you and me, and perhaps my dad; he likes football.'

'S'pose so . . .' said Ian, trying to smile at Phil. Despite all this he liked Phil a lot, but he didn't like him taking Janice away. She had been like a second mother to him since Mum died. He knew he mustn't cry; that would make him look stupid and babyish.

Janice decided to try and smooth things over. 'It might be ages before we find what we're looking for,' she said, 'and you'll be used to the idea by then, I promise you. This is what happens in families: people move away and nothing stays the same for ever. Phil and I were hoping you'd be pleased for us. We're going out tonight for a meal in town – just a little celebration, and we'd like you to come with us. Dad's coming, of course.'

'Where are you going then?' he asked, still a little sullenly.

'To the Lobster Pot. They do smashing meals there – all sorts of fancy things, but you can have fish and chips if you like.'

'Mmm . . . sounds OK,' he said. 'I won't have to get all dressed up?'

'No, not so long as you're neat and tidy,' said Alec. 'Janice and Phil really want you to be there. I shall be sorry when Janice leaves us, but we'll have a nice new place to visit in Yorkshire.'

'All right then,' said Ian. 'I'm going out now, though. We're having a kick around in the park, Gary and me and some others. What time are we going out?'

'We said we'd be there by seven o'clock,' said Alec. 'You'll be back ages before then, won't you?'

'S'pose so,' said Ian, then, as if aware that he sounded ungracious, he added, 'Yeah, I'll be back. See you later . . .'

'He'll come round,' said Alec when the door closed behind him. 'He just thought things would carry on in the same old way.'

'He misses Mum an awful lot,' said Janice. 'He didn't cry much when she died, if you remember. He just retreated into his shell and wouldn't talk about it. Maybe he's having a delayed reaction now. I'm pleased he's coming with us, though. I'd feel dreadful if he wasn't there.'

Fortunately the meal at the Lobster Pot turned out to be a happy occasion. It seemed as though Ian had decided to put his resentment to one side. He was rather quieter than usual, but he did his best to be amenable. None of them dressed up as they might do for a dinner dance or an important anniversary. They wore casual summer clothes suitable for the pleasant late spring evening.

Ian chose the ever-popular battered haddock and chips, served with fresh garden peas rather than the mushy chip shop variety, and tucked into his meal with relish. The others chose salad meals, Alec opting for fresh salmon and Janice and Phil for crab, a delicacy only eaten on special occasions. A bottle of sweet white wine, the house wine, was a pleasant accompaniment, and Ian, after a small glass of this, appeared to have forgotten his worries. After a delicious dessert of Black Forest gateau, with coffee to round off the meal, it was time to depart.

It was still only nine o'clock, and as Phil drove away out of the town Alec rather hesitantly suggested that as the night was still young – and if the others had no objections – he might spend an hour or two at the club he usually went to on a Saturday evening.

'Of course – why should we mind?' said Phil. 'How will you get home?'

'I might walk,' replied Alec. 'It's not all that far but sometimes I get a lift back. It just depends . . .'

The club was on the outskirts of the town where the shops gave way to large private premises, some of which were boarding houses or small hotels.

'See you later, maybe,' said Alec as he opened the car door. 'I won't be late but don't wait up for me. Thanks, Phil . . .'

Alec opened the glass door which led into the large lounge area. The aroma of cigarettes and ale drifted on the air but it was a comfortable, homely smell to Alec. A friendly game of darts was in progress at the back of the room and, in the annex beyond, a game of snooker. An attractive dark-haired woman behind the bar called out to him as she saw him enter the room. 'Hello there, Alec. We thought you weren't coming. You're later tonight, aren't you?'

'A family occasion,' replied Alec. 'My daughter's just got engaged and we've been having a little celebration. Anyway, I'm here now. I'll have a half of bitter, please, Norma.'

'Certainly . . .' She smiled at him in a friendly way. 'You go and sit down and I'll bring it over to you. We're quiet at the moment, so I'll have one with you . . .'

Six

By the end of July the garden of Sam and Val's home had undergone a transformation. Their house-warming party was to be held on the evening of the last Saturday in July. The invitations had gone out in good time while Sam and Val kept their fingers crossed that all would be ready.

It had been a mammoth undertaking but now, as Val remarked to her husband, 'Everything in the garden's lovely!'

They had hired a small firm of gardeners with a reputation for good work and a price that was not too extortionate. They did not object when Sam worked along with them with the more simple tasks in order to get the job finished more quickly. The basic layout was already there, but the previous owners, an elderly couple, had allowed the garden area to get overgrown and neglected.

The French windows of the living room at the back of the house opened on to a patio area of stone flags that were coated with the grime of many years. When they had been cleaned with a power hose their original colours of cream and pink were restored and they looked as good as new. Three stone steps, also in need of repair, led down from the patio to the long lawn where the grass had grown to several inches in height. A powerful mowing machine had worked wonders and grass seed had been planted in places that were worn and bare.

Ivy and clematis, and climbing hydrangea bushes had run riot on the fence that separated their garden from the one next door. They required only a little pruning, and the expanse of foliage gave a feeling of a wooded glade to the garden. The large ornamental cherry tree at the bottom end of the lawn, however, required a severe pruning, as did the lilac and the buddleia bushes.

One area that had thrived was the side bed of rose bushes – hardy plants that seemed to survive happily anywhere. After a little attention they were now a riot of colour: white, yellow and palest pink to deep crimson, scenting the air as the summer drew on. The gardeners had created a rockery at the far end of the lawn where alpine plants were already blooming. Bedding plants – geraniums, begonias, French marigolds and aubretia – made for a quick and simple display in large tubs and urns along the path by the garage.

Val had set her heart on a small summer house and Sam had agreed to this. It had a wooden floor, a pointed roof and a green painted door with room for a small table and a couple of chairs – an ideal place to enjoy the garden when it was not quite warm enough to sit in the sun. They had also purchased two reclining chairs but, so far, they had had little time to relax in them. Val could imagine herself sitting in the doorway of the little house – she thought of it as a fairy tale, Snow White sort of house – on a summer's day, reading a book and having a cup of tea or a glass of lemonade. After she had finished work, of course . . . She could visualize a pram on the lawn with a small baby asleep, or a toddler running around playing with a ball . . .

At the moment, though, life was busy both at work and at home. There was little time for relaxation as they settled in their new home, gradually putting everything to rights before entertaining a succession of visitors for Sunday tea or an evening meal. Sam's parents had come first of all; Val had been relieved when that visit had come and gone, although Beatrice had behaved very well and actually complimented Val on her cooking. Then Val's parents had come, followed by Jonathan and Thelma, then Cissie and Walter and both sets of grandparents.

The party on the coming Saturday would be a time for the younger folk to get together. A happy, relaxed occasion for friends of a similar age. Val was looking forward to it tremendously, although it did require a good deal of planning. She was hoping for good weather so that they could spend some time in the garden as they had planned to do.

When she looked through the bedroom window on the Saturday morning the sky was grey and overcast; there was no sign of the sun but at least it was not raining. It had been a typical British summer so far: hot one day then chilly the next. Val wondered if she was being too optimistic to believe that they might be blessed with a fine evening. She said a quick silent prayer, asking for good weather, although she was not really so naive as to believe that God might listen to and answer her request – not when there were so many other important things for Him to consider.

She went into town, quite early in the morning, to buy the requirements for the buffet supper. Sam had promised to see to the drinks, which would be delivered by a local off-licence store. She bought small bread rolls, fresh from the oven, from a bakery that was renowned for its produce, and two dozen of their small pork pies. Then she went to the busy market hall where she bought a selection of cooked meats

– boiled ham, tongue and thinly carved roast beef – and a pound of small pork sausages. She got a good chunk of Wensleydale cheese from the cheese stall, the tangy aroma drifting on the air all around, a variety of salad and two large punnets of strawberries from one of the many greengrocery stalls. Then, with two heavily laden bags, she took the bus back to Queensbury.

Sam had gone into work as he sometimes needed to do on a Saturday morning but promised he would be there in the afternoon to help prepare for the party. As she lugged the heavy bags up the garden path she thought again that she really must learn to drive. Thelma was able to drive, and even Cissie was now having lessons . . . from Walter! Judging by her friend's comments Val had decided that this was not the ideal way to learn to drive as it could lead to friction and arguments. When she had time, Val decided she would book a course of lessons with a driving school.

She unpacked her bags, putting the meats and salad into the fridge and the rolls into the bread bin. Thelma had offered to come and help her prepare the food in the afternoon.

'Only time for a quick lunch today,' she called to Sam as he came into the kitchen a little while later.

'Suits me fine,' he replied, giving her a hug and a kiss as he always did, even if he had been away only a few hours. 'What shall we have? Beans on toast?'

Val laughed. 'That's the usual stand-by. I'll start getting it ready while you sort out the table.'

Then the man from the off-licence arrived, delaying the lunch for a little while. Sam helped him to carry in the bottles from the van and Val looked in amazement at the array of drinks which took up most of the room on the kitchen worktop. There were bottles of beer, Double Diamond being the current favourite; small bottles of Babycham and Cherry B, both very popular party drinks for ladies; Coca-Cola; Britvic pineapple, orange and apple juice; a large bottle of Bulmer's cider and a bottle of sweet sherry.

'Gosh! There's enough there to satisfy an army of folk,' exclaimed Val. 'How many are coming? Twenty-four at the last count?'

'Don't you believe it,' said Sam. 'It'll all disappear, I can assure you. And I expect some of them will bring their own favourite tipple.'

'Well, we'll have to move it all into the living room. I shall need the space in the kitchen to prepare the desserts. I'll make them first before Thelma comes, then we'll see to the rolls and salad and everything else.'

'It's to be hoped the weather picks up a bit,' said Sam. 'No blue sky at the moment.'

'No rain either,' added Val. 'Let's look on the bright side, shall we? Whatever happens the show must go on, as they say.'

With the quick lunch eaten and cleared away, Sam went out into the garden – his pride and joy now that it was trans- formed – to do a bit of dead-heading and mow the lawn. Val set to work on making the desserts. She hulled the strawberries and sprinkled them with a dusting of castor sugar – served with ice cream, they would be one of the choices. She hoped that all the guests would not go for the same dish.

She also made a sherry trifle; a shop-bought Swiss roll moistened with ample sherry then topped with jelly, tinned peaches and ready-made custard from a tin. Later, she would add the cream then decorate the top with glacé cherries and strips of angelica. The third choice would be a lemon meringue pie – easily made from the ingredients in a packet – but a firm favourite, as it had been for several years.

When Thelma arrived they set to work cutting and buttering the rolls then adding the variety of meats. 'It's rather early,' said Val. It was only four o'clock, three hours before the first guests were due to arrive. 'I don't want the rolls to go hard.'

'They'll come to no harm. Trust your Aunty Thelma! I'm a dab hand at sandwiches. If we lay them out on large plates then wrap each one in a tea towel they'll stay nice and fresh.'

It had been Thelma's idea as well to spear tiny sausages on cocktail sticks, and likewise cubes of cheese, each topped with a pineapple chunk. This was a new idea to Val, but Thelma assured her they were all the rage now at parties.

They prepared large bowls of salad: lettuce, tomato, cucumber, radishes and spring onions, with salad cream in a dish for those who liked it. There was a dish of piccalilli too, and one of pickled onions to add a touch of relish to the rolls and pork pies.

'I won't put the crisps out till everyone has arrived,' said Val, 'or they'll go soft. I've bought a few packets of those new salt and vinegar ones as well as the ready salted. They seem to be very popular now.' She looked at the array of food and smiled with satisfaction. 'Let's cover it all up, then I think it's time for a cuppa, don't you?'

'Good idea,' agreed Thelma, 'then I'll have to get back and relieve Jonathan. He's looking after Rosemary; he doesn't mind, of course – he adores her. But he's not all that keen on changing her nappy!'

Val smiled. 'No, I suppose not . . .' She could not imagine the high and mighty Jonathan engaged in such a task, although he was far more amenable than when she had first got to know him.

'And then I've to get ready for tonight,' Thelma went on. 'My parents are babysitting for us; in fact, they're staying the night because I don't know what time we'll be back.'

'I don't know either,' said Val. 'We'll just have to play it by ear . . .' She was anxious for it to go well, hoping that the guests would not get bored or not get along with each other, although most of them were acquainted.

'Don't look so worried,' said Thelma, noticing her preoccupied expression. 'It'll be fine. There's plenty to eat and drink; quite a banquet, I'd say. Your garden's looking lovely . . . And look up there; the sun's decided to shine!'

Val looked out of the window and smiled. 'So it has,' she said happily. Her prayers had been answered after all and she offered up a quick 'thank you' in her head to whoever might be listening. The grey sky had given way to one of azure blue with just a few fluffy white clouds, promising a fine summer evening. They had been too busy all afternoon to notice the weather.

Sam, meanwhile, had been arranging the fold-up chairs that he had borrowed from the mill. He placed some on the patio area and some in the living room. With the chairs they already had there should be ample seating, although it was likely that most people would stand in groups and mill round, sitting down only to eat their supper. He'd also borrowed some bowls, spoons and glasses from the canteen. They would not need knives and forks, and Val had bought waxed paper plates and some jolly red and white striped serviettes from Woolworth's.

Thelma went home and Val and Sam looked at one another and smiled, Val somewhat nervously.

'All ready?' he asked.

'Yes, I think so but I've got butterflies fluttering around in my tummy. I hope it'll go well, Sam.'

'Of course it will! Why shouldn't it? Off you go and make yourself beautiful, although you are beautiful already, my darling.' He kissed her lovingly, then she went upstairs to bath and dress in her gladrags.

She put on the pretty pink, full-skirted dress that had been her going away outfit. She wore a pair of white high-heeled sandals and applied pink lipstick and a pale green eyeshadow that enhanced her dark brown eyes.

They did not expect any of the guests to arrive before seven o'clock; it was not the done thing to arrive early. The exception to this would be Janice and Phil. Val had invited them to stay the night – they would be the first people who had done so – as Ilkley was a fair distance away. It did not seem far in the daytime but late at night, especially after a few drinks, the moorland roads could be more difficult to negotiate. All the other guests lived in or very near to Halifax.

When they had suggested the overnight stay and Janice and Phil had said they would be pleased to accept the offer, Val found herself in rather a quandary.

'Do you think . . . will they share a room?' she said to Sam. 'I don't know whether they . . . well, you know what I mean, and it isn't the sort of thing we can ask, is it? I'm not sure what their relationship is like.'

Sam laughed. 'They're engaged, aren't they? And you and I . . . well, we had what you might call a satisfying relationship. I know it wasn't easy, but there were times . . .'

'Yes, I know,' Val interrupted, feeling a little uncomfortable as she recalled the odd times when her parents had been out and they were left on their own. 'But I was never all that happy about it, thinking that Mum and Dad might come back earlier. When Janice stays with Phil I'm pretty sure she has her own room, and Janice's new home is a bungalow. There won't be much room, but I'm sure they won't . . . er . . . sleep together. Phil probably shares with Ian. So . . . what shall we do?'

'Make up the bed in the spare room for Janice,' replied Sam, 'and suggest that Phil can sleep on the sofa. It's a nice long one and we can make it comfortable. Then it's up to them, isn't it? We don't want to lead them astray, do we?' He gave a chuckle. 'But I dare say they're as normal as other folk.'

Janice and Phil arrived just after six thirty, both with an overnight bag. After the usual hugs and kisses and handshakes of greeting Sam picked up Janice's bag to take it upstairs. 'You're in the guest room, Janice,' he said. 'You're the first guest to stay in it. And perhaps you can kip on the sofa in the lounge, Phil? Anyway, it's up to you, if you know what I mean.' He made the remark in a casual way, neither grinning nor hinting at anything.

Val noticed that Janice blushed and did not look at Phil. He just nodded and said, 'OK, that sounds fine. Thanks very much for putting us up. I must admit I don't drive around in the dark all that much, not on those moorland roads.'

Janice came into the kitchen to talk to Val when she had unpacked and made herself ready for the evening ahead. She looked pretty in a sundress with wide shoulder straps, covered with a matching green bolero.

'Thank you for inviting us to stay,' she began, a little hesi- tantly, 'and for being so tactful.' She gave an embarrassed little laugh. 'We've never shared a room,' she whispered, her cheeks turning pink. 'In fact, we've never . . . you know . . . made love, not properly. You don't mind me mentioning it, do you? There's nobody else I can talk to. My girlfriends from school are away at college and I don't know the girls on the course all that well.'

Val was rather taken aback. She did not know Janice anywhere near as well as she knew Cissie. She had been her friend for ever, since they were tiny girls, and there was very little that they had not confided to one another, especially with regards to Cissie's goings-on. She was very much an open book, whereas Val knew that Janice was much more reserved.

'I know how you feel,' Val answered, 'at least, I've some idea. It's difficult, isn't it, when you're both living at home? You could never suggest sharing a room. My parents would have been horrified at the idea! But then . . . you never know, do you? They were young themselves, once upon a time.'

'Yes . . . We would never go so far, not under my father's roof. And Ian's usually around; we don't get much privacy when Phil comes to stay. I've been wondering, though, about Dad. He's very secretive at the moment and he goes out more than he used to. I've been telling Phil that I think he might have a lady friend.'

'Oh . . . and how would you feel about that?'

'I'm not sure,' replied Janice. 'It's over a year since Mum died but that's not really all that long, is it? I'm glad that he's getting out and about and meeting different people. It's not so much me, though; it's Ian. I'm worried about how he might react. He's quite moody at the moment.'

'He's at a difficult age, I suppose. He's fourteen, isn't he? Not a little boy any more.'

'Yes; he's quite grown up in some ways, then at other times he acts like a little boy. He was quite upset when Phil and I got engaged. Not so much at that – he really likes Phil – but at the idea of me moving away. He thought I'd be around for ever.'

'Oh! Whatever am I thinking about?' exclaimed Val. 'I'm so sorry. I haven't even looked at your ring! I've been so busy with all this going on.'

She admired the pretty ring and remarked that the emerald matched the dress that Janice was wearing. 'We'll have a good chat later,' she said, 'then you can tell us all your news.'

'Yes, I'm hindering you,' said Janice. 'They'll all be arriving soon, won't they?'

'Not all at once; in dribs and drabs, I dare say,' said Val, 'but everything's just about ready.'

The food was laid out on the dining table, the covers to be taken off at the last minute, and the drinks on a separate small table. Sam and Phil came in from the garden where Sam had been showing off the results of the last few weeks' work.

'It's warm enough to be outside,' he said. 'In fact, it's better than it's been all day.' He opened the French windows and fastened them back to give easy access to the patio and garden. 'Aren't we lucky? But the sun shines on the righteous, so they say!'

The four of then stood around chatting idly about this and that for several minutes. 'I hope they'll all turn up,' said Val a trifle anxiously. 'It's quarter past seven . . .' She stopped when the doorbell rang.

'There you are, you see,' said Sam. 'Stop worrying!'

The first to arrive were Jonathan and Thelma, bearing a bottle of white wine. No sooner had they greeted one another than the bell rang again.

'I'll leave the door open – they can come straight in,' said Sam. He returned with the girls from Val's office with their partners. By seven thirty everyone was there. Most had come in cars. Two were parked on the driveway – fortunately there was ample room outside the house and on the avenue round the corner.

None of the guests had arrived empty-handed, although Val and Sam had stressed, 'No presents, just the pleasure of your company.' There were boxes of chocolates, a bottle of sherry, one of cider, gaily patterned tea towels, kitchen gadgets and a corkscrew with a painted head of a red-cheeked man.

Val tried to do a quick head count as they all milled around. She counted twenty-four, including herself and Sam. In a little while Sam tapped on the table with a spoon to get a moment's silence.

'Hush a minute, everyone,' he said, 'but I'm glad you're all getting friendly; that's what we want. I would just like to say that Val and I are pleased to welcome you to our home for what we hope will be a happy time together. There's plenty to eat and drink and room to move about in the house and garden, so just make yourselves at home. Music later and dancing if you wish. We have a wide variety of records and I see that some of you have brought some of your own along. So . . . grab a plate, tuck in and enjoy yourselves.'

Everyone clapped and cheered, then Jonathan raised his voice. 'I suppose it's up to me to say thank you to my little brother and his wife for inviting us to their home. So, come on, Sam; let's get these bottles opened and we'll have a toast. Grab a glass, folks, and choose your favourite tipple.'

There was a hubbub for several moments as Sam and Jonathan dispensed the drinks.

'Right then, everyone,' said Jonathan, raising his glass of ale. 'Let's drink a toast to Sam and Val. We've already done this at their wedding but let's do it again. Sam and Val . . . We wish you health and happiness in your new home, and we hope that soon there will be another little Walker to welcome to the family!'

Val felt herself blushing as they all raised their glasses, repeating, 'To Sam and Val . . .' She was very pleased, though, that Jonathan was showing his more amenable side.

'Thank you, Jon, and everyone,' said Sam, smiling at his wife. 'We're doing our best, I can assure you! Now, start eating and drinking and enjoying yourselves. Best to form a queue, I think, but there's plenty to go round.'

Some of the guests politely sat down, allowing the others to go first. Val went over to speak to Rita who had started work in the office a few weeks ago. She was to replace Pauline who was expecting a baby in September and would be leaving very soon. She was there with her husband, while Susan and Jill had come with their boyfriends. Rita, being unattached at the moment, had demurred at the invitation, although she was delighted to have been asked. But the other girls had insisted that she should go along with them.

'We won't be sticking to our fellers all night,' said Jill. 'We're not joined at the hip. We'll make sure you're not on your own, and it's a chance for you to meet some more people.'

Rita was a shy girl, eighteen years old and a little younger than the others. She was pleasant and friendly, in a quiet way, and good at her job.

'I'm pleased you could come, Rita,' said Val. 'I know it can be a bit overwhelming, meeting so many new people. It was pretty scary, believe me, joining the Walker family,' she whispered, 'but Jonathan's on his best behaviour tonight.'

'I know I'm being nosey,' said Pauline, 'but what he was saying, about another little Walker . . . Are you . . .?'

'No, I'm afraid not,' said Val with a rueful smile. 'Not yet, but we do want to start a family soon.'

'There's plenty of time,' said Pauline. 'You've only been married a couple of months, haven't you?'

'That's true,' agreed Val. 'I suppose I'm impatient . . . What about you? I expect you'll be glad to finish work, won't you?'

'Yes, I sure will. Only another two weeks. I shall miss the company, though.'

Pauline, at seven months, was looking attractive and smart in a loose-fitting pale blue silky dress, her bump not being obvious beneath the flowing skirt. She was quite tall and stately and carried herself well.

Val had noticed Cissie queuing for the food. She, too, was pregnant, as she had been telling everyone for ages. She was about four-and-a-half months into her pregnancy, a time at which, as a rule, it was barely noticeable. Cissie, however, was already dressed as though the birth was imminent, in a cherry red dress with white polka dots which flowed out from the high waistline. Her bright red earrings and lipstick of the same shade complemented her dress. It seemed that she was glorying in her condition, saying, 'Look at me!'

She was deep in conversation with Colin, one of Sam's friends whom she had met before at the tower ballroom in Blackpool. Colin's girlfriend, Carol, was looking rather bemused as the two of them laughed together. Cissie's husband, Walter, was not with her in the food queue. He was at the other end of the room talking to Brian, one of the young trainees that Sam had invited. Since Walter's promotion at the mill he was now regarded as almost one of the bosses.

Val was waiting politely until everyone had helped themselves to food before filling her own plate. She had felt so overwrought before they had all arrived that she had thought she would not be able to eat a morsel. But so far it was all going well and she was beginning to relax. The office girls and their partners joined the food queue and Cissie came to sit on the settee with Val.

'What a spread,' she said, looking down at her plate piled up with a little bit of everything. 'You've done us proud, Val.

But I'm eating for two, of course. The only thing I can't eat is pickled onions. They repeat on me something dreadful.'

Val smiled. 'You're keeping well, though?'

'Never felt better. The doctor's pleased with me; he says I can stay at home to have this one, if all goes well.'

'And how's Walter? Enjoying his step up the ladder?'

'Oh aye!' She sniffed. 'He reckons he's one of the bosses now. Your Sam had better watch out!'

'Don't be silly, Cissie. He's worked hard and he deserves his promotion.' Val had noticed a hint of frostiness when Cissie and Walter arrived. 'You've not fallen out, have you?' she asked, aware of Cissie's grumpy mood.

'Yes, I suppose we have, but he'll come round. He's very tetchy these days – flies off the handle at nothing. I wanted to drive here, you see, but he wouldn't let me. Said he wanted to arrive here in one piece and not end up in hospital! Of all the damned cheek! He offered to teach me to drive . . .'

'But maybe it wasn't such a good idea. It's no use if you're going to fall out about it, Cissie. Why don't you book some lessons with a driving school?'

'I don't think Walter would like it. He's in charge of the money, an' I haven't got me own now I'm not working, only what he gives me. I might not bother now till after the baby arrives. I'll be too fat to get behind the wheel, any road.'

'And afterwards you'll be too busy,' said Val. 'Look . . . Janice and Phil are over there. You haven't seen Janice's ring yet, have you? I think there may be a wedding quite soon.'

Before long everyone had served themselves with food and little groups were forming and reforming inside the house and on the patio and garden. A few had wandered down to the summer house and all their guests seemed to be happy and relaxed.

Sam had placed the record player near the French windows so that the sound could be heard inside and out. He put on a long-playing record of the songs from *My Fair Lady* as background music. He was in charge of this while Val stood at the table dishing out the desserts: the trifle, lemon meringue pie and the strawberries and ice cream. There was plenty to go round, although some opted for a little bit of everything rather than one choice.

The only things that would need washing up were the pudding bowls which she stacked together to deal with later. The paper plates were a godsend, easily disposable. Sam found her busy in the kitchen.

'Come along, darling,' he said. 'Don't bother with all that now. Come and join in the fun.'

'I'll just put these remnants in the fridge,' she replied. 'There's enough left for a pudding for us tomorrow. It's going well, isn't it, Sam? I'm so pleased!'

Seven

As the evening drew on the party became livelier and noisier. Many of the guests, enlivened by a drink or two and by the energetic pop music from the record player, were rocking and rolling on the patio and lawn as well as inside the house.

They jigged around happily and unrestrainedly to the strains of Elvis Presley's 'Hound Dog' and 'All Shook Up'. And when they heard Bill Haley's 'Rock around the Clock', everyone was on their feet.

'I hope we're not disturbing the neighbours,' said Val to Sam, trying to make herself heard above the noise. 'We don't want any complaints.'

'I think Mr and Mrs Coates are deaf,' he replied. 'Anyway, they're a nice old couple and I don't suppose they'll mind for once. It isn't as if we have a party every night.'

And the neighbours on the other side, a married couple a few years older than Sam and Val, Tim and Maureen, had been invited and were joining in the fun.

Val glanced at her watch. 'Gosh! It's ten o'clock already. How time flies . . .'

'When you're enjoying yourself,' added Sam.

The record came to an end and he put on Guy Mitchell's

'Singing the Blues'. 'Come on, love,' he said. 'Let's join the merry throng. The night's still young.'

The daylight was fading fast, though. Soon it would be too dark to remain outside and too cold as well, for a chilly little wind was getting up. The light from the French windows cast its glow across the patio and the upper part of the lawn.

Not everyone was dancing now. Here and there people who had not previously met were chatting and getting to know each another, which was just what Val and Sam had hoped would happen. Even Jonathan had relaxed sufficiently to chat to the office girls, particularly to Pauline, who would be leaving soon. They had planned a little office party for her on her last day, unknown to Pauline, and Val hoped he wouldn't let the cat out of the bag. She had worked at Walker's for six years and was a popular member of the staff.

Val noticed that Walter was sitting in a corner of the room chatting to Rita, the new office girl. She was smiling at him and looking more animated than she usually did. As for Walter, he was obviously listening with interest to what she was saying. There had been a big change in Walter recently. Since his marriage to Cissie he had become more approachable, despite his promotion at work. Val had feared that it might make him more aloof than ever but it seemed to have had the opposite effect. Val had never really liked him when he and Cissie were going out together, thinking that he was not suitable for her carefree and rather scatter-brained friend. But it had seemed at first that their marriage was a happy one, especially so after baby Paul arrived. Now, though, there were signs of strain between them. Val guessed that Cissie would be to blame, though, just as much, if not more than Walter. She hoped that their present ill feeling towards each other would soon come to an end.

After a few moments' pause from the music while people helped themselves to a drink or re-grouped, moving to talk to someone else, Sam put on an Elvis record and there was a complete change of mood. 'Love me tender, love me true,' he sang, and Val saw Cissie watching her husband with a grim expression on her face. Couples were starting to dance together with a partner now, holding one another close instead of jigging around energetically.

'Come along, Val,' said Sam, putting an arm round her. 'This is one of our favourites.'

She noticed Cissie walking purposefully across the room to where Walter was engrossed in conversation with Rita. She did not hear what was said but she hoped there would be no trouble. Cissie could be a little hell cat when roused.

'Excuse me, love,' said Cissie, looking pointedly at the girl sitting with Walter. 'I'd like to dance with my husband. Come along, Walter.'

He looked at her with barely concealed annoyance. 'Hold on a minute, Cissie. I was just talking to Rita. She's the new office girl replacing Pauline and we're getting to know one another.'

'So I see,' said Cissie, not smiling. 'I don't think I've had the pleasure. Hello . . . Rita.'

The girl looked a little nonplussed as she timidly replied, 'Hello.'

'This is my wife, Cissie,' said Walter. 'Cissie, this is Rita Johnson. Like I said, she works in the office. I've noticed her around but we've never actually met before.'

'Well, you have now,' said Cissie. She was very aware of the angry glint in her husband's eyes and she decided that she must try to be a little bit friendly although she was boiling up inside. She and Walter had scarcely spoken all evening but she had the sense to know that it was her fault as much as his, and she did not want to cause a rumpus in her friend's house.

'So are you enjoying working at Walker's?' she asked without much enthusiasm as she perched on the chair opposite to Rita.

'Oh, yes, I'm really loving it,' Rita replied. 'The girls are ever so friendly and they've made me really welcome. And it was so nice of Val to invite me to come tonight. The others have got husbands or boyfriends but I haven't. Still, they insisted I should come and I've really enjoyed it. Val's been ever so kind.'

'Yes, I know,' said Cissie. 'She would be. She's my best friend. She was my bridesmaid and I was hers. We've known one another for ages.'

'Yes, I've heard her mention you,' said Rita, regarding Cissie a little uncertainly. 'You used to work at Walker's, didn't you?'

'Yes; I worked in the burling and mending room, correcting the mistakes that the weavers had made. I started as a weaver, mind, but then I got promoted.'

'Oh, I see. I should think it's quite an important job, isn't it?' said Rita, still eyeing Cissie nervously.

'You have to know what you're doing,' said Cissie in a flat voice. 'Anyway, it's been nice meeting you, Rita.' Cissie knew that her tone did not exactly match her words. 'Come on, Walter. Are we going to have this dance or not?'

'Yes . . . Excuse me, Rita,' he said, standing up. 'I've enjoyed talking to you. No doubt I will see you around.'

He took hold of Cissie's arm, leading her, but not very gently, across the room. She knew he was dancing with her because he had no choice. Like her, he wouldn't want to cause a scene. She was beginning to feel a tiny bit ashamed but she would not admit it.

'Did you need to behave like that?' he hissed when they were out of Rita's hearing. 'That poor girl! I'm sure she was mortified. We were only talking. What on earth were you thinking of, carrying on like that?'

'Like what? I was perfectly polite to her. You've left me on my own all night, talking to your new cronies and then to her.'

'Don't tell me you're jealous?'

'Of course I'm not jealous! Why would I be jealous of a timid little mouse like her?'

'I know she's shy; that's why I went to talk to her, because I knew she'd joined the staff at Walker's.'

'Part of your new job, I suppose, now that you're almost one of the bosses?'

'Don't be like that, Cissie. You know I'm earning more money now. You don't need to be peevish.'

'Don't you call me peevish! I'm stuck at home all day while you're out meeting all sorts of new people.'

'I thought you liked being at home? You said you couldn't wait to finish work.'

'Yes . . . well, maybe I did. But I get fed up sometimes.' Cissie knew that what Walter said was true. She had wanted to stay at home, and when she had got over the early problems with Paul she had been very happy being a wife and mother. She knew she was being difficult. It had made her see red, though, watching Walter chatting to that silly girl and ignoring her, the mother of his children.

'Oh, come on, Cissie,' he said. 'Don't be ridiculous. Rita's only eighteen, just a kid really. But she's quite interesting to talk to, once she overcomes her shyness. She likes reading – books, I mean – listening to music . . .'

'Well, bully for her then!' said Cissie, who never read anything except the latest magazine.

'And she's a keen cyclist, would you believe?'

'No, I wouldn't, actually. So I suppose you've told her about your cycling club?'

'As matter of fact, I did. She's only recently moved to the area with her family and she didn't know anything about it.'

'But she does now . . .'

'Yes, she said she might come along . . . Oh, Cissie, this is stupid! You know that I love you. I'm sorry we argued about your driving an' all that. Let's forget about it, eh?' He held her close and she felt herself relenting.

'All right then,' she said in a small voice. 'I love you too, Walter. We are happy, aren't we?'

'Of course we are. I've never been happier.' The record had come to an end and there was a momentary lull. 'Come on; let's go and sit down and have another drink. You'd better stick to fruit juice and I'll do the same. I've got to drive home.'

'Cissie and Walter seem to be OK again now,' said Val, watching them walking hand in hand out to a secluded corner of the patio. It was a little colder out there now and the girls had put on white or pastel-coloured cardigans over their summer dresses.

'Well, you know Cissie,' replied Sam. 'She blows hot and cold. They'll get over it, whatever it was, and she's sure to be a bit temperamental in her condition. I'll put some more records on.'

There was an automatic change, if required, to the record player, and very soon Pat Boone was singing 'April Love', followed by Doris Day's 'Que Sera, Sera'.

'Whatever will be, will be,' they all sang happily. Everyone had come inside now but there was no sign that anybody wanted to leave. And when the Everly Brothers sang 'Wake up, little Susie' they nearly all got to their feet again.

The next-door neighbours, Tim and Maureen, were the first to leave as they had to relieve their babysitter. Cissie and Walter followed for the same reason, then Pauline and her husband, as she was feeling tired.

'One last record then, folks,' said Sam. 'I hope you've all enjoyed yourselves. It seems as though you have. We're so pleased you were able to come. For Val and I it will be one of those times we'll always remember.'

'Memories are made of this . . .' sang Dean Martin as Val and Sam danced closely together.

'I love you, darling,' he whispered. 'I hope you know how much.'

'I think I do,' she replied.

When all the guests had gone they looked round at the debris; the empty glasses and bottles, the full ashtrays and the chairs left higgledy-piggledy all over the room and the patio.

'It's not really all that bad,' said Sam. 'They were a very well-behaved crowd.'

'And we're here to help,' said Phil. 'Let's bring all the chairs in, Sam.'

'And we'll put the glasses and bottles in the kitchen,' said Val, 'then I suggest we leave it all till morning. Now, who's for a cup of tea before we turn in?'

They all agreed that was a good idea.

'It's been a lovely evening,' said Janice. 'We've enjoyed it, haven't we, Phil?'

'We certainly have, and it's a relief that I don't have to drive back,' added Phil. 'Janice is staying till Monday so she won't have to go straight back to Blackpool.'

'My course has finished now,' said Janice, 'but I shall have to start looking for a temporary job. I hope to get a position as an assistant chef at one of the big hotels. A girl from the course told me of one or two possibilities.'

'So, when are you two getting married?' asked Sam.

The engaged couple looked at one another and smiled. 'As soon as possible,' said Phil.

'But we have to be practical,' added Janice. 'Phil is looking for a business, with living accommodation if possible, for us to run together; somewhere in Yorkshire – not too far from Ilkley, so he'll do the searching and I'll get a job and try to save a bit of money. It will probably be next spring, I should imagine, before we can get married.'

'Yes, unfortunately,' said Phil. 'Janice feels that she has to ease her way rather gently. Her kid brother's being a bit difficult, isn't he, love?'

'Yes, he was at first when he realized we wouldn't be living in Blackpool once we're married. He seemed to imagine we'd be running a big hotel, though I don't know how he got that idea. But he's not mentioned it lately, so I'm letting things take their course. Time enough to tell him when we've found somewhere and fixed a date. Dad's OK, though; he's quite resigned to it.'

'You were saying you thought he might have a lady friend?' said Val.

'Yes . . . They all went on a day trip together to the Lake District – the members of the club. And he mentioned someone called Norma. He's dropped her name into the conversation once or twice, sort of casual, like. He might be dropping a gentle hint but I don't think Ian's noticed.'

'Ian will have to get used to the situation,' said Phil. 'To us getting married and to whatever Janice's dad decides to do. I know he's at a difficult age, but he's not a child and these things happen. Life has to go on and Alec's still quite young.' He noticed Val stifling a yawn. 'We're keeping you up, aren't we? And you've had a tiring day. I'll go and sort my bed out, shall I, Sam?'

'Yes; I'll come with you.' The two men went into the lounge, a much smaller room than the living-cum-dining room at the back of the house. There was a long three-seater settee that pulled down to make a bed, and Val had placed pillows, sheets and blankets in readiness.

'I'll be fine here,' said Phil. 'It looks very comfy and I never have much trouble sleeping anywhere.'

'Sorry the bathroom's upstairs,' said Sam. 'We haven't any facilities down here, I'm afraid. But you'll have already found the bathroom. And Janice is in the back room,' he added in a casual way with no hint of a smile. 'Goodnight then, Phil. See you in the morning.'

Val and Janice were at the foot of the stairs. Phil put an arm round Janice and kissed her gently on the lips. 'Goodnight, love,' he said. 'See you tomorrow . . . well . . . later today, I mean; it's already tomorrow, isn't it?' It was almost one o'clock.

Janice laughed. 'Yes, so it is . . . Goodnight then, Phil.'

He waited until everything was quiet, until the sound of the toilet flushing and the running taps had ceased, then he quietly crept up the stairs. The door of Sam and Val's bedroom was closed but Janice's was a little ajar.

'May I come in?' he whispered, tiptoeing across the room. 'You're not asleep, are you?'

'No . . . I'm not asleep . . .'

He sat down on the bed. 'Were you expecting me?'

'I'm not sure,' she replied. 'We didn't talk about it, did we?'

'No, but I think you feel as I do, don't you, darling? We've never really been on our own before. And I know you wouldn't like . . . well, the back seat of a car, would you? I think more of you than that.'

She nodded and smiled a little unsurely. The faint light through the curtains shone on her tousled fair hair and pale face. She looked so vulnerable and he loved her so very much.

'You're sure about this, aren't you?' he asked.

'Yes . . . but I want everything to be all right. I don't want to . . . well, to be like Cissie and Walter, getting married all in a rush. My dad would be so disappointed in me.'

'It's OK. Actually, I've taken care of that.'

'You mean . . .?'

'Yes; I'm prepared. Nothing will go wrong.'

You were assuming, then, that I would . . .?'

'I hoped so . . . Oh, Janice, love, don't look like that!'

At that moment she looked crestfallen and unsure of herself.

'I'm not taking you for granted, really I'm not. We love each other, don't we?'

'Of course we do . . .'

'Well, that's all right then, isn't it . . .?'

She smiled and nodded and he drew her into his arms.

Their lovemaking was gentle and tender at first, becoming more urgent and passionate as they adjusted to one another. It was the first time for Janice, so she was prepared for a certain discomfort, but it was surpassed by the pleasure and the delight she felt that they were now complete as a couple.

She guessed that Phil might not be quite as inexperienced as she was but she made no comment. She didn't really know, and he was sure to have known other girls before herself. He had served his time in the RAF, a young man away from home.

'Are you OK?' he asked as he held her close to him.

'Yes, of course . . .' She was not sure what else to say. Did he intend to stay all night? she wondered.

He answered her unspoken question. 'I'll stay a little while then I'd better get back to my own bed. Not that I feel guilty, and Val and Sam wouldn't say anything.' He chuckled. 'It's probably what they were expecting! But I think it would be best – save any embarrassment all round.'

'It will probably be our only chance for a while,' said Janice. 'There won't be any opportunity, will there?'

'That's why I want us to get married as soon as possible,' said Phil. 'But don't worry about it; we're a properly engaged couple now.'

Janice smiled contentedly. 'So we are . . . I think you'd better go now, Phil, straight away. We might both fall asleep.' She glanced at her little alarm clock which she always took away with her. 'Gosh! It's turned two o'clock; there's not much of the night left.'

'Yes, you're right,' said Phil. 'Goodnight, love. Sleep well; see you in the morning.' He kissed her gently then tiptoed from the room.

Janice's head was in a whirl. She felt excited yet a tiny bit guilty, wondering what her mother would have thought about it and her father. She guessed she might feel self-conscious, too, wondering if people would be able to tell there was something different about her. In a little while, though, her mind stilled and she fell asleep.

Val and Sam had also been awake. Val had scarcely been able to keep her eyes open after the busy day and the lovely evening which had fulfilled all her expectations. The guests had all gone home saying how much they had enjoyed it. But she quickly came to life when Sam put his arms around her.

Their lovemaking was urgent as well as tender that night. They both felt the longing for each other and the sense of fulfilment that followed. Val reflected that surely this time it would result in what she so badly wanted. There was only a week or so to wait, then she would know if it was, at least, a possibility.

They heard muffled footsteps on the landing, then the creak of the third step from the top – it always did that – as Phil made his way back downstairs, or so they guessed.

Sam laughed quietly. 'I might have known, and who can blame them? They're a great couple, aren't they? I hope everything works out well for them and that they'll be as happy as we are.'

'Yes; it would be the first time for Janice,' whispered Val. 'She told me, in confidence, that there's never been the opportunity. She seemed rather concerned about it. I hope she's OK . . .'

'Of course she'll be OK. Why shouldn't she be? I'm sure Phil's an understanding sort of chap. Anyway, it's none of our business, is it? Now, you get off to sleep. You were fit to drop when you came upstairs; but then . . . well, you know . . .'

'I've no regrets,' said Val with a laugh. 'Night night, Sam. It's been a lovely evening, hasn't it?'

'Terrific!' He kissed her then snuggled down beneath the bedclothes.

As it was Sunday morning and, because they had visitors, Val decided to make a special cooked breakfast. First of all, though, she took a cup of tea to Janice in the upstairs bedroom and Sam did the same for Phil in the lounge.

'Did you sleep well?' asked Val, a rhetorical question but it was what one always asked.

'Oh, yes, thank you, very well,' replied Janice. 'It's a very comfy bed.' There was a slight flush to her cheeks and her voice sounded a little breathless.

'Good,' said Val with a smile. 'Breakfast in about half an hour. I won't do the eggs until we're all ready.'

'Lovely! You're spoiling us.'

'Not at all. It's fun having guests to stay. Like I said, you're the first ones to stay overnight.'

Sam asked the same question of Phil.

'Yes, I slept like a log,' Phil replied, 'eventually . . .' He raised his eyebrows, grinning at Sam.

Sam winked at him. 'Jolly good. Val's cooking breakfast, so just appear when you're ready.'

They ate in the dining room rather than the kitchen, which was where Sam and Val usually had breakfast. They had done a quick tidy up and would get everything back to normal when their guests had left.

'I hope the breakfast's OK for you two culinary experts,' said Val. 'I've tried not to make a mess of the eggs. I think fried eggs are one of the hardest things to do. I usually break the yolk then it runs all over the place.'

There was grilled bacon, sausages and tinned mushrooms as well as the eggs, and the empty plates were all that Val needed to prove that her meal was a success.

'You've done us proud,' said Phil. 'I couldn't have done any better. Fried eggs are the very devil to cook.'

'So you're off on holiday soon, then?' said Janice. 'Val has been telling me about your trip to Paris. How exciting!'

'Yes, we're off to "Gay Paree",' said Sam. 'We had only a few days' honeymoon because we were anxious to get the house in order, so I promised Val that we'd go further afield later in the year.'

'The mill closes down for the second week in August,' said Val. 'You remember; that was when we all met, two years ago.'

'And what a lot has happened since then,' said Janice. 'I'm sure you must be excited about going abroad, Val. Are you flying?'

'Yes, from Manchester,' replied Val. 'I get colly-wobbles when I think about it but Sam assures me that you're safer up in the air than you are in a car. I wish I could believe him!'

'You'll be fine, honestly,' said Sam. 'I promise you, and I never break my promises, do I?'

'My first flight and my first time abroad,' said Val.

'It would be for me as well,' added Janice. 'I've never been out of England, not even to Scotland. Phil's been to Jersey with his parents; I don't know whether that counts as abroad but my parents were never so adventurous. Anyway, Mum was always busy with the hotel.'

'Never fear, our turn will come,' said Phil. 'I shall make sure, when we have our own business, that we have our holidays as well. All work and no play . . . you know what they say.'

Janice smiled at him. 'You're looking a long way ahead.'

'Not all that far, I hope. This time next year we might well be up and running. And well and truly married by then, of course.'

'Where will the wedding take place?' asked Val. 'Will it be in Blackpool?'

'We haven't really discussed it,' said Janice. 'I suppose it should be in my own parish. But Phil lives over here, and so do some of our friends. But we'll let you know and hope you'll be there with us.'

'Of course we will,' said Val. 'We'll send you a card from Paris . . . It's been really good seeing you again this weekend.'

'And we'd better get off before long,' said Phil, 'and leave you two to settle down again. Work tomorrow, I suppose?'

'Yes, work as usual,' said Val. But not for much longer, I hope, she thought to herself. It was by no means easy running a home and doing a full-time office job. She seldom took advantage of her position as wife of one of the bosses as she might have done. She had hardly ever taken any time off in case it should be thought that she was not pulling her weight.

Janice started to clear the pots from the table but Val stopped her. 'No, you get yourself ready. Sam and I will wash up and we've got all day to clear away. Off you go and make the most of your time together.'

There were handshakes and hugs and kisses again when Janice and Phil were ready to depart.

'See you soon . . . Take care now . . . Enjoy your holiday . . .'

Janice waved until they turned the corner of the avenue and were out of sight. She gave a sigh of contentment. 'I've really enjoyed it. We've had a lovely time, haven't we, Phil?'

'I'll say we have!' he replied with a meaningful smile.

'Oh, Phil; I didn't mean just that!' Janice knew she was blushing. 'Do you think your parents will know?' she asked. 'Will they be able to tell that we've . . . I feel . . . different, somehow.'

Phil burst out laughing. 'No, you silly goose! Of course they won't know, not unless we tell them and we won't do that. Just act normal and try not to get all confused. Anyway, I think that parents are a good deal more perceptive than we give them credit for and more understanding as well. They were young themselves once, you know.'

'Let's not go straight back. My dad's given me the whole weekend off. We'll have some lunch at a pub, then we could have a stroll on Ilkley Moor, just as though we're visitors . . .'

Eight

Val could feel the butterflies dancing around in her tummy as she and Sam crossed the tarmac to board the aeroplane that was awaiting them for their journey to Paris. This was despite the brandy and ginger that Sam had persuaded her to drink in the airport lounge bar.

'There you are,' he said. 'That will settle your nerves, although there's nothing to worry about. You'll enjoy it once we've taken off.'

Jonathan had driven them to the airport and she had tried to hide her anxiety from him. She felt, at times, that he still looked on her as one of the hoi polloi, unused to such things as foreign travel. It was good of him, though, to offer to take them to Manchester before returning home to begin his own holiday, touring in Scotland with Thelma and little Rosemary.

The plane did not look as big as she had imagined, neither from the outside nor inside the cabin. A smiling air hostess in a neat blue uniform with a jaunty little cap greeted them cheerfully at the top of the steps, pointing them to their seats.

'You sit by the window,' said Sam, 'then you'll have a good view.'

Val didn't think she would dare to look out of the small window. It all felt rather claustrophobic with the seats crowded closely together.

'OK now?' asked Sam when they had stowed their hand luggage in the rack above their heads and sat down.

'Yes, fine, thanks,' she replied. She realized she was being silly and that there was nothing to fear. Look on it as an adventure, she told herself; the start of what promised to be an exciting week.

She was hugging a little secret to herself and she tried to think about that instead of dwelling on her fear of flying. She was almost sure that their ardent lovemaking following the house-warming party had resulted in what she so badly wanted. She was well over a week late now, something that very rarely happened. She hadn't said anything to Sam, though. It was too soon, and the 'time of the month' was not something that she talked about, not even to her husband. She had been brought up to believe that it was a private matter, not to be discussed openly.

The air hostess stood at the front of the plane, telling them about emergency exits and oxygen supplies. 'Just routine,' said Sam, taking hold of her hand. Then they were told to fasten their seatbelts ready for take-off.

The aeroplane started to taxi along the runway, then there was a loud whirring sound as the propellers turned and the plane increased its speed. It went faster and faster until they were airborne. Val held on tightly to Sam's hand then relaxed as the plane steadied on to a straight course. She felt her ears pop and she sucked hard at the boiled sweet that the air hostess had given them all. Sam told her it was to help to relieve the pressure.

She began to breathe more easily and even dared to peep out of the window. She could see the wing of the plane stretching out to the side of them, and beyond that the blue of the sky above the clouds. Through a break in the cloud she could see, far below, streets of houses and patches of grass, looking like a miniature toy village. Then, in just a few minutes, they were flying over the sea, crossing the English Channel.

Val was surprised that the journey was so short. No sooner, it seemed, had they seen the sea far below them than they were flying over the rooftops of northern France. It was just over an hour after take-off that the aeroplane made its descent. Seatbelts were fastened again for the landing. Once again Val gritted her teeth and held tightly to Sam's hand. She was aware of the change in air pressure as her ears popped, then there were a few minor bumps as the plane touched down on the runway.

The air hostess said she hoped they had enjoyed the flight and that she would see them again. They made their way across the tarmac to the airport buildings. If Val had found Manchester Airport confusing, this one was much more so – crowded and noisy with voices chattering in a language she did not understand. The signs, too, meant nothing to her. She did not have even a smattering of schoolgirl French like some of her contemporaries who had gone to a different school.

Sam, though, a grammar school lad, understood the language well enough to get by. He guided her through passport control and the reclaiming of their luggage, then out on to the fore-court where, after a short wait, they boarded a taxi.

Sam had visited Paris once before with his parents and brother. He had decided to book at the same little pension in Montmartre. It had been clean and comfortable and in an ideal location; he hoped it would not have changed.

It was all bewildering but so thrilling and different from anything that Val had seen before. They began a steep climb up the cobbled streets of the district that Sam told her was Montmartre. She had seen pictures of the Sacré-Coeur and there it was in front of them, the dome of the great church outlined against the blue of the summer sky, towering over the rooftops.

Sam paid the taxi driver then dealt with the formalities at the reception desk in the small foyer. The proprietor helped them carry their cases to the lift, an antiquated cage-like structure which took them past several floors, almost to the top of the building.

'I asked for a room on the fourth floor,' said Sam as he

humped the heavy cases into the room, 'and this is why. Come and look, Val.'

She gave a gasp as she gazed through the window at the vista of Paris stretching away into the distance. 'Look; there's the Eiffel Tower!' she cried in delight.

Sam pointed out a few other places that he knew: the domes of the Grand Palace, the Pantheon and Les Invalides, although his knowledge of the city was not extensive. They were looking forward to exploring it together.

There was a washbasin in the room but the bathroom and toilet were along the corridor. It was late afternoon by now, and after unpacking the cases and a quick wash and tidy up they set off to find their way around. Sam had bought a comprehensive map and he told her that the best way to see Paris was on foot with the occasional journey on the Metro.

They wandered along the cobbled streets of Montmartre, watching the artists at work. The hotel provided only bed and breakfast so they were free to dine wherever they wished in the evening. That night they dined early, as they were both hungry, at a little bistro where paintings by local artists hung on the walls. They dined by candlelight – the room was dark in contrast to the brightness of the street – on tender chunks of beef in a rich wine sauce with tomatoes, onions and peppers, followed by a dessert of chocolate profiteroles. They enjoyed half a litre of wine, with coffee to follow. Val had never enjoyed a meal quite so much; it was a memorable start to their holiday and the first of several more enjoyable meals.

They retired early to bed on the high mattress covered with a lightweight duvet, Val's first experience of the continental style of bedclothes. She snuggled down contentedly after their tender lovemaking, feeling that she must be the happiest girl in the world.

Breakfast was served in the downstairs dining room, a rather bare, functional room where several more guests were already seated. The continental-style meal, however, was delicious. Freshly baked rolls with creamy, unsalted butter – the sort one rarely tasted at home – and homemade black cherry jam. Fragrant dark coffee was served in thick white cups with either milk or cream as desired.

Val was thrilled with all the places they visited during their five-day holiday. They rode on the metro to the Place de la Concorde then walked the length of the Champs-Élysées to the Arc de Triomphe. She was delighted by the elegant shops on the Rue de Rivoli, where Sam bought her her first bottle of Chanel perfume, and the lovely Tuileries Gardens where they stopped a while to rest their aching feet.

They visited the Louvre – one just had to see the *Mona Lisa* – and took a boat trip along the River Seine. They ascended the Eiffel Tower, though not to the very top, for the most spectacular view of the city with the Sacré-Coeur in the far distance, near to their own hotel. They explored the Latin Quarter, then the peaceful Île de la Cité, and admired the magnificent stained-glass windows of Notre Dame.

On their last evening they dined again at the little bistro in Montmartre where they sampled the famous French dish *pot de feu*, a delicious concoction of meat and vegetables; a hearty meal once eaten by poor people but now a speciality dish.

No visit to Paris would be complete without a visit to one of their famous stage shows. Sam decided to forgo the pleasures of the Folies Bergère or the Moulin Rouge, concerned about what Val's reaction might be. He chose a small theatre close to their hotel where they were entertained for two hours by a dazzling spectacular of girls, scantily clad in satin and sequins, with plumed headdresses; conjurors and acrobats; ballet dancers and folk groups. The fantastic costumes, changes of scenery and lighting effects had the audience gasping in wonder. The French certainly knew how to put on a show.

The time for leaving Paris seemed to come very quickly. Val knew she would always remember her first trip abroad but it was really rather nice to be going home.

'It's been great, hasn't it, darling?' said Sam as they settled in their seats for the return journey.

'Wonderful!' she replied.

'And you're not nervous this time?'

'No,' she said, smiling happily. 'I'm a seasoned traveller now.'

She was still hugging the same little secret to herself. It

had been more than two weeks and there was still no sign of anything to dash her hopes. She was really starting to think that she might be pregnant, but it might be better to be absolutely sure before she said anything to Sam.

By the beginning of September she was almost certain. Why else would she have missed two periods? She did not feel sick, though. She had heard a great deal about the dreaded morning sickness but it did not seem to be happening to her. But her breasts felt a little tender and she knew it was time to visit the doctor and make absolutely sure.

Sam was delighted at her news. 'Clever girl!' he said. 'That's wonderful.'

'I didn't do it all on my own,' she reminded him. 'I think the pair of us have been rather clever.'

She arranged to see their family doctor the following Monday morning. She told a white lie to the girls in the office, saying that she had a dental appointment, but she hoped that she would soon be able to share her good news with them.

She woke very early on the Monday morning, aware of a familiar dragging pain in her abdomen, the sort of pain she most certainly did not want to feel right now. She crept out of bed, quietly so as not to disturb Sam, and went to the bathroom. And there her fears were confirmed. She was bleeding.

Tears filled her eyes as she sat there. The loss of blood was quite severe and she was feeling quite poorly as well as miserable. She made herself comfortable, trying to hold back the tears as she returned to the bedroom.

Sam was awake and sitting up in bed. She burst into tears, unable to contain them any longer. 'Sam, I'm not . . .' she cried. 'I'm not pregnant. I'm so disappointed and I don't feel well at all.'

'Oh, my poor love!' He put his arms around her. 'I'm so sorry, but never mind. There's plenty of time. How long have we been married? Only five months. That's no time at all.'

'But I was so sure, Sam . . .'

'Well, it wasn't to be, was it? You get back into bed and I'll go and make us a nice cup of tea.'

She nodded glumly. 'And can you bring me some Anadins, please, Sam? This pain is quite severe.'

The tablets eased the pain but she was unable to get over the fear at the back of her mind that there might be something wrong with her. She knew, deep down, that she was probably being silly. As Sam had reminded her, they had been married only a short while. She had never been a hypochondriac and had always tried to make light of any aches and pains, but she now decided to keep her appointment with the doctor. Sam drove her there on his way to work, although he could not understand why she needed to go.

'Cheer up, darling,' he said, kissing her as she got out of the car. 'Don't come in to work today, I'll tell them that you're not well. I hope you're feeling better by the time I get home.'

Dr Spencer had been the Walker family's doctor for many years. He did all he could to set Val's mind at rest.

'I'm sure you have nothing to worry about, my dear,' he said. He had taken her blood pressure and her pulse rate. 'You are a fit and healthy young woman. What has just happened . . . it may have been a very premature abortion; nature's way of clearing the womb of something that, maybe, was not quite right. There is no reason why you should not conceive. Just relax and try not to worry about it – that only makes things worse. It will happen in time, my dear. I'll give you some tablets for the pain, and you should take a couple of days off work. Goodbye for now, Valerie . . .'

She took a bus back home after collecting her prescription at the chemist's. She was feeling much better by the afternoon and decided to make a special meal for Sam that evening; his favourite, steak and chips. She supposed she might have been something of a misery that morning and knew she must snap out of it.

Cissie was sailing through her pregnancy with no problems. She looked positively radiant, with a rosy glow to her cheeks and a spring in her step despite her considerable bulk. She made no secret of the fact that they would both like a daughter this time. Val hoped that she would get her wish.

What did it matter, though? thought Val, so long as the

child was healthy. She was still doomed to disappointment as summer came to an end, followed by the shorter days and darker nights of autumn. A dismal time of year, or so it seemed to Val. Some people loved autumn: the vibrant colours of the foliage, the mistiness in the air and the looking ahead to the Christmas season. But Val thought it was a dreary time; she knew, though, that it seemed so because the months were passing and there was still no sign of what she so badly wanted. October, November then into December. Val sensed a certain constraint in their relationship, although neither of them put the feeling into words. She feared that their lovemaking had lost some of its former joy and spontaneity, and she knew that this must be largely her own fault. She was so anxious to conceive that it sometimes felt as though they were just going through a routine.

Early in December she received a letter from Janice – the first one for several weeks – together with an invitation to the wedding to be held in Blackpool on 12 April. Janice was now working as an assistant chef at one of the large hotels on the north promenade and still living at home with her father and Ian. Phil was still looking for a suitable business venture but they had decided they could not go on waiting indefinitely before planning their wedding. Hence the springtime marriage, after which Janice would live with Phil and his parents until they found a place of their own.

'Something for us to look forward to,' said Sam. 'We can have a weekend in Blackpool. That will cheer us both up . . . I do understand how you feel, darling, but I keep trying to convince you that we have plenty of time and there's nothing to worry about. I want to start a family as much as you do, but why the rush? We're very happy, aren't we? Just the two of us?'

Val nodded. 'Yes, of course we are . . .' But seeing Cissie with little Paul and Thelma with Rosemary convinced her that a child would make their marriage complete.

Cissie gave birth to a baby girl on Christmas Day, and by then Val was once again keeping her fingers crossed. She was ten days overdue.

Nine

Janice had found employment quite soon after finishing her catering course. There were hundreds of hotels along the promenade, and many more, some still known as boarding houses, in the streets just a little way inland, particularly in the area near the tower. Many of them were looking for staff.

Streets such as Adelaide Street and Albert Road were part of the boarding house hinterland near to Central Station, where many of the same visitors came back year after year. If you should walk along these streets, and many similar ones, in the late afternoon, you would see, in every window, the tables laid, almost identically, ready for 'high tea'. A three-tiered cake stand held bread and butter, maybe scones, and a selection of 'fancies' – cream cakes, iced buns, almond slices, jam tarts . . . There would also be a large cruet set, a bottle of salad cream and maybe tomato or HP sauce, depending on what the meal consisted of that teatime.

Many boarding houses and smaller hotels still served three meals a day: cooked breakfast, midday dinner – the main meal of the day – and 'high tea', which might be salad and boiled ham or fish and chips.

Many of the larger hotels, however, now provided bed and breakfast and an evening meal, leaving the visitors free for the whole of the day and also giving staff more time to prepare the three-course evening meal.

It was at one of these larger hotels that Janice was working throughout the summer and the autumn of 1957. It was not as prestigious or as well known as the Imperial, the Metropole or the Savoy hotels. It was a family concern which had passed through three generations and Janice loved the friendly atmosphere that pervaded the place. The staff were happy, working in congenial surroundings, and so the guests were happy too, enjoying a holiday which was almost a home from home but with that touch of luxury that one did not get in the smaller establishments. To Janice it felt almost like working back at home in her mother's hotel, the Florabunda. Lilian Butler had always created a happy atmosphere, but here at Summerlands it was slightly more splendid.

The proprietors were Mr and Mrs Summers. George Summers was the chef and his wife, Evie, was in charge of the management and accounts. They also employed an assistant chef – a man in his mid-twenties – and they were pleased to employ Janice as an additional chef to bring new ideas for pastries and puddings, although she had explained that she might not be there for very long. Mr Summers seemed keen to encourage her in her ambition to become more proficient in her particular skill. During the summer months they would be serving fancy gateaux and pastries, and he was looking to Janice to expand this side of their cuisine. And she, of course, was delighted to be working at something she really enjoyed, and this time being paid to do so.

The hotel was on the promenade close to the North Pier, and she cycled there each morning or afternoon, depending on which shift she was working – early morning to mid-afternoon or afternoon till ten thirty at night. Her work was flexible; she helped to cook the breakfasts, occasionally served in the small bar area and assisted with the preparation and serving of the suppertime drinks for those guests who enjoyed the comfort of the lounge in the evening.

The only snag to her otherwise ideal working life was that she hardly ever saw Phil. He had been to Blackpool a few times as he could more easily be spared from his work at the Coach and Horses. His father knew he was only marking time there anyway. Janice had only managed one weekend in Yorkshire at a time when Summerlands was relatively quiet.

Phil was still looking for a suitable business but so far had found nothing that would suit their requirements.

'We can't go on waiting for ever, love,' he said as they strolled along the promenade one night in October. Janice had been on an early shift and they were taking advantage of her free time to take a look at the illuminations, which stretched from Squire's Gate in the south of town up to Bispham at the north end, where there was a spectacular display of tableaux on the cliffs.

'No, we can't,' agreed Janice. 'We said we would arrange our wedding when we had found somewhere to live and work, but it's taking too long.'

'Far too long,' said Phil, drawing her close to him and kissing her. 'We never have the chance to be really alone, do we? Not like when we went to Val and Sam's party . . .'

Janice smiled to herself. That had been wonderful, but since then there had not been an opportunity for them to be together in that way. They felt restricted by the presence of parents, even though they were engaged and waiting to be married.

'There's no sense in waiting any longer,' Phil went on. 'We could get married now . . . well, as soon as we can arrange it. And then you could come and live at our place, just for the time being. We could both look for somewhere, together.'

'Yes, I think we should,' said Janice. 'We must! Or else we could carry on like this for ever. It's all gone very quiet at home. Dad never asks me about our plans, and as for Ian . . . Well, you can see what he's like, can't you?'

'Yes; he's not all that happy about everything, is he?'

'He cheered up, though, when he knew you were coming this weekend. He looks on you as a big brother, you know, and that's the way it should be. But he never asks me when we're getting married. Maybe he thinks that if he doesn't talk about it it will all go away and everything will just carry on the way it is now.'

'Norma won't go away, though, will she?' said Phil. 'That's something that Ian will have to get used to, I'm afraid.'

'I suppose you can't blame him,' said Janice. 'He was quite happy, just him and Dad, and me there, of course, to look after them. I know he still misses Mum but he did seem to be getting more used to her not being there.'

'Let's see; it's about eighteen months since your mum died, isn't it?'

'Yes, thereabouts. I must admit I was rather surprised myself when Dad started talking about this Norma. Just casually at first, then I realized there might be something going on. Dad's still young, though. He's not fifty yet, and I suppose we can't expect him to stay on his own for ever.'

'Do you think he will marry her?'

'I've no idea. He sees her at the club and they go to the cinema occasionally. She's only been to our place once but I think Dad spends quite a bit of time at hers. She lives not far away, just off Whitegate Drive. Anyway, you'll meet her yourself tomorrow. Dad's invited her for Sunday tea, seeing that I'm on early shift. I suppose he thinks there's safety in numbers!'

Janice had met Norma Williams for the first and only time a month ago. Alec had been very guarded about mentioning her coming round that Sunday at first, then he had decided to take the bull by the horns.

'I've invited a friend for tea on Sunday,' he had said to Janice late one night when Ian had gone up to bed. 'Er . . . you know I've got quite friendly with a lady at the club, don't you, love?'

'Yes, Dad,' she'd replied. 'I've heard you mention her. She's called Norma, isn't she?'

'Yes, that's right. She's just a friend, that's all. She's widowed, like I am; about the same age as me. She's very nice and friendly. I think . . . well, I hope you'll like her.'

'That's OK, Dad,' she'd replied, not over-effusively. 'I'm on an early shift so I'll make us a nice tea. I'm making special gateaux for the guests for Saturday so I'll bring some pieces home . . . there's always far too much. We must make a good impression, mustn't we? And there's a tin of roast ham . . .'

'You don't mind, do you, Janice?'

'No, of course not. Why should I? I know you'll always love Mum, won't you?'

Alec's eyes had misted a little. 'Your mother was one in a million. I could never replace her. But I can't be sad for ever, love. Lilian wouldn't have wanted that.'

Janice had nodded. 'I'll leave you to tell Ian.'

It had not gone down too well with Ian. Alec had told his son he had invited a guest for Sunday tea.

'Oh, who is it?' Ian had asked. 'Is it somebody I know?'

'No . . . It's a lady I met at the club. A very nice lady who works in the bar there . . .'

'A barmaid?'

'No, not really. She just helps to serve the drinks. She's a member of the club. A lot of ladies are members as well as men. Some of them come with their husbands but she's on her own, like I am.'

'But you're not on your own, Dad, are you? You've got me and Janice.'

Alec had sighed. 'You know what I mean, Ian. Look . . . she's just somebody I've got friendly with. You invite your friends home, don't you? And so does Janice.'

'OK, then,' Ian had said with a shrug. 'It's all right, I suppose. I'll be playing football on Sunday afternoon, though.'

'Well, don't be late then. Janice will have tea ready for five o'clock.'

Alec had then had a quiet word with Janice. 'I feel there might be trouble with Ian. I don't think he would be rude to Norma – he's never been that sort of a lad – but I sense a feeling of resentment.'

'It's only to be expected, Dad, if you think about it.'

'Yes, maybe so. I'm trying to understand but I don't want Norma to feel uncomfortable. Do you think you could have a word with him?'

'I'll try, Dad,' she'd answered.

Ian had been very non-committal when she'd spoken to him. 'I've told Dad I'm playing football. I don't see why I should stop what I'm doing just because he's invited this woman to tea.'

'I know that, Ian . . . and I agree with you. But don't be late back, will you? And just try to be polite. Dad's had a bad time and he misses Mum just as much as we do.'

'Doesn't seem like it . . .'

'Well, let's just see what she's like, shall we? Dad's a quiet sort of chap and I'm sure he wouldn't make friends with someone who wasn't . . . well, suitable, if you know what I mean.'

Janice had prepared a good meal for that Sunday tea. There was always a tin of roast ham in the cupboard which made a satisfying meal with salad: lettuce, tomatoes grown locally on Marton Moss, cucumber, radishes and hard boiled eggs. Bread and butter, both brown and white, homemade scones which Janice had baked during the little spare time she had and a choice of coffee or strawberry gateau with fresh cream – the same that was being served to the guests at Summerlands. They were using the best lace tablecloth and the china tea service which was only used on special occasions.

Norma Williams had arrived at half past four in her own little Morris car. Janice, busy in the kitchen, heard her father welcome her and take her into the front room – the best room, used to entertain guests at Christmas or on occasions such as this.

After a moment or two Janice had taken off her apron and gone to meet her father's friend. She'd had no idea at all what to expect. When she entered the room her father had stood up, smiling broadly. 'Janice,' he'd said, 'this is Mrs Williams . . . Norma, this is my daughter, Janice.'

The woman had stood up as well. She looked, as her dad had said, very nice and friendly, as far as one could tell from a first glance. She'd held out her hand. 'Hello, Janice. Your dad has told me a lot about you and it's good to meet you . . . at last.' She'd smiled, raising her eyebrows slightly as she spoke the last two words. Janice guessed her father had been shilly-shallying for a while.

'Good to meet you too, Mrs Williams,' she'd replied.

'Oh, that sounds very formal! Please, call me Norma.' She had not seemed at all shy, and she'd squeezed Janice's hand as if to reassure her that everything was OK. She was dark-haired with brown eyes, and Janice was glad that she did not resemble her mother, who had had been fair and blue-eyed. She was slim and possibly a shade taller than Alec. Not beautiful – her features were rather angular – but certainly most attractive and smartly dressed in a dark red silky rayon suit with high-heeled patent leather shoes.

'Er . . . sit down and get to know one another,' Alec had said.

They'd chatted together easily enough. Janice had learnt that Norma worked as a chief assistant in the dress department of RHO Hills, one of the town's leading stores. She was interested in Janice's choice of career and the plans that she and Phil had for the future.

'So you'll be getting married soon?' she'd enquired.

'We're not sure. It all depends . . .' Janice had stopped talking as Ian burst into the room. Janice wondered how he would react.

He'd looked at the newcomer. 'Oh . . . hello,' he'd said, nodding at her.

'Ian, this is Mrs Williams,' Alec had told him. 'Norma, this is my son, Ian.'

Norma had looked up and smiled at him but had not stood up and held out her hand as she had done with Janice. Maybe she'd sensed a certain reticence in the lad and had not wanted to draw attention to it. 'Hello, Ian,' she'd said in a pleasant voice.

'Hello,' he'd repeated abruptly. 'I'm just going to take off my mucky things or I'll be in trouble.'

'Been playing football?' she'd enquired.

'Yeah, that's right. What else?' There'd been an awkward silence for a moment as he left the room.

'Do you have any children, Norma?' Janice had asked, rather diffidently.

'One daughter, that's all,' she'd replied. 'She's married and lives down south so I don't see a great deal of her.'

'Ian's a good lad,' Alec had said defensively. 'At a difficult age, though, or so people tell me. He's fourteen; he's a clever lad, doing well at school, but he lives for football. That's OK, so long as he does his homework and everything.'

'Tea's almost ready.' Janice had changed the subject. 'I'll go and brew the tea and give Ian a shout.'

That first tea had not been a rip-roaring success. Janice had done her best to support her father and to make Norma feel at ease. She'd asked her about her job at the department store, which Norma seemed to enjoy very much.

'I've been there for ten years,' she'd said. 'I've always done shop work, ever since I left school. One bonus at Hill's is that we get a discount on the clothes we buy.'

Janice had admired her suit and told her that she looked very smart and modern. Ian had taken no notice, eating his way unconcernedly through the ham and salad and the strawberry gateau.

Norma had tried, unsuccessfully, to bring him into the

conversation. 'This is all girls' talk, isn't it, Ian? You go to watch Blackpool play every Saturday, I suppose?'

'Yeah, most of the time.' He had scarcely looked up from his plate.

'So . . . who's your favourite player? Stanley Matthews, I suppose?'

'No, Stan Mortensen,' he'd answered briefly.

'And what about you? Would you like to play for a team like Blackpool?'

'No, of course not!' he'd said scornfully. 'I'm not a stupid little kid. It's just something I do with my mates.'

'And you play football at school?'

'No . . . they play rugby,' he'd answered resignedly, as if to say, 'anything else you'd like to know?'

Janice had been glad when the meal came to an end. Ian had gone out again, almost at once, to play chess with his friend, Gary. Norma had offered to help with the washing up but Janice had refused. She'd been glad to be on her own. It had been rather a strain and she'd felt sorry for her dad.

Now, a month later, Norma was invited for tea again. This time Phil would be there as well. But before that, quite late on the Saturday night, they told Alec about their marriage plans.

He looked rather taken aback at first, although it surely could not have been a great surprise. 'What do you mean by quite soon?' he asked. 'Before Christmas?'

'Well, not quite as soon as that,' replied Janice. Phil would have liked it to be as soon as possible but she did not really want a wedding in the coldest time of the year.

They settled on Saturday, 12 April, which seemed a long way away, but weddings – and her father had insisted that she have a really good one – could not be arranged in five minutes. Easter Sunday would be on 6 April, a time when the hotels in Blackpool would be busy, then there would be a slight lull until Whitsuntide.

'I knew you'd have to leave sometime,' said Alec, 'and it makes sense for you to go and live in Ilkley until you find somewhere of your own. I'll miss you, though, and so will Ian . . . very much. But he'll have to get used to changes, won't he?'

Janice was working the early shift the following morning. Mr Summers let her finish at twelve o'clock as he knew that Phil was in Blackpool. When Janice told George and Evie that they had fixed a wedding date, they suggested at once that they should hold the reception at Summerlands. 'That is, if you want to, of course,' added Evie. 'George and I would be delighted.'

'That's a wonderful idea,' said Janice, and her father and Phil agreed.

Ian went silent when Janice told him they had fixed their wedding date. He stared down at the floor then looked at her pleadingly. 'I don't want you to go,' he said gruffly. He was dry-eyed, though; Ian seldom cried.

'Oh, come on, old pal,' said Phil. 'You knew it would happen sometime. And we've told you, you can come and stay with us, watch Leeds United and Sheffield Wednesday . . . We won't be all that far away. Janice and I can't wait for ever, you know.' He spoke to him confidingly. 'You'll know, one day, when you have a girlfriend. I love Janice and we want to be together.'

'Yes, I know that,' said Ian. 'But you know why, don't you?' He lowered his voice although his father had gone out into the garden. 'It's Dad . . . and her!'

'Norma's a very pleasant lady,' said Janice. 'I can understand how you feel but Dad would never do anything to hurt you. He'd never neglect you; you know that, Ian.'

'But he's different now . . .'

Janice sighed. 'He's happier now, Ian. He goes out more, I know that, but you don't want him to go on being miserable, do you?'

'Well, I just don't like her!' said Ian. His mouth was set in a grim line. 'I know you think she's very nice but I don't want her here!'

'Well, she's coming for tea,' said Janice, 'and I have to go and get it ready. Ian . . . just try to be reasonable and polite, will you, just for me? Please . . . I do understand, really I do.'

'OK, then,' he replied with a shrug.

And, to her relief, he was as good as his word. The meal passed without any overt silences or awkwardness. The conversation was mainly about the forthcoming wedding. Norma was keen to know all the details, which Janice and Phil were not yet sure of themselves, and she even offered to help Janice choose her wedding dress.

Ten

'Oh, isn't she beautiful! She's more like you than Walter this time,' said Val, peering at the baby lying in the carry-cot at the end of the bed where Cissie was sitting up, smiling happily.

She had given birth to the baby girl two days earlier on Christmas Day. Val had come round as soon as she was able, anxious to see the new member of the Clarkson family.

'Yes, she's lovely, isn't she?' said Cissie contentedly. 'It wasn't much trouble either, having her. I messed up everybody's Christmas dinner but it couldn't be helped. An' it's nicer being at home than in hospital.' Cissie had insisted on a home birth, and as her last confinement had been trouble free, the doctor had agreed. 'A lot of the work's falling on Walter, of course. He doesn't seem to mind, though, and his mother comes round to help. My mam's not all that much use, you know, when it comes to dirty nappies an' all that. She just likes the easy part, when they're all clean and smelling nice.'

'I'd like to pick her up but I won't,' said Val. 'She's fast asleep so I won't disturb her. I can see she's got your fair hair – quite a lot of it, too – and I expect she'll have blue eyes, like you. I've brought her a little present. I'm not the world's best knitter and I know she'll have lots of matinee jackets and things like that, so I've brought you a dozen little bibs. I know they go through a lot, don't they, when they start on more solid food?'

'Oh, those are real cute,' said Cissie, admiring the bibs, all edged in pink and depicting nursery characters like Bo Peep and Humpty Dumpty. 'Paul used at least two a day an' he's still a messy eater.'

'And this as well; I couldn't resist this,' said Val, presenting

Cissie with a little pink teddy bear, just the right size for a baby to cuddle.

'Oh, isn't he gorgeous!' said Cissie. 'Well . . . it's a she, I suppose, not a he, though we always call teddy bears he, don't we? How clever of you to get a pink one; you must have got it before Christmas?'

'Yes; actually I bought one of each, a pink one and a blue one; it will come in useful sometime.' Val smiled coyly. 'I must tell you . . . I'm trying not to get too hopeful but I think I might be pregnant. I haven't told anyone yet, except Sam, because I've been disappointed before, but this time I really think I am.'

'Gosh, that's great!' said Cissie. 'We'll be able to push our prams out together. When will it be?'

'I'm not sure yet. I'm only two weeks overdue but that's a lot for me. So, if I'm right, it would be early in August. Too soon to think about it, really, so don't go telling anyone. I haven't even told my mum yet. And I'll have to wait a few weeks before I see a doctor and make sure. Anyway, what about you? Are you feeling OK?'

'Yes, fine, thanks. I'm feeding her myself, like I did with Paul, for as long as I can.'

'And has she got a name yet?'

'Yes; we're going to call her Holly. It's a nice Christmassy name. They was a choir on the wireless just after she was born, singing "The Holly and the Ivy". An' you'll be godmother again, won't you, Val?'

'I'd be delighted,' said Val. 'Thanks for asking me, but isn't it someone else's turn?'

'Who else would there be? You're still my best friend. There have to be two godmothers, though, 'cause it's a girl, so I think I'll ask Brenda, a girl I got friendly with at the clinic. And Walter can choose the godfather – one of his cycling mates, perhaps.'

Val did not stay too long. Despite Cissie's cheerful manner it was obvious that she was tired. Val kissed her cheek; she smelled faintly of milk. 'Look after yourself and that lovely little girl. I'll see you again soon.'

'Yes, please do. Ta-ra for now, Val. Love to your Sam . . .'

Walter was downstairs playing with Paul on the hearthrug, his toy cars spread all around. Several nappies were airing on a clothes horse near to the fire, which was surrounded by a sturdy fireguard. The room was reasonably tidy, considering that it was still the Christmas period. Val knew that Walter liked everything to be spick and span and would try to keep it that way. Christmas cards were hung on strings on the wall and a few paper streamers decorated the ceiling. Their small Christmas tree was in the front room. Val had seen its lights twinkling as she knocked at the door.

'You're got your hands full now, Walter!' she remarked.

'You can say that again!' he replied, standing up as she entered the room.

'You've got a lovely little girl . . .'

'Yes, she's gorgeous, isn't she?' He gave a small laugh. 'I hope Cissie will be satisfied now. One of each is enough, as far as I'm concerned. And this one's a real live wire.' He ruffled his son's dark hair. Paul was becoming more and more like his daddy – dark-haired and of a wiry build. 'He's a good lad, though, aren't you, Paul, helping Daddy to look after Mummy and the baby?'

'You've got a new baby sister, haven't you, Paul?' said Val.

The child nodded. 'Holly . . .' he said, stumbling a little over the strange new word. At eighteen months he was tearing around and into everything, and talking just a little.

'Here's a new car to add to your collection,' said Val. She knew that children sometimes felt overlooked when there was a new arrival but that didn't seem to be the case with Paul.

'Bus . . .' he said, smiling in delight at the big red bus. 'Yes,' laughed Val. 'I stand corrected. It's a bus, isn't it, not a car?'

'Say thank you to Aunty Val,' said Walter.

'Thank . . . you,' he repeated. He crouched down again, making 'brrm, brrm' noises as he whizzed the new bus along the carpet.

'Back to work on Monday,' said Walter. 'I can't say I'm sorry.' He laughed. 'I'll be glad to get back for a rest!' Christmas Day had been on Wednesday, and it was now Friday.

'How will you manage then?' asked Val.

'My mum's coming round to help with Paul and to see to

the meals, but Cissie should be up and about in a few days' time. I know she'll want to get back to normal. Thanks for coming, Val. You're a good friend to Cissie . . .'

'The baby's lovely,' Val enthused to Sam when she arrived home. 'She looks just like Cissie: blonde hair and a lovely fair complexion. She's asked me to be godmother again. They're calling her Holly.'

'I expect all babies look lovely to their mothers, don't they?' said Sam. 'No matter how red and wrinkly they are. Some look like little monkeys.'

'Sam, how can you say that! I think she's beautiful and I'm not her mother.'

'Yes, I'm sure she is beautiful, but do try not to get too excited, love – about your condition, I mean. I don't want you to feel all let down again. I keep telling you it's early days and we've got plenty of time.'

'OK; I'll try not to think about it too much,' said Val, 'and I won't keep talking about it.'

However, the weeks passed and by the beginning of February Val felt sure that there could be no doubt about it. Her breasts were tender and she was starting to feel a little queasy, though not always in the morning.

She went to see the doctor, who confirmed that she was expecting a baby. It – he or she – would be born, all being well, in early August, which was the date that Val had worked out herself.

'You are fit and healthy, Valerie,' the doctor told her. 'Just carry on normally but don't overdo things. There's no reason why you should not go on working for a few months. And you'll be expected to go to the hospital for a check-up. I would prefer you to go into hospital as it's your first child.'

Val was delighted, and so was Sam, to have their hopes confirmed. They decided she should carry on working until the end of April, which was about normal for a pregnant woman. She did not want people to say that the boss's wife was being given preferential treatment. The girls in the office were very pleased although they would miss her pleasant company.

Pauline's baby boy had been born in September and was

now five months old. The girls made a great fuss of him when Pauline brought him into the office to show him off.

'Your turn next,' they said to Val. She couldn't wait to have her own bundle of joy.

Plans were going ahead for Janice and Phil's wedding in April. They had booked the time, twelve o'clock, at the parish church, with the reception to follow at Summerlands at one thirty.

Phil was still looking for a suitable workplace, with living accommodation, so that they wouldn't need to travel each day. This was not proving easy, as many of the places had a flat above that was already occupied. His search in Ilkley and nearby Otley and the environs had been fruitless so far, so Phil suggested to Janice that they should look a little further afield.

'Knaresborough's a nice place,' he told her when they spoke on the phone one evening in late February, 'and so is Harrogate. They both get more tourists than Ilkley; holidaymakers and day-trippers, as well as the local folk, of course.'

'I haven't been to either of those places,' said Janice. She had not seen Phil for three weeks but was due to go to Ilkley the following weekend. Mr Summers had given her some time off as the hotel was quiet.

'Right then; we'll go there on Saturday,' said Phil, 'and who knows? We might find just what we're looking for.'

The February day was cold but the sky was clear and there was no sign of rain when Phil and Janice set off for their day out. Janice had arrived late on Friday afternoon. Saturday would be their only full day together as she would have to leave on Sunday afternoon to start work again on Monday.

They drove across the moors to Knaresborough, where Phil parked in a side street off the main road. The town was busy with Saturday shoppers as it was market day. They walked through the market square along narrow, cobbled streets to the area where the ruins of the medieval castle stood. Since the early 1900s the castle grounds had been used as a public park which provided a magnificent view across the valley.

Janice gasped with delight when she saw the view, one which featured on picture postcards and railway posters. Below them were the rooftops of the town and the viaduct crossing the River Nidd against a background of moorland. A train was crossing, puffing smoke into the clear air.

'What a stupendous view!' she said. 'I had no idea it was such a picturesque place.'

'It's Knaresborough's hidden gem,' said Phil. 'Come along; let's go down and look at the river.'

They wandered down a steep path then crossed the railway line by the level crossing. A further steep path led them down to the level of the river. After a short walk they passed the entrance to Mother Shipton's cave. She was a famous Yorkshire witch, born in the fifteenth century, who had prophesied future events such as the Great Fire of London, the defeat of the Spanish Armada and even the end of the world! The cave was a popular tourist attraction because of the nearby petrifying well. There, everyday objects left by tourists – even a handbag left by Agatha Christie – were turned to stone by the action of the chemicals in the water. At the time of Mother Shipton local townsfolk had believed that the well was magic and feared that if they touched the waters they would be turned to stone.

They did not linger there, taking the steep climb by road up to the main part of the town. The couple of estate agents they visited had nothing of interest to show them. There were cafes a-plenty along the main street but they dined at the one they had seen previously, close to the castle.

'This would be an ideal place for us,' said Janice as they tucked into the tasty ham sandwiches and apple pie.

'It's thriving, though, and I don't suppose the owners have any intention of leaving,' said Phil. 'We'll press on to Harrogate. There will probably be more scope there.'

It was only a few miles to the town; in fact, the towns were often linked together as Harrogate and Knaresborough.

'It's quite a posh place, isn't it?' said Janice as they approached the outskirts of Harrogate.

'Yes; I suppose genteel is the word for it,' replied Phil. 'A lot of people retire here as it's a very congenial sort of place to live. It's a spa town; people used to come to take the waters, as they called it in the Georgian and Victorian times. But I've heard that the water actually tastes bloomin' awful because of the sulphur content.'

'Ugh! How ghastly. Like bad eggs, I suppose. I think we'll give that a miss.'

'We sure will. I don't suppose many of today's visitors come to taste the waters.'

They were driving up a steep road which led from the valley to the centre of town. 'That's Betty's Tea Rooms,' said Phil, pointing to a busy-looking shop on the corner of two streets, facing the war memorial. 'They're more likely to want a cup of coffee at Betty's than a drink of spa water.'

There was quite a crowd of people outside the shop and cafe. 'It's a very popular place,' he went on. 'A bit pricey, mind, but folks come from all over to sample the toasted teacakes and cream cakes.'

'Would there be any point, then, in us opening up our own place here?' queried Janice. 'We couldn't compete with Betty's.'

'Nor would we try to,' said Phil. 'Harrogate's a big place so I'm sure there'd be room for us as well. There are lots of other tea shops and restaurants and they have their own clientele. Just as we shall have.' He turned to grin at her. 'Let's park up and have a look around.'

Phil parked the car in a side street, then they walked along a road lined with shops and hotels opposite a wide stretch of grassland.

'That's what they call the Stray,' he told her. 'It's quite unique and I should imagine that's why a lot of people come to settle in Harrogate. Where else could you find so much open space surrounding a town?'

He told her that the Stray consisted of two hundred acres of grassland encompassing the town. By an act passed in the eighteenth century it could not be built on and the restriction was still in force. At one time animals such as sheep and cows were allowed to graze there and the land was enclosed. Now it was a public park for the enjoyment of the residents and the many visitors. The only animals were dogs as it was an ideal place for them to run free.

'Thanks for the history lesson!' said Janice, laughing. 'It's very interesting, though. I'd no idea it was such a lovely place. It's like being in the country, and yet you're not.'

There were stretches of secluded grassland with trees and bushes and banks of flowers, then they came upon a row of shops in front of a residential area about half a mile from the town. They wandered away from the grassy area to take a look at the shops.

'Look!' cried Janice. 'There's one for sale, or is it to let? Oh, Phil, how exciting! Let's go and see.'

It was a row of shops such as one might find in any residential area. A newsagent's shop, a hairdressing salon, an off-licence, a ladies' clothing shop and a florist's. The shop at the end was empty. They made a beeline for it.

The notice in the window showed that it was for sale, enquiries to be made at an estate agents in Harrogate. It was not clear what sort of shop it might have been but they looked at one another and smiled. It seemed to be just what they had been looking for.

'That's exactly what we want, isn't it, Phil?' said Janice. 'Shall we go back now and look for this estate agents? I can hardly believe it, after all the time you've been searching.'

'But not searching in the right place, obviously,' he replied. 'It seems ideal, as far as we can see, but you never know what snags there might be, or lots of other people interested in it. Don't get your hopes up too much, love. But . . . well . . . yes, I think we must at least go and make enquiries.'

As it was a corner property they walked along the street at the side. The property stretched back quite a long way and it seemed that there would be ample space for their requirements. They had not yet decided exactly how they would organize their business. A tea room, a shop with a cafe, a restaurant . . . It would depend on the scope of the premises before they made up their minds.

They walked back to the parked car but left it where it was while they looked for the estate agents. Their office was in a side street leading off the Stray, just a little way from the town centre. But they were closed on Saturday afternoons.

'Oh, damn!' exclaimed Janice, unable to hide her disappointment.

'I suppose we might have known,' said Phil. 'They don't always work shop hours. Never mind; it's not all that far away. I'm sure Dad will give me time to come over again on Monday.'

'But I won't be with you . . .'

'You can trust my judgement, can't you? And we both thought it was what we wanted, even at a first glance.'

There was a photo and a notice about the shop in the window. 'Vacant possession and open to offers', it declared. The price seemed a little above their budget but not too improbable.

'Come on,' said Phil. 'We won't have long to wait. Let's walk down to the valley gardens before we head back home.'

The valley gardens, as the name implied, were down in the valley, reached by one of the steep roads that led down from the town. They had been developed in the early nineteenth century when the town was becoming famous as a spa. Visitors could stroll there as part of their health regime after taking the waters. The waterside walk, with flowers and trees in abundance, became a favourite place for promenading and socializing. The facilities were extended to include a tea room and a bandstand. It was still a very popular venue for residents and visitors, although on that February afternoon there was a lack of flowers.

They wandered through the pathways and into the colon-nades that had been opened some twenty years ago. Although it was wintertime there were hardy climbing plants inter-twined among the trellis work making a leafy arbour above them. The late-afternoon sun cast dappled light and shadow around them as they strolled hand in hand through the walkway. There was scarcely another person in sight as the day drew towards evening.

They walked back to the car almost in silence, each engrossed in their own thoughts.

'I can't tell you how much I hope this works out for us,' said Janice as they drove back.

'I think I can guess,' Phil replied. 'But there'll be another one if this doesn't work. I feel sure.'

Phil's parents were pleased to hear their news and his father agreed that he must drive over again on Monday. If all was well Janice would come over again as soon as possible.

Their parting at the railway station on Sunday afternoon was not as poignant as usual as they had high hopes for the near future. Janice decided not to say anything to her father about the property they had in mind until she had heard from Phil. Ian seemed pleased to see her home again. He was quiet these days, spending a good deal of time at the homes of his mates playing chess, as it was too dark for evening football.

Norma still visited occasionally but Alec continued to spend more time at her place than she did at his. He said nothing of his future plans, and Janice did not ask. She could tell that Ian was doing his best to ignore the situation, although he was polite enough to Norma when they met; polite but . . . aloof.

Janice waited on tenterhooks for Phil's phone call. She was on an early shift so he had promised to ring on Monday evening.

'I'll go,' she said as the phone rang in the hallway. 'It'll probably be Phil.'

'Good news, darling,' he said as soon as she answered. 'Dad went with me today; I thought we could do with an expert opinion. We had a good look round the property with the estate agent and . . . it's just what we want!'

'Oh, that's wonderful!' she cried. 'Tell me all about it.'

'Plenty of room for whatever we decide to do, good living accommodation and quite a modern kitchen and bathroom upstairs. And the price is OK. They came down a bit because – would you believe? – it's been on their books for quite a while. We'll need a mortgage – a small one, I hope, but we can go ahead with our plans.'

'That's wonderful!' she said again. 'I'll come over again soon if it's all right with Mr Summers.'

'Yes, that would be great. I won't talk any more now; I'm running up the phone bill. Ring me later in the week. Bye for now, darling. Love you . . .'

'Bye, Phil. Love you too . . .' she whispered.

'What's all the excitement?' asked Alec. 'I could hear you were pleased about something and I expect I can guess what it is, can't I?'

'Yes, I dare say you can.' She told him about the property they had found and that their plans could now go ahead.

'You mean . . . you've found somewhere to live?' asked Ian. He had been doing his homework in his attic room and had come down to see what was going on.

'Yes, that's right. We won't be able to move in straight away, but after we're married I shall be there to help with all the planning.'

'And it's only – what is it? – seven weeks till your wedding,' said Alec. 'It's all happening, isn't it?'

Ian went upstairs again without a word. He never wanted to talk about the wedding.

Eleven

'Come in,' called Janice, hearing a timid knock on her bedroom door.

She was not surprised to see Ian, looking a little sheepish. 'Sure I can come in?' he asked.

'Of course you can,' she answered. 'I'm quite decent! I'm just getting ready to meet Jean and Kath. They're going to be my bridesmaids and we're having a meal together at the Lobster Pot. But I've got plenty of time.'

Her brother flopped down on the bed, then looked at her with soulful brown eyes. 'Don't you miss Mum?' he asked.

Janice sat down on her Lloyd loom chair and reached out a hand to briefly touch Ian's. 'Of course I do,' she replied. 'You don't really need to ask, do you? I miss her like mad, especially now.'

It was the week before the wedding and by now the arrangements were finalized. Janice's greatest regret – the only one, really – was that her mother would not be with her to share the most important day in her life. She was busy and excited, of course, and looking forward to being Phil's wife, at last, but there was an ache deep inside her when she thought about her mum and how she would have loved to share in this occasion.

She had not wanted to refuse Norma's offer to help her to choose her wedding dress and she was getting a good reduction on it as well. It would have been churlish to refuse but the thought had been with her all the time: my mum should be doing this.

She tried to explain this to Ian. 'Every girl should have her mother with her on her wedding day but we can't change what has happened, can we, Ian? I know it's all very sad but life has to go on. That's a worn-out phrase if ever there was one, but it's true. It would do no good to wallow in misery and Mum wouldn't have wanted that, would she?'

'No, I suppose not. But Dad seems so . . . . carefree, as though he's forgotten all about her.'

'I can assure you he hasn't. You've heard him say that no one could ever replace Mum, but he has a right to be as happy as he can be.'

'D'you think he'll marry her?'

'I don't know, Ian. Try not to think about that just now. I'm glad you've agreed to be a groomsman at our wedding. It means a great deal to Phil and me.'

Ian grimaced. 'I shall feel a real twit with a flower in my buttonhole. And a new suit an' all. But Dad insisted and at least he's paying for it.'

'Just be thankful we're not having morning suits – top hats and all that, like they did at Valerie's wedding.' Janice and Phil had decided that it should be a fairly informal occasion with the men in ordinary lounge suits, although the ladies always liked to have an excuse to dress up.

'I'll leave you, then.' Ian stood up. 'I just wanted to talk to you. I was feeling a bit fed up, like . . . I'll miss you, you know,' he added, a little embarrassed.

'I'll miss you, too, but let's not get all sad and mopey.' Janice smiled at him. 'It'll be a happy day, I'm sure, and we must try not to dwell on what might have been, OK?'

Ian nodded. 'OK, I'll try.'

Phil and his parents stayed at Summerlands the night before the wedding, along with an aunt and uncle from Yorkshire and Phil's best man, Brian – an old school friend – and his wife.

Alec's brother and sister and their spouses, who lived in Burnley – Alec's home town – were travelling over to Blackpool for the day; relations that Janice seldom met but it was obligatory to invite them. There was also Janice's uncle and aunt – her mother, Lilian's brother and his wife – who lived near Blackpool. That was the sum total of relations; the other guests were friends of Phil and Janice.

There were thirty-five people gathered at Summerlands for the reception that followed the midday marriage. The service at the parish church, where Janice attended occasionally, was simple and reverent without a great deal of ceremony; the way Janice and Phil wanted it to be.

She had chosen, with Norma's assistance, a traditional dress in ivory satin with a lace bodice and long sleeves and a gently flared skirt that flowed to her ankles. Her short veil was held in place with a pearl coronet and she carried a small bouquet of white lilies and narcissi. Her bridesmaids wore dresses of hyacinth blue, knee length, in a simple style that could be worn on other occasions.

It was a happy day and it was good to see relations that they met only occasionally, at weddings such as this, and, sadly, at funerals.

It was traditional that the parents of the bride and groom sat at the top table with the bridesmaids, best man and groomsmen. Janice felt a pang of regret to see Norma sitting with her father. But then, where else could she sit? She was Alec's friend and it was right that she should partner him rather than sitting elsewhere.

Mr and Mrs Summers had done them proud with a three-course meal of prawn cocktail, roast chicken and sherry trifle. Janice's friend, Pat, whom she had met on the catering course, had made the two-tier wedding cake. After the cake had been ceremoniously cut and the happy couple toasted in champagne – Alec had insisted on this for his only daughter – the guests mingled together, meeting old friends and getting to know those who were strangers to them.

Janice was pleased to see her friends Val and Cissie again, with their husbands. They had driven over together in Sam's car rather than use two vehicles.

'So we're all married now,' said Cissie excitedly. 'Isn't that lovely? Who'd have thought it when we all met at the Winter Gardens! I had my doubts about Val and Sam, but not any more I don't. And Janice and Phil, you two are made for one another, aren't you?'

Phil smiled at his new wife. 'We certainly think so.'

'And me; I went back to Walter here,' said Cissie, linking his arm. 'But we've no regrets, have we, love?'

'None whatsoever,' answered Walter with an ambiguous smile.

'And how's your family?' asked Janice. 'I'm looking forward to seeing your baby girl – Holly, isn't she? I'll be able to see you more often now I'm living in Yorkshire.'

'Holly's doing fine, isn't she, Walter? She's four months old now. And our Paul will be two on the first of June. Little tinker he is, into everything. Walter's mam and dad have got them today. And what about our Val, eh? Doesn't she look well!'

Val smiled complacently. It was just becoming obvious that she was pregnant, a fact that she did not try to disguise. She was wearing a lightweight woolen costume in a raspberry pink shade which suited her dark hair and rosy complexion. She looked radiant and happy.

'I'm glad you're keeping so well,' said Janice. 'Everything is going to plan, is it?'

'Yes, fine thanks . . . touch wood,' she replied, reaching out to touch the back of a chair. 'The baby's due in August; only four months to go.'

'I won't ask whether you want a boy or a girl,' said Janice. 'A silly remark really, isn't it? We just hope all goes well for you, don't we, Phil?'

'Indeed we do,' he replied. 'We're pleased that we'll be quite near to you when we move to Harrogate. We hope you'll be there at the grand opening?'

'And when will that be?' asked Sam.

'Not for a little white. The property needs a fair bit of

renovating, although it's in quite good condition. Late summer, we hope. We'll let you know, of course . . . Come along . . . Mrs Grundy,' he said to his new wife. 'We'd better go and circulate before it's time for us to depart. We're off to the Cotswolds for a few days. We'll see you all again before long. Thanks for coming . . .'

Janice and Phil set off for their honeymoon towards the end of the afternoon. The guests waved them off, showering them with confetti again as they got into the car to drive along the promenade. What the majority of the guests did not know was that they would drive around the Fylde area for a little while before returning to Summerlands for their first night. Then they would do their journey to the Cotswolds in a leisurely way the following day.

Phil drove south, past the tower and the Pleasure Beach, to St Annes and then on to Lytham. He parked the car near the vast expanse of grassland beyond which was the Irish Sea. The rival seaside town of Southport could be seen in the distance across the estuary of the River Ribble. They walked hand in hand along the path near to the sea. They felt, strangely, that they had little to say to one another after the events of the day; they were just happy to be alone together.

They stood looking out across the ocean. It was a peaceful scene, away from the hubbub of Blackpool. Phil turned to kiss his new wife. 'Let's head back now, shall we?' he said. 'They'll have all gone by now.'

Just a few people were in on the secret: Alec and Norma, Ian, the bridesmaids and Phil's parents, but they, too, would have gone home by now to leave Janice and Phil on their own.

George and Evie had reserved one of their best rooms for the honeymoon couple. There was a snack meal of ham sandwiches and pork pie awaiting them on their return. There were only a few guests staying at the hotel the weekend after Easter. Some of them were in the visitors' lounge but Janice and Phil did not feel like socializing with strangers. They spent the evening with George and Evie Summers in their private sitting room, chatting and idly watching a variety show on the television.

George poured out glasses of their best sherry for their own toast to the newlyweds, wishing them every happiness and success in their marriage and their new venture. Janice had become a popular member of the staff during the nine months she had been working there. They were sorry to lose her but she promised to keep in touch and visit them when they came to see her father.

Evie made supper drinks for the few guests who wanted them and after they, too, had finished their cups of tea, Phil and Janice looked at one another. Janice felt a little embarrassed as they stood up to say goodnight and depart to their room. George and Evie, though, had the good sense not to make any facetious remarks.

'Goodnight . . . See you in the morning,' they said, but did not add 'sleep well'.

Janice felt suddenly shy and unsure of herself. There had been very few occasions when they had been alone like this. There had been only one, in fact, when they had taken the opportunity, after Val and Sam's party, to express fully their love and desire for each other.

But now they were married and Phil soon put an end to any restraint that Janice was feeling. This time there was no sense of guilt or worry that something might go wrong. They came together gently and lovingly at first, then more passionately, as they had denied themselves for so long.

Janice lay awake for a little while. She felt happy and contented but there were a couple more thoughts on her mind. She wished her mother could have been there to share in her happiness and she hoped so much that Ian would settle down to living with his dad without her own bolstering presence, and that he would adapt to the situation if her father decided to marry Norma. But her thoughts were mainly of how lovely and right it felt to be married to Phil. And so she fell asleep . . .

Following a hearty breakfast – the same fare as the other guests received – they set off for their journey south. The Cotswold hills was an area of England that was not familiar to either of them but the pictures and descriptions in the guide books had appealed to them and they found that the reality was even better.

They arrived mid-afternoon at Stow-on-the-Wold where Phil had made a reservation at an old coaching inn in the market square of the picturesque town. They had driven along leafy lanes where the trees and hedgerows were bursting into full springtime green, further advanced than those in the north. Sheep grazed on the steep slopes of the hills. The area, in the Middle Ages, had been the centre of the wool industry which, since that time, had moved to Yorkshire. The rich wool merchants had built many of the impressive churches – very large for the size of the villages – and the stately manor houses of Cotswold stone. The mellow golden-hued stone was unique to the area, so different from the red brick of Lancashire and the grey millstone grit of Yorkshire which were so familiar to them. It was an idyllic part of the country in which to spend the first few days of their married life.

They stayed for five days, visiting the other charming olde-worlde places in the area: the elegant town of Cheltenham; the lovely village of Bourton-on-the-Water where the River Windrush flowed through the main street, crossed by low stone bridges; and Chipping Camden with its Jacobean market hall.

The weather was kind to them; just the occasional April shower which did nothing to dampen their spirits or their joy in being together.

Then they were back in Ilkley to what was a new home for Janice. She had no job to go out to each day but there was plenty to occupy her at the Coach and Horses until such time as they set up on their own. Phil continued with his work as a chef and Janice filled in wherever she was needed: waitressing, serving in the bar or helping in the kitchen, where she was able to put into practice her skill at pastry and cake-making, which would be one of her main occupations when they opened their own place.

A firm of builders and joiners was contracted to make the necessary alterations. After a good deal of deliberation and assessment as to how to make the best use of the property, they decided that the front part of the premises should be a cafe, open during daytime hours. In the morning, from ten o'clock, they would serve coffee and tea, toasted teacakes, pastries and cakes, and light lunches for two hours at midday, then afternoon tea, closing at five thirty.

To make more use of Phil's talents as a chef they proposed to open in the evenings for small parties, preferably pre-booked. These ideas were still taking shape in their minds. They would need to wait and see how their proposals worked out once they were open. Then they could build their business up according to the response of their customers.

They hoped the cafe was near enough to the town centre to attract both residents and visitors. They would advertise in the local papers and send out leaflets to various groups and organizations, then trust that their reputation would do the rest. They realized it might be thought a chancy venture – there were other such places in the vicinity – but they planned to have their own individual style.

They learned that the shop had once been a small bakery with much of the produce made on the premises. But over the years they had suffered from competition from larger firms. The elderly couple who ran it had not kept up with modern trends and they had no family to take it over so the business had declined. The couple had retired to a bungalow in Knaresborough, leaving the one-time baker's shop in the hands of the estate agents.

Because of the nature of the business there was a fair-sized kitchen on the ground floor but the ovens and the sink were dilapidated and would need replacing. There was a room at the rear of the small shop which had possibly been used as a storeroom; the wall could be knocked through to make the front area larger. When this was done they estimated that the cafe would accommodate up to twenty people. This might be a tight squeeze but time would tell and they would learn by experience.

The living quarters upstairs were adequate, though in need of decorating. A large living-cum-dining room at the front, a smallish kitchen and a bathroom which, surprisingly, were quite modern, and two bedrooms, one much smaller than the other. A place which was affordable, especially with the windfall from Phil's aunt. They required a mortgage, however, which did not prove to be a problem. It was amazing, though, how the necessary requirements – the alterations to the structure, the joinery, repainting and decorating, plus the new ovens and up-to-date plumbing – were eating away their money. And then they would need to furnish the cafe and purchase crockery and cutlery.

The work was progressing well, though, with no snags so far. Phil and Janice drove over a couple of times a week to see how the work was going along.

Two things happened, though, while the preparations were going ahead. Neither of them caused Phil and Janice to alter their plans or hindered the ongoing work but both gave them pause for thought. During the first week in May, Sam rang them to tell them that, unfortunately, Val had suffered a miscarriage. Janice felt so sad for her friend, knowing how disappointed and upset she must be.

Then, in early June, Alec rang to tell his daughter that he and Norma were to be married at the end of the month.

Twelve

Val woke suddenly with severe abdominal pain. It was a Monday morning at the beginning of May, the start of her last week at the office. She had been looking forward to finishing work as she was getting rather tired, but apart from that she felt fit and well and was still very active. She knew that she would miss the company of her friends. Looking forward to the birth of their baby, though, would more than compensate for the lack of companionship.

She sat up in bed and nudged Sam, who stirred sleepily. 'What? What's the matter? It's not time to get up, is it?'

'No . . . but I think there's something wrong, Sam. I've got such an awful pain.'

Instantly, he was wide awake. He glanced at the alarm clock which went off at seven o'clock. It was half past six.

'You're not . . .? You don't think it's the baby, do you? It's far too soon.' She still had fourteen weeks or so to go. He looked at her in alarm. 'Shall I go and make you a cup of tea? It might only be a twinge; perhaps it will go off.'

'Yes, please . . .' she murmured. The pain did seem to be subsiding a little.

By the time Sam came back with the tea, though, it was obvious that something was amiss. The pain was recurring regularly and Val's face was ashen.

'I'd better get you straight to hospital,' he said. 'Do you want to get dressed?'

Val shook her head. 'Best not to, I think.' She was quite scared by now. 'I'd better just go as I am. Oh, Sam . . . do you think we're losing the baby?'

'Let's hope not, love. You've not . . .? There's no blood or anything?'

'No, just this pain . . .'

Sam dressed quickly and drank the tea that Val had left after taking a few sips. She was still wearing her nightdress with a dressing gown over it, and had put on a pair of briefs to make her feel more comfortable. There was nothing much on the roads and they were soon at the hospital at the other side of the town,

When they arrived she was helped into a wheelchair and taken straight to the maternity ward. Sam kissed her gently before she was wheeled inside. 'You'll be all right, darling; they'll take good care of you.'

Val could only smile feebly at him as she grasped at his hand. Sam waited in a small room outside the main ward for what seemed like hours and hours. It was, in fact, less than an hour, but he could tell when the doctor came in and spoke his name that the news was not good.

'Mr Walker . . . I'm very sorry; your wife has had a miscarriage. We did all we could but I'm afraid she's lost the baby.'

'And what about Valerie?' he asked. She was really his main consideration. 'Is she all right?'

'Yes, she will be in a little while. She's lost a lot of blood and it's a traumatic experience to go through but she will be all right. She's sedated at the moment and I'd like her to rest now. Perhaps you could come back later in the day. You don't need to wait for visiting hours.'

'Thank you, Doctor,' said Sam. 'Could you tell me . . .?
What was the baby? A boy or a . . .?'

'It was a boy, Mr Walker.'

Sam felt his eyes mist with tears but he knew it was nothing
compared to the heartache that Val must be feeling. She had
been so anxious to have this baby.

He went into work mid-morning; he had phoned his
father to say he would be late as Val was not well. He broke
the news to Joshua, who was truly sorry. He had become
very fond of Val and had been looking forward to another
grandchild.

'It would have been a boy,' Sam told him, 'not that I was
too concerned about the sex of the child but I expect you
would have liked a grandson, eh, Dad?'

'Maybe,' replied Joshua. 'But never mind, lad; better luck
next time. You and Valerie are still young and strong. These
things happen for a reason, you know. There may have been
something wrong and it's nature's way of not letting it go
on. You take the rest of the day off and give my love to that
lovely wife of yours and your mother as well. She'll be sorry
to hear about it and she's got quite fond of the lass, you
know.'

'Yes, I do believe she has . . . I'll go and tell the girls in
the office. Val was due to start her last week there.'

'Aye; I passed on the message that she wasn't feeling too
good. They'll be sorry to hear the news. She was a good
worker there as well.'

The office girls were all dismayed at the news and Rita, the
youngest one, shed a few tears.

'Oh, how awful for Val! She was looking forward to it so
much. We knew we would miss her, though. She was real
nice to work with.'

Sam wondered, then, if it might be best for Val to return to
work but he did not mention it, nor would he say anything
to her, not yet. Rita had fitted well into the post left by Pauline.
Susan, who was slightly senior to Jill, was due to take over Val's
post as senior clerk but a replacement had not been found yet
to do her own job.

'Thanks for your kind messages,' said Sam. 'I expect Val will be home in a day or two and she'll no doubt come in to see you when she feels up to it. Bye for now . . .'

Sam drove into town to buy a large bunch of early roses for Val and a box of her favourite chocolates. Little consolation, he knew, but he must do something to cheer her up. He made himself a quick lunch of scrambled eggs on toast before driving to the hospital in the early afternoon.

Val was in a small private room. He wondered if it might be better for her to have the company of other women in the general ward, but then he realized that might not be such a good idea as they all had their babies with them in cots at the end of the beds. Val was sitting up in bed looking very forlorn. She smiled when she saw Sam, but when he went to put his arms around her she burst into tears.

'Oh, Sam! Isn't it dreadful? We've lost the baby . . .'

'Never mind, darling. So long as you're all right, that's the main thing at the moment. You are feeling OK, aren't you? As well as you can be, I mean? I know you're very upset about it, of course.'

'Yes, I'll be OK.' Val sighed. 'I've to stay here for a day or two . . . But you must be so disappointed with me, Sam. This is the second time, isn't it? Suppose we can never have a baby?'

'Don't be silly, darling. How long have we been married? Little more than a year, that's all.'

'And during that time I've had two miscarriages . . .'

'We don't really know about the first time; it was only a few weeks. But this time, yes, I know it's heartbreaking for you, for both of us. We'll talk to the doctors – the one here and our own doctor. I'm sure they'll tell us there's nothing to be concerned about. And then we'll just have to relax and let things take their course.'

'You're right, I know you are,' said Val, still sounding tearful. 'I'll try not to get upset each month when nothing happens.'

Sam kissed her cheek. 'Yes, that's right. We mustn't spoil these first years of our marriage by worrying. We couldn't plan a holiday in August, could we? But now we'll be able to so that will be something to look forward to. And then there's the opening of Janice and Phil's cafe. All sorts of nice things are happening.'

Val was a little more cheerful by the time he left her, and when she came home in two days' time she seemed more resigned to what had happened. Both doctors told them it was too soon to have any real concerns. Perhaps if nothing had happened by the end of the year it would be time to investigate further.

As Sam had predicted, Val found that time hung heavy when she was at home day after day. She had plenty of time to fulfil her desire to be a perfect housewife but she also had more time to brood, and she had promised Sam she would try not to do that.

When he suggested, tentatively, that she might consider going back to work, she agreed readily. The vacancy had not been filled and she was happy to let Susan continue as chief clerk and take a subsidiary role herself. She trusted that it would not be for very long.

Janice was pleased to be able to further her friendship with Val now that she was living in Yorkshire. Her school friends from Blackpool were all away at training college or university and she had missed them during the term times. She had no regrets, though, that she had been unable to go to university as had originally been planned. It had been her own decision when her mother was taken ill to give up her college place and stay at home to keep the hotel going to the best of her ability. Phil had worked along with her for a while, leaving his home and work in Yorkshire to make use of his talents as a chef at the Butler family hotel. It seemed to her now that fate had played a hand when she had met him at the Winter Gardens on that memorable night in the August of 1955. Now they were married and looking forward to starting their own business and living in their own home.

Phil drove her to Val's home one Saturday in early June. He was off to Harrogate to see how the work was progressing on their property and would call back for her later.

Janice was pleased to see that Val was quite cheerful and optimistic following the great disappointment of losing her baby the previous month.

'It's done me a world of good going back to the office,' she told Janice. 'I was looking forward so much to being at home but I found that I didn't settle to it at all. I was so used to going off each morning and being busy that I couldn't get used to having all that free time. And I also had too much time to think about everything. Anyway, it's great to see you, Janice. So . . . have you any news?'

'Well, I'm getting on OK with my in-laws!' replied Janice. 'I knew it would work out all right, though. Patience and Ralph have always made me feel welcome, but it will be nice to get into our own place. It'll be a couple of months, though, yet. We must try not to be impatient. I do have some other news, though. My dad is getting married at the end of this month. He rang to tell us last week.'

'Oh . . . I see.' Val looked taken aback, as though she did not know whether to say how nice it was . . . or not. 'So how do you feel about it?' she asked.

'It was not really a surprise,' answered Janice. 'I think we had been expecting it. Norma is a very pleasant person; nothing like Mum, though, which is just as well. She's certainly been good for Dad. He's cheered up and he's out and about a lot more and made new friends. Yes, it's . . . good.'

'How long is it since your mum . . .?'

'It's two years now so we can't accuse him of rushing into it. I'm much more resigned to it than Ian, though. I've tried to talk to him and tell him that Dad loves us as much as ever and that he'll never forget Mum. But I suppose I can understand his feelings.'

'You'll be going to the wedding, of course?'

'Yes; it's on the last Saturday in June at the registry office. I think Dad wants it to be a quiet occasion. They're having a "do" though, afterwards, at the club they both belong to. They probably couldn't get out of that; all their friends will insist on making merry, no doubt. I hope it will be a happy occasion for Dad, and for Norma, too. I do like her and I feel sorry about the situation with Ian. She's doing her best to be tolerant with him. He's not really rude to her or unpleasant, just not very welcoming . . . Anyway, enough about me. How's Cissie getting on? I won't have time to see her today. Give her my love, won't you?'

'Yes, I'll do that. She's very busy with her little ones. I don't see her as much as I did at one time. We used to walk home from work together when our shifts coincided and we always went to the pictures at least once a week. That was in the days before we were married, of course. Now, as I say, she's too busy with her home and her children; the children above all. I never thought she would settle down to motherhood as well as she has done.'

'And she and Walter . . . They're getting on well together?'

'Yes, I think so . . . I hope so. Why do you ask?'

'Well, there was a bit of a spat at your party, wasn't there? I know it's a while ago but I remember how she had a go at Walter because he was chatting to a girl from your office.'

'Oh, yes, Rita. The poor girl was really upset – Rita, I mean. Walter was only being friendly because she was new to the firm but Cissie got it all wrong. Rita wouldn't say boo to a goose. She was really shy at first when she came to work with us but she's coming out of her shell now. Walter mentioned to her that he was a member of a cycling club and she joined it soon afterwards. We believe she's got a boyfriend there now but she doesn't say a great deal about him . . . To get back to Walter and Cissie – I think they're getting on OK. I never had much time for him, to be honest, before they were married, but he's changed a lot. He's much more friendly and chatty. I did wonder, though, when they got married how it would work out.'

'Yes. She had a bit of a fling with a lad in Blackpool, didn't she?'

'She did, but he let her down and she turned back to Walter, her old flame.'

'And now they've got two children . . .'

'Yes, and I think there'd be more if Cissie had her way! I really think she should devote more time to her husband. I'd better say no more, though. I'm speaking out of turn . . . Tell me about your cafe, restaurant – whatever it's going to be. Do you have a name for it yet?'

'We might just call it "Grundy's". It's short and to the point.'

'Like "Betty's", eh? They do well with just the one word. You may become as famous as they are!'

'Oh, we're not setting up in opposition,' Janice hastened to assure her friend.

'I was only joking . . .'

'Yes, I know, but I wouldn't want anyone to think we were. Phil says there's plenty of room for all of us. There are already a lot of cafes in Harrogate, so we'll have to try to be a bit different.'

She told Val of their plans to open in the morning for coffee or tea, followed by light lunches, then afternoon teas. 'Nothing too adventurous at first.'

'It sounds like quite enough to be getting on with,' remarked Val. 'Are you having a grand opening?'

'It's not large enough to invite everyone. Just family and friends and special guests, maybe, for a private "do" before we open to the public.'

'Well, Sam and I will be away the second week in August, when the mill closes down. We'll plan a holiday in Scotland, probably, seeing as there's nothing else on the agenda . . .' She looked pensive for a moment. 'And I expect Walter and Cissie will be away that week with the children.'

'If things go according to plan it may well be before that but we'll let you know in good time.'

Sam came in from the garden where he spent most of his Saturday afternoons. Val put the kettle on and by the time it had boiled Phil had arrived back from Harrogate. Over a cup of tea and a sample of Val's homemade Victoria sponge cake, Phil reported that all was going well and he hoped they would be able to open the cafe by the end of July.

Thirteen

A bright and sunny morning with not a cloud in the sky boded well for the wedding of Alec and Norma at midday.

It felt strange to Janice to be waking up in her old bedroom with Phil at her side. They had driven there the previous night so that Janice could spend some time with her father and, of course, with Ian, who she guessed would be feeling rather mixed up and unsure of himself. She had been pleased to see, however, that he seemed more resigned to the situation.

'It's all change, though, isn't it?' he remarked to his sister when they managed to snatch a few moments together. Alec was showing Phil the attempts he had made with the small garden area. 'It's all happened at once: you getting married and now Dad. But I s'pose I'll get used to it.'

'You must try to get along with Norma, you know, Ian. If it wasn't for her Dad might still be feeling sad and sorry for himself.'

'Yeah . . . She's all right, I suppose,' Ian admitted, rather to Janice's surprise. 'Quite nice actually but she's not like Mum.'

'And that's just as well,' said Janice. 'We're all different and you can't make comparisons.'

'Mum was a smashing cook, though, and I don't know what she'll be like – Norma, I mean. She's made us a few meals since you left; Dad was pretty hopeless in the kitchen, you know.'

'Yes, I know that. He never helped with that side of things in the hotel but he helped in other ways.'

'Norma's meals were OK. She made a quite decent steak and kidney pie and a toad-in-the-hole. She even got Dad helping a bit, 'cause he's had to manage when she's not there. But she'll be there all the time soon, when they come back from Wales or wherever they're going.'

Alec and Norma had planned a few days' honeymoon in north Wales at a small hotel in Llandudno. They would be travelling in her car as she was an experienced driver. That was something that Alec had never learned.

'So I have to go and stay with Uncle Len and Aunty Jean while they're away,' said Ian, a trifle grumpily. 'I don't know them all that well. We haven't seen them so much since Mum died.'

'Len's very busy with the garage,' said Janice, 'but he's OK is Uncle Len; very easy to get on with and so is Jean. She's a good cook, too, from what I remember.'

Leonard Cartwright was Lilian's younger brother who owned a garage on the outskirts of Blackpool. He had said that either he or Jean would drive Ian to school each morning and he would catch the bus back at the end of the afternoon.

'It'll be all right, I suppose,' said Ian with a shrug, 'but I'd rather come and stay with you and Phil.'

'And we'd love to have you,' said Janice. 'It just isn't possible at the moment. We're not in our own home so we can't really invite guests to stay. Anyway, you would have to miss school and that's not a good idea, especially with exams coming up. It's only a few weeks, though, before you break up for the summer holiday, so you can come and stay with us then. We should be up and running before then with a bit of luck.'

'Gosh! That'd be great,' said Ian, his face lighting up at the idea.

Alec and Phil came in from the garden at that moment.

'I was just saying to Ian that he can come and stay with us during the summer holidays, can't he, Phil?' said Janice.

'Sure he can,' answered Phil. 'We could find him a job. Can't have him staying for nowt, can we?' He winked at Janice.

'Could you? Could you really?' said Ian, looking even more delighted. 'Super! Is that OK, Dad? Can I go and stay with Janice and Phil?'

'Of course you can, son,' said Alec. 'It's a very good idea. You're always at a loose end during the school holidays, aren't you? You can't play football all the time and you're still too young to do a holiday job at a hotel here but it'll be different at Phil and Janice's place.'

'What could I do, though?' asked Ian.

'We'll think of something,' said Phil. 'There'll be stacks of washing up, for a start.'

'Aren't you going to get a dishwasher?' asked Ian, looking as though washing up was not a good idea.

'Yes, but it will want loading and cleaning, and they don't wash absolutely everything. Maybe you could wait on at the tables,' suggested Janice. 'How about that?'

'That sounds better,' said Ian with a smile.

'You'll have to look presentable, of course,' added Janice. 'No scruffy old jeans or trainers. A nice, clean white shirt and black trousers. There'll be plenty of jobs for you to do. And we'll pay you, of course, won't we, Phil?'

'Of course we will. We won't expect you to work for nothing and there'll be tips if you're a waiter!'

'Great!' Ian looked happier than he had in a long while. 'I'll be able to save up for those new football boots I want.'

Janice noticed that her father looked pleased and relieved at the change in his son. She hoped that Ian's good mood would continue, especially during the following day.

There was just a small gathering of people at the registry office. Norma's sister, Kathleen, who was her bridesmaid – or a witness, as they were called at a civil wedding – Jeff, who had introduced Alec to the social club and was acting as his best man, Jeff's wife, Kathleen's husband, Janice, Phil and Ian.

Norma looked most attractive in a pale pink silk dress with a matching feathery hat perched on top of her dark, curly hair. She carried a small posy of roses in a darker pink shade, and the men sported buttonholes of similar flowers. Alec had bought a new grey suit for Janice and Phil's wedding so he had decided to wear the same one again. Ian, too, wore the suit he had worn for his sister's wedding.

After the simple ceremony, which was what they had both wanted – no fuss or palaver, as Alec had said – they drove in their own cars to the social club, which was not far away.

As Alec and Norma had anticipated, and had had to agree to, there was a rousing welcome for them from quite a large crowd of people. Not all the members of the club were there but there was a good number including the darts team, the bowling team and personal friends of Alec and Norma, most of whom Alec had not known when he was married to Lilian.

He had not invited his brother and sister who lived in Burnley. He saw them very rarely, but they had sent their good wishes by telegram. He had, however, invited Lilian's brother and his wife. He had always been on good terms with them, and they were sincere in their congratulations to him and Norma. They knew what a devoted husband he had been, and were pleased that he was able to find happiness again.

The buffet meal was the usual fare for such an occasion. An assortment of sandwiches, chicken 'drumsticks', pork pies, sausage rolls and crisps, with sherry trifle or ice cream to follow. The wedding cake was just one tier, which had been baked and expertly iced and decorated by Norma's sister, Kathleen, who had studied the art at night school.

The cake was cut by the bridal pair and photographs were taken by a few amateur photographers. Their health and happiness was toasted in Bristol cream sherry and Jeff made an appropriate speech wishing them well and saying how pleased all their friends were that Alec and Norma had decided to tie the knot. They were held in high esteem at the club and at their places of work, and he hoped they would spend many happy years together.

There was very little ribaldry or joking as there might have been with a younger couple. The guests were all aware that Alec had had a previous happy marriage, had been widowed for a comparatively short time and that his immediate family were, no doubt, experiencing mixed feelings about the occasion. Norma had been a widow for several years but her marriage, also, had been a happy one.

Norma had been abstemious, only drinking the sherry for the toast then keeping to fruit juice as she knew she had a long way to drive to their destination in Wales. Alec, too, who had never been a hard drinker, had kept within the limits he set himself. Janice was pleased to see him laughing and joking with his pals. It had been difficult for her at first but she now understood her father's situation and was pleased that he had found someone so compatible as Norma. She knew, deep down, that the memories of her mother would always be there for all of them. But now they were starting a new chapter and must try not to look down memory lane too often.

Ian was coping very well. He had stayed close to Phil as there were no other younger people there. Janice watched him talking politely to some of Alec's friends who made themselves known to him. He was more cheerful when he had drunk the sherry and the half of lager that his Uncle Len had bought him (strictly on the quiet) but there was no one who would be bothered enough to report the misdemeanour.

When it was mid-afternoon Alec and Norma decided it was time for them to depart. Alec kissed his daughter's cheek and gave her a hug.

'Thanks for being here, love,' he said. 'It means a lot to me and to Norma.'

He was not normally a demonstrative man but he hugged Phil as well. He was very fond of his son-in-law.

Ian stood to one side, looking a little unsure of himself. Norma, very guardedly, kissed his cheek.

'We'll be back soon,' she said. 'It's just a few days' holiday. It will be a nice change for you to spend some time with your aunt and uncle, won't it?'

Ian gave a weak smile. 'Sure . . .' he replied.

His dad hugged him. 'Bye for now, son. See you soon . . . I'm very proud of you, you know,' he added in a whisper.

'Bye, Dad,' said Ian. 'Er . . . Have a nice holiday.'

The guests followed them out into the street where the car was parked, and they were unable to dodge the flurry of confetti as they got into it. Then they were away, with everyone waving until they turned the corner.

It was time then for all the guests to say their goodbyes. Len put an arm round Ian's shoulders. 'Come along, lad,' he said. 'We'd best get going.'

Ian nodded. 'OK,' he said, looking a little forlornly at his sister.

Janice and Phil came over to him. Janice kissed his cheek, just a little peck. 'Now, don't forget, you'll be coming to stay with us soon. He'll be our first guest, won't he, Phil?'

'First to stay in our guest bedroom, sure he will. There'll be all sorts of jobs lined up for you, Ian. Washing up, peeling spuds, scrubbing the floor! And we might let you be chief waiter if you shape yourself!' Phil punched him playfully on the cheek. 'Off you go, and have a great time with Len and Jean. We'll see you soon . . . You know, Ian, things are not always as bad as they seem,' he added in a quiet voice. 'Just look forward to the summer holidays, eh?'

'Sure,' said Ian again, trying to smile at Janice and Phil, though his eyes had lost the sparkle that had been there earlier in the afternoon. 'See you soon . . .'

Fourteen

If all went according to plan, Phil and Janice's cafe was due to open at the end of July. They had debated what they should call their premises. 'Tea room' sounded very staid and old-fashioned; 'coffee shop' was not strictly correct as they would be serving all sorts of beverages. 'Cafe' seemed to fit the bill, so long as people did not think it was a greasy spoon sort of place. They aimed to have a high standard both in cleanliness and in the food and drinks they served.

Eventually they decided they would call it simply Grundy's, which was what they had thought of in the first place. They hoped that before long the name would become known in the area and that their reputation for good food in a comfortable environment would spread.

They knew, though, that they must start in a comparatively small way and not be too adventurous. They had to balance their budget and not borrow more than they felt they were able to pay back or spend too freely on items that were not necessary.

They were pleased with the way things were taking shape. They had wondered at first when the walls were knocked down and old fittings and fixtures removed if it would ever come right, but a couple of months' work had completely transformed the place.

The kitchen area where all the work and preparation would take place was spacious and well equipped with up-to-date electric ovens and grills, a large stainless-steel sink, dishwasher, refrigerator and freezer, and working surfaces and cupboards in pale blue Formica.

The cafe area was roomy enough but not over-large. It would seat twenty in comfort, or so they estimated; five tables with four settings at each would leave room to dine with space to move around. But it was difficult to judge when the place was empty as it was at the beginning of July.

Janice had a fancy for circular tables but was persuaded that they might be impractical. Phil's father recommended a warehouse that he knew near Leeds and they purchased six square tables and twenty-four light oak wheel-backed chairs, all in a simple and practical design and, most importantly, at a reasonable price – so much so they were able to get an extra table and chairs, just in case they might be needed.

They had debated, too, about the style, the decor and the general theme of the cafe. No red-checked tablecloths, Janice had stressed – too ordinary and reminiscent of a fish and chip shop – or pristine white cloths which would be difficult to keep spotless and were rather mundane, or lace-edged cloths which were too genteel and old-fashioned.

Phil decided that Janice should have the final say regarding the decor. He guessed it would be mainly women who would frequent the place during the daytime, apart from visitors, of course, and elderly retired couples. There might be more men there at the weekends or in the evenings for the special pre-booked occasions but that was something to be considered in the future. They would start with morning coffee (or tea), light lunches, and afternoon teas, as they had originally planned.

The cafe area had been decorated in wallpaper of a neutral cream colour, slightly embossed, which would tone with any shade, and the paintwork was ivory. Janice had visited the local markets and in the large Halifax one she had purchased tie-on flat cushions for the chairs in a variety of floral designs. Then she had spotted some material which would be ideal for long curtains at the window; she had not really known what she wanted until she had seen it but now she could picture how it would appear – bright and cheerful, modern in design but with a touch of old-world charm. The background was bright yellow with a scattering of blue and white flowers in a heavy rayon which would hang well at each side of the window, reaching to the floor. The stall holder took the measurements and promised that the curtains, with golden ties and tassels, would be ready in a fortnight.

'It's about time you learned to drive,' Phil told her good-naturally, 'then you could do these expeditions on your own.'

'All in good time,' she promised him. She knew it might be a good idea. Her father was learning to drive and so was Val. Cissie was too, but as far as she was concerned it seemed to be causing endless arguments between her and Walter. She had not passed a test yet despite a couple of attempts.

The trip to Halifax had been fruitful as Janice had also bought tablecloths – a dozen of them so that there were always spare ones – in a delicate shade of lemon rayon. And so the colour scheme and theme of the cafe were taking shape. Flowery and summery, predominantly yellow and gold, giving a feeling of the countryside and sunny days.

There was crockery to be bought as well. Cups and saucers, large and small plates, fruit dishes, soup bowls, teapots, coffee-pots, serving dishes . . . The list seemed endless. Not to mention cooking utensils: pots and pans, cake tins, mixing bowls – the thousand and one things it seemed one needed to stock the kitchen.

They could not afford expensive china – Shelley, Coleport or Crow Derby – nor would it be practical. But the market stalls sold lots of oddments of cups, saucers and small plates. Janice decided that as long as the cup matched the saucer it would not matter if a variety of colours and patterns were used.

As well as combing the markets in the area herself, Janice enlisted the help of Norma and Patience. It was surprising what bargains could be found: oddments of cups and saucers, plates and fruit dishes in many kinds of floral patterns. She decided that they should keep to the floral designs rather than abstract or stripes and spots as they would add an incongruous note. And she preferred china rather than the heavier pottery for the morning coffee and afternoon tea sessions.

Some of the items they managed to find were from well-known china firms: Shelley, Rockingham, Aynsley and Wedgwood. Others were unmarked or from the lesser-known factories but they were all in good condition with no chips or cracks, and they all blended well together.

Phil had stressed, however, that the plates and dishes on which they would serve the snacks and light lunches at midday must be of sturdy pottery rather than china and that they should all be of the same plain design. Phil's father, once again, was able to help, recommending a retailer he had dealt with himself. They purchased large and medium-sized plates, soup bowls and dishes in cream-coloured pottery – perfectly plain but with an attractive sheen – at a reasonable price. The same firm met all their requirements for the kitchen, including labour-saving mixers and blenders and a coffee machine.

While the premises were being equipped and finishing touches added to the decor, Phil and Janice had been engaging their staff. Adverts in the local papers had brought a fair number of applicants whom they interviewed at the new place of work. The exterior had been painted in a leaf-green colour and a sign over the door simply stated Grundy's.

Janice was to be in charge of the morning and afternoon sessions, when the menu would consist mainly of cakes and pastries in the morning, and the addition of dainty sandwiches, toasted teacakes and crumpets in the afternoon. Phil would be responsible for the light lunches: homemade soup of the day, more substantial sandwiches with a side salad, various items on toast including scrambled and poached eggs, baked beans and creamed mushrooms, Welsh rarebit and omelettes with a choice of fillings.

Janice required someone who was competent at baking and cake-making, and Phil an assistant chef for the savoury dishes. The number of waitresses needed might vary from day to day, so they decided to start with just two, as they had to balance their wages budget, and see how things progressed. They engaged two cheerful and friendly-seeming women in their mid-thirties who would alternate with morning and afternoon shifts. Then there would be Ian helping out for a few weeks in August, and an advert for students who were looking for a holiday job brought a flurry of applicants.

Janice, who had left school herself only a few years ago, employed four girls – sixteen-year-olds from a local school who had finished their O-level exams and were waiting to go into the sixth form. They would share the work on a part-time basis and were willing to fit in and do odd jobs as well as waiting on the tables.

By the end of July it had all come together, as they had hoped, and they were ready to open. They had planned a small party for family members and friends on the last Saturday afternoon in July, then the cafe would open for business the following Monday morning at ten o'clock. This was the week before bank holiday Monday. They would, of course, open on all the bank holidays, as those would be the times when folk were out and about, making the most of their leisure time.

They would not open on Sundays. The day was still regarded, by and large, as a day to be set apart, whether from a religious conviction or the feeling that one day in the week should be a day of rest. There were exceptions, of course. Hotels and boarding houses could not take the day off, as Janice well remembered. This also applied to the Coach and Horses; Phil's father found that Sunday was one of their busiest days.

All the other shops in their row were closed on Sunday, and for a half day on Wednesday, which was the norm for most of the shops in the town. The exception was the newsagents, which opened on Sunday mornings to sell newspapers and anything else customers required but closed at midday. Janice and Phil knew they would be thankful for their day of rest.

A comparative rest, at least, as preparations would need to be made for the week ahead. It would be an early start for both of them each morning. They planned to rise at six o'clock to start baking the cakes and pastries that must be freshly made each day. Janice's assistant, a married woman in her forties who was experienced in that line of work, would join her at eight, and Phil's assistant, a young man of similar age to himself, would do so later in the morning.

One thing they had decided not to do was to bake their own bread; this would take too much time and effort. They made arrangements with a local bakery to deliver, each day, the required number of loaves, teacakes, crumpets and crusty rolls to be served with the soup.

They would deal with the financial side themselves with the help of an accountant from time to time. There was a small cash desk in a corner where Janice would write the bills and deal with the payments with the help of the waitresses. Janice hoped that all the baking would have been finished by the time the cafe opened so that she could deal with other matters. She guessed there would be very little time to themselves until they closed at five thirty.

It was agreed that tips should be the prerogative of the waitress – or waiter when Ian joined them – who had served the customer, not put into a general pool to be shared, as was the case in some places. Janice hoped that this would encourage service with a smile and a desire to please.

A smallish group of less than twenty gathered at Grundy's on the Saturday afternoon for the opening party. Ralph and Patience had driven over from Ilkley, leaving the inn in the competent hands of their staff. Alec, Norma and Ian drove from Blackpool while Sam and Val, Cissie and Walter did so from Halifax. The rest were friends of Phil and Janice and neighbours whom they had met recently – the newsagent and his wife, and the lady, a middle-aged widow who owned the florist's shop next door.

She brought a bouquet of sweet peas and roses still in bud, which delighted Janice. She put them in a cut-glass vase on the cash desk at first, then she would keep them in a cool place so that they would be fresh for the opening on Monday. The others had brought gifts of chocolates and wine; they had also received several cards with good wishes for their new venture.

As it was a private party in what was their own home, they started the occasion with a glass of sherry. They would not be permitted to serve alcohol on the premises but Phil intended to ask for a licence when they started catering for evening parties – something to think about in the future.

'This calls for a toast,' said Ralph, rising to his feet and raising his glass. 'I'm sure we would all like to wish Phil and Janice every success with Grundy's – what could be a better name than that! – and every happiness as they continue their married life together. We've already said that at their wedding and that was only three months ago. But what a lot they have achieved in that short time, and I'm sure they'll go on from strength to strength. So will you all please raise your glasses to . . . Phil and Janice.'

'To Phil and Janice,' they all echoed, standing as one.

Then there was a round of applause and a few cheers from the younger folk. Janice felt tears in her eyes as Phil stood to reply.

'Thank you for that, Dad,' he said, 'and thank you all for coming. It means a great deal to Janice and me to have you here today. But I'm not going to say any more as there's work to be done. Janice and I have the pleasure of waiting on you today.'

The guests dined on sandwiches of fresh salmon, roast ham, chicken and egg and cress, cut into dainty fingers, and small homemade sausage rolls. These were followed by a selection of the cakes that Janice intended to serve to the clients. There was Yorkshire tea bread, rich with fruit and delicious spread with butter, and three large cakes cut into slices: cherry and almond, coffee cake with buttercream icing and walnuts, and a lemon drizzle cake.

It was Janice's idea to have three such cakes, of different varieties, each day, to be cut as required, and small 'fancies' as well. For today's guests she had made tiny meringues with fresh cream, strawberry tartlets and small chocolate eclairs – an experiment as she was trying to perfect the art of making choux pastry. Fortunately they had turned out well so she was encouraged to make them again.

The tea, served in stainless-steel pots to keep it hot, was Yorkshire tea, the blend preferred by most true Yorkshire folk. Janice decided they could not go wrong with that, although she knew the posher varieties, such as Earl Grey, might be served in other places in town.

They were using the china oddments of cups, saucers and plates they had acquired from market stalls, second-hand stores and antique shops. There was a wide variety of floral designs: red roses, bluebells, primroses, bold daffodils and tulips, dainty forget-me-nots and fuchsias. They added a pleasing splash of colour to the summery theme of the cafe.

'You've created a lovely setting,' Norma said to Janice. 'There's such a nice, happy feeling to the place and I love the pictures on the walls. They're the perfect finishing touch.'

Janice laughed. 'Thank you; yes, I'm rather pleased with them myself. We couldn't afford expensive pictures – even prints are quite pricey. These are from old calendars. Phil's mum had one from last year with all different views of places in the British Isles, and I bought one of Yorkshire views from a second-hand shop. The frames are the cheapest we could find.'

'Well, they're really effective,' said Norma. 'They make you think of summer holidays.'

Janice had chosen the spring, summer and autumn views from the calendars, avoiding the snowy winter scenes. There was one of the North Yorkshire moors, purple with heather; the harbour at Whitby and the quaint fishing village of Robin Hood's Bay. And from other counties, a Cotswold village with trees in their autumn glory; a pretty thatched cottage surrounded by flowers; trees heavy with apple blossom in Kent; the grandeur of the mountains depicted in Scotland's Great Glen and Snowdonia in Wales.

'Talking of summer holidays,' Norma continued, 'your dad and I are off again for a short break in August. We thought we'd have a few days away while Ian is staying with you. He's not old enough yet to be left on his own so we thought it was a good opportunity.'

'That's a good idea,' agreed Janice. 'Where are you going?'

'Not very far, actually; your neck of the woods. We thought we'd visit the Yorkshire Dales, maybe travel up as far as Richmond. We've not booked anywhere; we'll just trust to luck with bed-and-breakfast places. And it will be a good chance for your dad to practise his driving!'

Janice smiled. 'How's he getting on?'

'Oh, he's getting the hang of it pretty well. He's having a few lessons with a driving school as well as going out with me. It's not ideal for a wife to try to teach her husband! Although we've not come to blows . . . I'm only joking! Your dad's very even-tempered.'

'Phil's trying to persuade me to learn,' said Janice. 'I really think I must but there doesn't seem to be much spare time at the moment . . . By the way, how are you getting along with Ian? I do understand.'

Norma nodded. 'Not too badly; it's improving. He's not quite so wary of me now. I try not to monopolize Alec and to include Ian in what we do. But he spends quite a lot of time on his own up in his room. He's got his mates he plays football with, and chess – that's something he enjoys. I know he's looking forward to coming to stay with you.'

'Yes, we're looking forward to having him for a few weeks. I'm so pleased you're here today, Norma,' Janice said as she saw Val and Cissie coming towards her.

'Well done, you!' said Val, flinging her arms round Janice. 'This place looks wonderful, doesn't it, Cissie? I feel sure you're going to do ever so well.'

'Yes, we're real impressed,' said Cissie, giving Janice a hug, 'and we've had a real good nosh-up.' She patted her stomach. 'I feel ready to burst.'

Janice reintroduced them to Norma, whom they had met only briefly at her and Phil's wedding. Then Norma moved away to join her husband.

'Yes, it's all splendid,' said Val, 'and we'll tell all our friends about you. Have you some special VIPs coming on Monday for the opening?'

'No, nothing like that. We've just advertised in the local press and we hope the word has got round. We'll just wait and see what happens. I expect folk will come for a nosey, and if they like it maybe they'll come again. Anyway, I'm pleased you've come, all four of you. You came in Sam's car?'

'Yes,' replied Val. 'There was no point in using both.'

'We've left the kids at home with Walter's mam,' added Cissie. 'We're both learning to drive, you know, Val and me, aren't we, Val?'

Val smiled. 'Trying to. I've not had many lessons yet, but Cissie—'

'I've been learning for ages,' Cissie broke in again. 'I've failed me test twice but I'll pass next time, you'll see! I stopped going out with Walter; he's too bloomin' critical. My instructor's a lot more patient with me.'

'Well, better luck next time then,' said Janice. 'I intend to learn eventually but we're too busy at the moment.'

The conversation went on to the forthcoming holiday in August when Walker's mill closed down for a week.

'We'll be having a few days in Scotland again,' said Val. 'We had a lovely holiday there before we got married. We'll go further north this time, up as far as Inverness.'

'And are you and Walter going away?' Janice asked Cissie.

'No . . . well, maybe for a day or two when Walter gets back. He's going on a cycling trip with some mates from the club. He asked if it was OK with me so I said yes, it was all right. It's more trouble than it's worth taking the kids away. Holly's only seven months old and we need to take so much stuff with us. Next year we might manage a holiday. I don't mind, though. I'm quite happy being at home with 'em.'

Janice was surprised at how complacent Cissie had become. She obviously thought the world of her two children; it seemed that her life revolved round them, but was it to the exclusion of Walter? Janice wondered. Cissie was still as lively as ever but did not seem to have the pride in her appearance that she had once shown. She appeared dishevelled, in a floral dress that was slightly crumpled, and her blonde hair was more than ever like a bird's nest. She wore her usual make-up, though: bright pink lipstick and pink nail varnish on her fingers and her toes, which peeped through her open-toe sandals. It must be difficult to be always well groomed, Janice supposed, with two young children to care for.

By six o'clock most of the guests had departed with promises that they would spread the word about Grundy's and that they would certainly come again themselves.

Alec, Norma and Ian were among the last to leave.

'Can I stay now?' Ian asked Janice in a quiet voice while his dad and Norma were talking to Phil. 'We've done all our exams at school.'

'I don't think that's a good idea,' she replied. 'You haven't got your stuff with you and Phil and I need a bit of time to get started and see how it's all going. There are sure to be a few problems at first. Let's get the bank holiday weekend over, then you can come the second week in August and stay till the end of the month. How's that?'

'Yeah . . . that sounds great,' he admitted.

It was decided that he should travel by train and get off at Leeds, where Phil would meet him, so that he would not need to change trains. He looked much happier when they said goodbye and waved cheerily as the car pulled away.

Fifteen

By the time Ian returned three weeks later Grundy's was attracting new customers day by day and getting a name for prompt and cheerful service and good food in pleasant surroundings.

There were a few teething problems such as learning to cope with a temperamental coffee machine and estimating how many cakes would be needed each day. Some varieties were more popular than others, although this varied from day to day. One morning it might be the coffee gateau that had all gone; another time the almond tarts. There were at least three large cakes to choose from, however, and a few sorts of small cakes so the choice was quite extensive.

Phil and Janice had known that it would be hard work; they were quite prepared to feel tired at the end of each day and they most certainly did. They had the evening to themselves, though, making sure they closed by five thirty. Then they prepared a meal for the two of them – three when Ian joined them. They enjoyed their times of relaxation in their new home and had no wish to go out of an evening. Maybe in a little while they would do so, they promised themselves. There was little time to visit their friends and families. Sometimes on a Sunday they drove to Ilkley to see Ralph and Patience. And Alec and Norma had said they would call to see them when they were on their tour of the Yorkshire Dales.

Ian had settled down happily with his sister and brother-in-law and was eager to pull his weight with all kinds of work. He made a valiant attempt at whatever he was asked to do. He had hardly ever entered the kitchen when they lived at the hotel except, maybe, to raid the cake or biscuit tin. His mother had not expected him to help with culinary matters, nor had she expected Alec to do so. She had been brought up to regard the kitchen as the woman's province. Alec had had to learn, though, and Ian was learning now.

He was becoming more skilled at peeling the potatoes that were needed each lunchtime for the meals served with chips. The actual preparation and cooking of the light meals was done by Phil and his competent assistant chef, Toby. There was washing up to be done – an endless line of pots and pans and dishes as the dishwasher could not cope with everything, but Ian helped cheerfully with the chores. He also took his turn at cleaning the small room with the toilet and washbasin so it was always in pristine condition for the use of the customers.

Ian's favourite job, though, was waiting at the tables at any of the three sessions where there was a need. He looked smart in black trousers and a crisp white shirt and was proving very popular with the customers. Janice soon realized that he tried to organize his shifts to coincide with those of Sophie, one of the four students they had engaged.

Janice persuaded him to phone home quite regularly, assuming that he would not want to write letters.

'You'll be seeing Dad and Norma quite soon, though,' she told him. 'They're going to pay us a visit when they're touring in the Dales.'

Ian grimaced, though jokingly; at least she hoped it was a joke. 'Oh, crikey! I thought I'd seen the last of them for a while,' he commented.

'Oh, come on now; things aren't too bad, are they?' she queried. 'I thought you were all getting on OK.'

'Yeah, I suppose we are,' he admitted. 'It's different, though.'

He had told her soon after his arrival about the changes that had been made in the bungalow since Norma moved in.

'Mum and Dad's wedding photos have been moved,' he said. 'You know the one that was always on the sideboard? Well, it's gone; I don't know where it is.'

Janice nodded. 'Well, I suppose that's understandable, Ian, and I know that Dad wouldn't mean any disrespect to Mum. But he's married to Norma now, isn't he?'

'At least he hasn't put up any of their wedding,' he replied. 'But they didn't have a lot of photos taken, just those that friends took. And there's still one of the four of us – you, me and Mum and Dad – that someone took years ago, but it's in a different place.'

'Well, there you are then,' said Janice. 'We're not forgotten.'

'And she's brought some of her own stuff. You know, those china ladies in fancy dresses – they're all over the place. And some different vases, and a big mirror over the fireplace.'

'Well, she does live there,' said Janice, 'and it's usually the women who make the home feel . . . well, homely. Men aren't always bothered about that sort of thing; they leave it to their wives but they appreciate it when it's done. You've got your own room upstairs, though, and you can do what you like there, can't you? Have it just the way you want it.'

'Yes, I'm glad I'm up in the attic,' he agreed.

But now Janice had told him about his dad and his new wife touring around Yorkshire, Ian looked disgruntled again.

'He never went away on holiday with Mum, did he? They've already been away on their honeymoon or whatever, and now they're off again. And they go out a lot in the evenings, to the club and to the pictures. He never took mum out, did he?'

'Yes, I know what you mean,' said Janice, 'but there was never really the opportunity, was there, when we had the hotel? Mum was working all the time, right till the end of the illuminations, so they couldn't go on summer holidays. But we all went to London for a few days, one year close to Christmas, remember? And they made sure we went on school trips and outings, even if they couldn't go themselves.'

'Yeah . . . S'pose so . . .'

'And they were happy, Ian, just being together in their home. Mum must have been exhausted sometimes when she'd finished her day's work and Dad was always there for her. We had a very nice home, you know, away from the hotel side of things. I'm finding it's like that now, and so is Phil. We're dead tired when it comes to half past five and it's so good to have our own home to relax in . . . There's nothing to stop you going out though, Ian. You won't want to stay in with us every night. Not that we mind,' she added. 'We love having you here.'

'Yeah . . .' Ian shrugged. 'But I've nobody to go with, have I?'

Janice gave a quiet smile. 'I've noticed you're getting quite friendly with Sophie,' she said. 'Why don't you ask her if she'd like to go to the pictures or . . . just for a stroll around, maybe. I know you can't go in pubs but there are coffee bars in town and it stays light till quite late in the evening.'

Ian blushed a little. 'Yeah . . . she's pretty, isn't she?' he said with a shy smile. 'She's older than me, though; she's taken her O-levels.'

'Well, a year isn't much and you'll have a lot to talk about with you both being students.'

'I'm not used to girls,' he said, 'being at an all boys' school. There were some girls at the youth club I used to go to but I've not been there since we moved to the bungalow.'

'Well, nothing ventured, nothing gained,' said his sister. 'Sophie seems a nice girl. I like her very much. Just you think about it.'

'Yes, p'raps I will . . .'

Janice experienced a fleeting moment of concern. What was she doing, encouraging her little brother to take an interest in girls?

'Don't be daft!' Phil reassured her when she told him. 'I'm pretty sure that Sophie is well aware of Ian. He's a good-looking lad; a bit shy, mind, but I'm sure they'll get on well. They're all very nice girls. You've chosen well there but I think Sophie is probably the pick of the bunch.'

Phil and Janice had both been highly satisfied with the staff they had engaged. As well as Sophie there were three more sixteen-year-olds – Sharon, Julie and Dawn. They were all competent and eager to please; they turned up on time each day and worked cheerfully while they were there. They agreed among themselves which shifts they would work on a part-time basis. But, as Janice had noticed, Sophie and Ian often seemed to be on the same shift.

The two full-time waitresses were Brenda and Jessie, women in their late thirties who had children who were able to fend for themselves if their mum was not there. There was no evening work, as yet, so they did not need to worry about leaving their families at night. There were always two people serving at the tables – either Jessie or Brenda and one of the students (which included Ian), or sometimes three if they were extra busy.

Phil's assistant chef was called Toby. He was a young man – older than Ian but not yet thirty – who had worked in a couple of places previously and had good references.

Janice's assistant was a woman old enough to be her mother, and Janice had taken to her straight away. She was a widow with grown-up children and was able to work early in the morning then return in the afternoon to make preparations for the following day. Janice had felt unsure about giving orders to Marjorie, as she was called. She was a much older woman who was also more experienced in the art of cake-making than Janice. But her new assistant said how pleased she was to be working in such genial surroundings.

'You mustn't be scared of telling me what you want me to do,' Marjorie told her. 'I've been used to giving orders myself.' She had worked for a confectionery business at one time and had been in charge of a large group of women. 'Some of the lasses could be real stroppy and I wasn't all that good at first at telling 'em what to do. It's nice now to be the one that's not in charge, so don't start feeling all embarrassed about it.'

They had got on well together from the start, and Janice looked to the older woman for advice and help with the more difficult skills.

'I learned a lot from my mother,' Janice told her new assistant, 'but she was largely self-taught; she'd learned it all from her own mother and then she'd done just a few night-school classes.'

'I'm sure she was as good in her own way, as are many of these top chefs,' said Marjorie.

'She certainly was. Visitors used to come back year after year to our boarding house.' Janice laughed. 'That was how my gran always referred to it – a boarding house. She would never call it a hotel, but when she died Mum decided it should be called that. Most of our neighbours' places were. And Mum gave it a name as well, something my gran would have called getting too big for your boots! She called it Florabunda, partly because my gran's name was Florrie and because she liked the Florabunda roses.'

'I know you miss your mum,' said Marjorie, 'but I'm sure she would be proud of you, the way you're coping with your new work.'

'Yes, I think she would,' Janice agreed. 'She badly wanted me to go to university and I was going to do so to please her and dad. So I hope she'd be happy about the way things have worked out.'

With Marjorie's help they perfected the trickier skills and were soon producing faultless chocolate eclairs, meringues, choux buns filled with cream and a variety of iced 'fancies', of which very few were left at the end of the day.

Ian did not take very long before acting on his sister's advice to further his budding friendship with Sophie. After all, he was only there for a few weeks so there was no time to be lost. They were working together on the lunchtime shift and he plucked up the courage to speak to her when they were clearing away. He was not sure, though, how to begin.

'Er . . . Sophie,' he said, 'I was wondering . . . are you doing anything tonight?'

She smiled at him, not with any surprise. 'Why?' she asked.

'Well, I thought, perhaps, we could do something . . . together; have a walk into town and have a cup of coffee or . . . something. If you'd like to . . .'

She smiled even more. 'Yes, I'd like to very much, Ian. I wasn't planning on doing anything like washing my hair. That's the usual excuse, isn't it? But I'd really like to – honest, I would.'

'That's great then,' he said, feeling a flood of relief. He had been dreading her saying no but she seemed quite keen to go with him.

She lived only a few minutes' walk away from the cafe, but as it was further away from the town they agreed to meet outside Grundy's at seven o'clock.

'Good for you,' said Janice and Phil when he told them.

'I won't know what to say to her, though, what to talk about . . .'

'Oh, you'll think of something,' said Phil, 'and I should imagine Sophie will have lots to say.'

And that was the way it turned out. Conversation flowed easily once they got started, and they found they had a good deal in common.

Ian felt a faint fluttering in the region of his chest – was it his heart? – when he saw her walking towards him. It had been a warm day and the sun was still shining. She was wearing a pretty floral dress with a flared skirt in shades of pink and blue, and a pink cardigan. Her dark hair waved gently over her forehead and round her ears. She wore just a touch of pink lipstick and a trace of green eyeshadow over her hazel-brown eyes. Not that Ian noticed all the details at first; he was just pleased that she had come and not changed her mind.

They strolled along the paths bordering the Stray, towards Harrogate, a mile or so away. It was Sophie who started the conversation, seeming to know that Ian was a little unsure how to begin.

'Tell me about living in Blackpool,' she said. 'It's a fun place, isn't it? Do you have a lot of fun?'

He laughed. 'Not all that much really. I don't think you do when you live there, not like the visitors do. The Pleasure Beach is the fun place. We used to go there when we were younger, Janice and me, when there was time, 'cause Mum was always busy. Yeah, we went on the Big Dipper and the Ghost Train and the bumper cars an' all that, but I've not been for ages. I watch Blackpool play – the football team, I mean. I go every Saturday in the season. They'll be starting again soon. And I kick around with some lads; we go to Stanley Park, the big park near where we live now. We used to live near the sea when we had the hotel but then . . . Mum died and we moved to the bungalow.'

'Yes, I know about your mother,' said Sophie. She and her friends had heard that Mrs Grundy – who liked to be called Janice – had helped to run a hotel in Blackpool after her mother died. 'It must have been awful for you and your sister.'

'Yeah, but Janice moved away to Ilkley, then she married

Phil only a few months ago. I like Phil, he's a great guy, but I miss Janice a lot. We always got on well, though she's a few years older than me.'

Sophie also knew that his father had remarried. 'I know how you are feeling,' she said, 'about your dad getting married, because the same sort of thing happened to me.'

'Did it really?' he said. 'You . . . lost your mum?'

'Oh, no, it wasn't as bad as that. I've still got my mum and my dad, but they're divorced. Dad got married again three years ago and I live with my mum, with her and Graham, 'cause she got married again as well. I didn't like him at first; well, I told myself I didn't, but he's not so bad. At least I've still got my own name. There's a girl in our form at school whose mother remarried and she changed Anne's name as well. Anne's real upset about it but there's nothing she can do, at least not yet. It's hard to get used to my mum being Mrs Davis but I'm still Sophie Miller.'

'And what about your dad? Do you see him?'

'Oh, yes, most weekends but not so much lately since I've been working. Actually, it was all his fault, I suppose. He got friendly with a young woman in the office where he works – in a travel agency. She's a lot younger than him and . . . well . . . you can guess! So he and Mum got divorced and now Dad and Carol have got a little girl called Wendy. She's four years old and she's a little love. And Carol's OK but I have to be careful what I say to Mum; she doesn't want to know.'

'Oh, gosh!' said Ian. 'It must be difficult for you.' He was relieved in a way to know that he was not the only one with a similar problem. 'I was just the same,' he admitted. 'I pretended not to like Norma but she's OK. And Dad's happy, I suppose.'

'And it's nice for you to be staying with your sister. When are you going back?'

'Oh, I don't want to think about that yet! We start school the second week in September so I'll see if I can stay almost till then.'

'Yes, that's when we start. I'll be in the sixth form then if I pass my O-levels! The results are out next week. I'm dreading it!'

'I'm sure you've no reason to be. You'll do well, won't you?'

'I hope so. What I mean is I'm dreading not doing as well as I should. I've taken eight subjects and I'd like to get Bs in most of them . . . or As, of course. What about you? You've not taken them yet, have you?'

'Er . . . no.' It was a sore point with him that he was only just fifteen. 'I'll be taking them next year. Actually, I'm doing them a year early. I've only been at the grammar school for three years but I was already twelve, one of the oldest in the class. So when I'd been there a year I skipped a year and went into the express stream, me and a few more lads, so we'll take the exams next year.'

'Oh, you clever clogs!' said Sophie.

Ian grinned a little sheepishly. 'Well, I don't know about that. I was doing OK with the work and we've caught up with the others.'

'So . . . what subjects are you taking?'

'Oh, the usual. Maths, science, French, Latin . . . ugh! History, geography, English language and English lit.'

'And what do you want to do when you leave? Go to uni?'

'Dunno. I've not really thought so far ahead. I stayed with my uncle a little while ago – he owns a garage – and I got interested in the cars and engines an' all that. You don't need to go to uni to be a mechanic and my sister's done well without going, but I don't know yet.'

'Is it an all boys' school?'

'Yes . . . That's why I'm not all that used to being with girls.'

Sophie held on to his arm for a moment. 'You're doing OK,' she said, smiling at him. 'Actually, it's the same with me. Ours is an all girls' school. They haven't got round to what they call co-ed yet. P'raps they will before long. I haven't decided either what I want to do. But I shall go into the sixth form – Mum wants me to – and you can drop the subjects you don't like so it won't be too bad. Just imagine, no more Latin or maths! I'm hopeless at maths. Anyway, that's enough about school, isn't it?'

They had arrived at the end of the Stray where the town centre began. They soon found a coffee bar that was not too crowded.

'Do you want coffee or would you like something else?' asked Ian. 'I'm paying,' he added, feeling very grown up to be saying so.

'OK.' Sophie grinned at him again. 'So you should, seeing as you asked me,' she said pertly. 'But my treat next time, eh?'

'Yes, fine,' he replied, 'if that's what you want . . .' He was delighted to think that there would be a next time.

They decided on strawberry milkshakes and iced cherry buns.

'They're OK,' said Ian, 'but not as good as my sister's.'

'Yes, she's an amazing cake-maker, or whatever you call it,' said Sophie.

He nodded. 'My dad's very proud of her . . . and Mum would be too.'

Sophie changed the subject. 'Would you like to go to the pictures on Saturday? There's one of those doctor films with Dirk Bogarde on in Harrogate. I like him and it's one I've not seen.'

Ian agreed that that would be great. He paid the waitress, who smiled at them both understandingly.

Dusk had fallen when they went out and coloured lights were twinkling around the square. Ian felt happier than he had for ages. Very bravely, he took hold of Sophie's hand as they strolled back along the tree-lined paths. She chatted about her friends who worked with her. Dawn was her special friend and had a boyfriend who was in the sixth form at the boys' school. And she, Sophie, had been friendly with a boy there but he'd now met someone else.

'I'm not bothered, though,' she said. 'There's more fish in the sea, as my mum says.'

Ian knew it would be polite to walk Sophie home. He couldn't let her wander around in the dark. They stopped at a semi-detached house halfway down a leafy avenue.

'Well, this is me,' she said. 'Thanks, Ian. We've had a lovely time, haven't we?'

'Yes, we have,' he answered. 'Er . . . thanks for coming.'

She laughed. 'The pleasure is all mine, as they say.'

They looked at one another then she leaned forward and kissed him on the cheek. 'You can kiss me if you like,' she whispered.

He did so, carefully and gently placing his lips on her slightly open ones. It was a new experience for him but one he would like to try again. But not just now; he already had quite enough to think about. 'Goodnight, Sophie,' he said quietly. 'See you tomorrow.'

'Yes . . . see you, Ian. Bye for now.'

He did not linger in the living room where Janice and Phil were watching the television, his arm around her as they sat on the settee.

'Had a good evening?' asked Phil.

'Yeah . . . great, thanks,' said Ian. 'I'll just go up to my room and read for a while.' He did not feel like talking, not that he thought Janice and Phil would quiz him but he wanted to be on his own with his happy thoughts.

Sixteen

'Ian enjoyed his stay with us, didn't he?' said Phil to Janice as they sat together relaxing after the day's work. 'And he worked jolly hard as well. He looked a bit downcast when I saw him on to the train but he seems to be in a better frame of mind about everything now.'

Ian had stayed a week longer than originally had been planned, and had only returned to Blackpool on the Saturday to start school again on the Monday.

'Getting friendly with Sophie has done him a world of good,' said Janice. 'Finding out that her mother − and her father − had remarried made him realize he's not the only one in that situation. And he says he's going to write to her. But it remains to be seen, doesn't it, how long that will continue?'

'Yes, they're only kids,' said Phil with all the wisdom of his twenty-four years. 'All the same, you can never tell. We were only young ourselves, weren't we, when we met?'

'What do you mean?' said Janice with a smile. 'We're still young, aren't we? I sometimes feel amazed at just how lucky we've been at our age. Our own business and our own home;

some young couples have to struggle like mad to get on their feet.'

'Yes, we've got off to a good start,' agreed Phil, 'and it's down to us to try to make sure it carries on that way. There may be something of a lull now that the summer season is almost over. It's not like Blackpool where it carries on till the end of October. I'm thinking it might be time to start with evening meals.'

Janice agreed that they could give it a try, and they decided to put an advert in the local paper and a notice in their window to say that they would be taking bookings for evening parties, but they must be pre-arranged.

Their new venture started quite slowly but it was enough for them to cope with until they saw how it worked out. Their first engagement was for a silver wedding anniversary party, a smallish family group of twelve. Phil gave them a choice of four different menus, asking them to choose two options – more than two would be difficult to cope with – for each of the three courses. Toby, and Janice as well, helped Phil with the starters of homemade chicken soup and grapefruit cocktail, main courses of roast beef and fresh salmon (with appropriate vegetables in season), and raspberry pavlova and sherry trifle as the dessert options. A fairly standard sort of menu, but he did not want to run before he could walk. He hoped to be more ambitious as time went on.

An added bonus was that Janice was asked to make the celebratory cake, which she decorated with pink and white icing, pink ribbons and miniature silver bells, with a small silver vase containing freesias on the top.

This October meal was a success, and bookings followed at the rate of at least one a week. The daytime trade, as they had anticipated, had dropped off slightly, but the evening bookings made up for it. In mid-October Janice had a phone call from Val.

'Guess what?' said her friend, not waiting for an answer. 'I've passed my driving test, first time!'

'Well done,' said Janice. 'You clever girl! I didn't know you were so far on with your driving.'

'I had some private lessons and Sam took me out as well.

He was very patient. Anyway, we're coming over to see you on Saturday and we'll have lunch at your place. It will give me a chance to drive on a long stretch of road. We might stay for afternoon tea as well; we'll see how it goes 'cause I want to look at the shops in Harrogate – they're a lot posher than the ones we have here.'

'We'll look forward to seeing you,' said Janice. 'You're making me feel guilty. I've not even started to learn how to drive yet.'

'Well, you haven't had time, have you?'

'No, that's very true. We've been busy here. Anyway, we can discuss all the news when we meet. See you Saturday . . .'

Janice made sure she had time to chat to her friends that Saturday after they had enjoyed their lunch. The lunchtime session was largely Phil's province, giving Janice a little time to herself. They closed for an hour to give them a short respite before the afternoon teas started at three o'clock.

Janice was pleased to see that Val looked well and happy. Neither of them mentioned Val's miscarriage earlier that year. Val did make an oblique reference to it, though, when she talked about being back at work.

'I didn't realize I'd missed the girls so much,' she said, 'while I was at home. I must admit I really enjoy office work and I'm not in charge any more. Susan took over my job when I thought – well, I hoped – I'd be leaving for good. And I don't mind a bit about being replaced. It's less responsibility for me and I'm still hoping I won't be there for ever.'

'How's Cissie going on?' asked Janice. 'Do you see much of her now?'

'Not as much as I did, but we still keep in touch, of course; we've been friends for so long. Oh . . . I nearly forgot. She's passed her driving test as well. She failed twice but she was determined to carry on. She can be real determined, can Cissie, when she sets her mind to something. Anyway, she's done it and she's as pleased as punch.'

Sam laughed. 'I only hope I'm not on the road when she's anywhere around!'

'Oh, Sam, don't be like that,' said Val. 'I'm sure she'll be OK. And the examiner wouldn't have passed her, would he, if she wasn't good enough?'

'Oh, I don't know so much. She'd flutter those big blue eyes at him. I'm only going by what Walter says. He's a bit worried about her going out on her own.'

'Well, I don't think she'll be able to do much driving while she's got the children to look after. She just wanted the satisfaction of knowing she could do it. She's probably improved a lot since she stopped going out driving with Walter. I know he used to get exasperated with her; that's why she had lessons.'

'Are Cissie and Walter getting on all right?' asked Janice. 'Apart from the driving, I mean?'

'Yes, as far as I know,' answered Val, a little warily. 'Why . . .?'

'Well, I sensed there was a bit of tension between them the last time I saw them. And there was that scene at your party . . .'

'Oh, yes, with Rita,' said Val, remembering only too well. 'He was only being friendly because she had just started working there. She's a very shy girl – at least she was at first, and he wanted her to feel at home. I think Cissie realized she'd been too hasty. Yes, Cissie and Walter are OK. They think the world of their children but I've tried to tell Cissie that she must spend more time with her husband when she can. She's so wrapped up in the kids that I wonder sometimes if Walter might feel rather left out of things.'

Val had heard a little rumour which she hoped was not true. She certainly wasn't going to spread it around. She was not a gossip and neither was Janice. She knew that Janice was only enquiring because she liked Cissie.

'Yes, she was such a fun-loving girl, wasn't she?' said Janice. 'It's odd to think of her as a housewife with two children.'

'Well, she seems happy,' said Val, 'but now I've passed my test I'm going to suggest that I babysit one evening so she and Walter can go out.'

'I'd better come with you,' said Sam. 'We could both babysit. I don't want you driving around in the dark on your own.'

'Honestly! You're as bad as Walter!' said Val. 'You must realize that we girls are perfectly capable of looking after ourselves.'

'You're quite right, Sam,' said Phil, who had just joined them after the lunchtime session. 'I would be just the same if it was Janice driving.'

'Well, it looks as though that might be a long time ahead,' said Janice, 'so you don't need to worry about it just yet.'

Val and Sam decided to walk to Harrogate to see the shops before returning for afternoon tea.

'It's great to see those two doing so well,' said Sam. 'They're really making a go of it, aren't they?'

'Most certainly,' agreed Val. 'I was wondering if we could come and have an evening meal here quite soon. What about us coming when it's your birthday?' Sam's birthday was at the end of November, in about six weeks' time. 'We could invite Jon and Thelma to come with us. What do you think?'

'Yes, good idea. They never have any trouble finding a babysitter. My parents or Thelma's are always pleased to look after Rosemary. We'd probably have to stay the night, though, and there's no room at Janice and Phil's place.'

'There are hotels nearby,' said Val. 'See . . . There's one there.' It was a prosperous-looking place overlooking the Stray, close to the town centre. There were other similar ones and Sam made a note of them to phone nearer the time after he had asked his brother and wife if they would like to come.

They had a quick look at the shops, although time was limited. They were grander than those in Halifax and Sam bought Val a shoulder bag in soft brown suede that he saw her admiring.

'You're so good to me,' she said. 'You mustn't buy me every-thing I say I like; it isn't good for me.'

'Why not?' He smiled at her. 'Make the most of it, darling. The time will come when we shall have . . . other priorities.'

They did not often discuss the family that they both wanted, having decided it was better to just let things take their course.

'You seemed a little wary when Janice mentioned Cissie,' he said to her as they walked back. 'You've not heard anything, have you? That Walter might be . . . playing away from home?'

'Nothing definite,' she said. 'I know he spends a lot of time with his cycling club and that's something Cissie has never taken part in. I think she should make more time to be with him on his own without the children but Paul and little Holly are everything to her at the moment. Why, have you?'

'Er . . . yes. I've heard a little rumour,' said Sam, 'but I try not to get involved in gossip. After all, it's none of our business.'

'It is if it involves my friend,' said Val. 'Let's hope that it's something and nothing.'

It was not long, though, before they were to learn more about it.

Cissie parked the car close to the entrance to Walker's mill. She had seized the opportunity she had been waiting for when Walter decided to cycle to work that morning, a bright sunny morning at the end of October. He was obsessed with keeping fit at the moment.

She had left the children with her mother who was pleased to look after them, but not for too long. That was why she had decided to take the car. Holly was OK on the back seat in her carry-cot, with Paul at her side to keep an eye on her. To walk to her mother's and then to the mill and back again would take too long.

She sat there for a few moments but not because she was having second thoughts. She knew the time had come to act on what she had heard.

She had been in the market hall last week, with Holly in her pram and Paul at her side, when she had seen Marlene, a young woman she had once worked with at the mill.

'Hello, Cissie,' she greeted her. 'How nice to see you; it's been ages, hasn't it?' Marlene had left the mill a few years ago. Her little boy was now at school but she had not returned to work. 'You look just the same, well, nearly the same. I heard you had two kiddies; time flies, doesn't it? Actually, I thought I saw you last week but when I got near I realized it wasn't you.'

Cissie looked at her quizzically.

'Er . . . perhaps I shouldn't be telling you this, but on the other hand you've got a right to know when it's about your husband.'

Cissie knew that Marlene had always loved to gossip and had often been guilty of spreading rumours far and wide. Nevertheless, she wanted to know. 'Come on then,' she said. 'What's all this about Walter?'

'Well, I was in the Fox and Hounds one night last week, with Sid, and I caught a glimpse of Walter at the other side of the room. He was with a blonde girl and . . . well, of course I thought it was you. Who else could it be? So I say to Sid that I'll just go and have a word with you. But when I got near I realized it wasn't you at all. So I turned round and went away again. I didn't speak to Walter. He might not have remembered me; any road, it was nowt to do with me who he was with. Happen it was his sister, eh?'

'He hasn't got a sister,' said Cissie. 'So . . . what was she like, this . . . blonde girl?'

'Well, she wasn't really like you at all; it was just the hair, y'see. She was a lot slimmer than you. Sorry, Cissie, no offence meant, but she was. Quite a scrawny-looking girl actually, not much meat on her bones. Looked as though a puff of wind 'ud blow her away. Quite pretty, though, and delicate looking.'

Cissie guessed at once who it must be. Her mind went back to the young lass that Walter had been talking to at Val and Sam's party all those months ago. Rita, that was her name. Walter said he was just being friendly because she had come to work in the office. She was keen on cycling and said she might join the local club . . .

'Thanks for telling me, Marlene,' she said. 'I know who she is. She belongs to Walter's cycling club but there's nowt in it. There'd be a few of the others there an' all. They meet at the pub now and again but I can't go 'cause I have to stay and look after the kids.'

This was not true, and probably Marlene would know that, but Cissie was damned if she would give her the satisfaction of thinking she'd caused trouble. She'd never liked Marlene anyway – spiteful little cow!

'Ta-ra for now. Be seeing you . . .' But Cissie hoped that she would never set eyes on the interfering madam again. She walked away quickly, tears of anger and hurt brimming up in her eyes.

She had been boiling up inside ever since but had tried to act normally in front of Walter. It was time now, though, to tell that scheming little hussy just what she thought of her.

Seventeen

Cissie knew her way around the mill and no one would question her being there. She had sometimes popped into the office to see Val but not so much recently since Holly was born. The office was just a few yards from the front entrance and there was nobody around as she flung open the door and went in.

The girls sitting at their desks looked up from their typing. Val stood up, smiling.

'Cissie, what a surprise! How nice to see you . . .' Her voice petered out as she became aware of the angry expression on her friend's face. 'Er . . . do you want something?'

'Do I want something? You're damned right I want something . . . or somebody. I'm looking for the little minx who's pinched my husband.' Her eyes darted round the room past Val and the other two girls, focusing finally on the little blonde girl who was staring wide-eyed at the intruder.

'There she is!' cried Cissie. She strode across the room and grabbed hold of Rita by her shoulders, pulling her to her feet.

'It's you, isn't it?' she yelled, shaking the girl till her head wobbled back and forth. 'It's you what's got your grubby little paws on my husband. Well, you can just leave him alone. Do you hear? We were happy till you came along, so just lay off him.'

The other young women stood up and moved towards them, aghast at what was happening.

'I'm not! It's not me, honest it's not!' cried Rita.

Cissie gave her a vicious shove, sending her crashing into the filing cabinet. 'Not you? Of course it's you. Who else could it be?' yelled Cissie, reaching out to grab a handful of the girl's hair.

Val and Susan pulled her away. 'Stop it, Cissie!' shouted Val. 'You've no right to barge in here, making accusations. What's come over you?'

'Her! She's what's come over me!' yelled Cissie, pointing at Rita who was cowering in a corner, tears streaming down her face. She was still crying, 'It's not me!'

Susan put her arm round the sobbing girl. 'Come along, Rita, it's all right. We know it isn't you. You've got it all wrong,' she said, looking sternly at Cissie. 'You'd better clear off, right now, before I ring the police and have you arrested for assault. Rita isn't interested in your husband. She has a boyfriend. I've seen her with him several times, haven't I, Rita?'

The girl nodded. 'Yes, he's called Jimmy,' she whispered. 'I don't go with married men. I wouldn't, not ever.' She started sniffling again.

'Just go, right now,' said Susan, 'before I get somebody to see you off the premises.'

Cissie looked a trifle abashed. 'There's somebody, though,' she muttered. 'If it isn't her then it's somebody else and she knows jolly well who it is . . . Who is it?' she shouted at Rita. 'Who is it that's messing around with my husband?'

'I don't know! I can't tell you! I won't tell you!' said Rita. 'Please . . . just leave me alone.'

'I think Rita deserves an apology,' said Susan. 'You coming in here and making ridiculous accusations.'

'They're not ridiculous and I know it's true,' Cissie insisted. 'He's been seen with a blonde girl and she looks like her.' She pointed at Rita.

'Well, we know that it wasn't Rita,' said Val. 'You'd better go, Cissie,' she said more gently, concerned that her friend was so agitated. 'Go and sort it out with Walter. That's the best thing to do. It will probably turn out to be something and nothing. By the way, where are your children?'

'I've left 'em with me mam,' said Cissie. 'I'll go and pick 'em up now.' She glanced sheepishly at Rita. 'Sorry, then . . .' she mumbled. But she couldn't resist a final retort. 'But you'd better tell whoever it is that I'm on to her.' She marched out of the room, still angry and clearly ready to do battle when she found out who was to blame.

'I'll make a cup of tea,' said Carol, the fourth member of the staff. 'I think we could all do with one. Your friend is quite a firebrand, eh, Val?'

'I'm afraid so,' Val replied. 'She's always been hot-headed but I've never seen her in such a rage as that. I'm sorry, Rita,' she said to the disturbed girl. 'Do you know anything . . . about Walter?' Her voice was gentle. 'I must admit I've heard a little rumour myself.'

The girl nodded. 'Yes . . .' she said in a tiny voice. 'There is somebody but I don't like to say.'

'Well, you don't need to,' said Val, 'not if you feel you shouldn't. It's up to Cissie to sort it out with Walter.'

Rita was silent for a moment then she blurted out: 'I'll tell you. I've got to tell somebody. I'll go mad if I don't. It's . . . it's my sister, our Linda. She looks just like me, actually – same blonde hair and everything. People sometimes think we're twins but she's two years older than me.'

'And . . . she's friendly with Walter?' asked Val.

Rita nodded again. 'Yes . . . I've told her it's wrong, that he's married, but she won't listen. There's nothing much going on, not . . . like that, at least I don't think so. But she likes him a lot and he seems to like her. She joined the cycling club just after I did and they got friendly. Happen she'll realize now what I keep telling her – she shouldn't be egging him on.'

'You haven't mentioned her very much,' said Val. 'I knew you had a sister but that's about all I knew. Where does she work?'

'At a jeweller's shop in town. She likes all sorts of fancy things and nice clothes. She likes the men an' all, does our Linda. She's not quiet and shy like me. Mum says we're like chalk and cheese. I suppose she's like our dad and I'm more like Mum.'

Carol brought her a cup of tea. 'I've put plenty of sugar in,' she said. 'It'll do you good. Are you feeling a bit better now?'

'Yes, I'll be OK,' said Rita. Peace reigned for a little while as they all drank their tea.

'I hope Cissie has calmed down,' remarked Val, 'but it's heaven help Walter when he gets home tonight!'

Cissie sat in the car trying to stop her limbs from trembling and to put an end to the jumbled thoughts buzzing around in her brain. She had been so sure that she was right. Who else could it be but that scraggy little blonde girl in the office? She fitted Marlene's description exactly and Cissie knew she was a member of the cycling club. If she was wrong, though, she had made a fool of herself and no doubt Walter would find out what she had done. But that didn't matter. It was Walter who was in the wrong – he was going to pay for it. And she was still determined to have it out with the girl when she found out who she was.

She put the key into the ignition and started the car. She'd go and collect the kids, then she'd call at the corner shop on the way home and treat herself to one of their nice meat and potato pies for dinner. She'd have to cook a meal for Walter and herself when he got home from work, though she didn't have much food in. She could call at the butcher's as well and get half a pound of sausages. She'd make chips and open a tin of beans. She was trying to think of other things to take her mind off her all-consuming worry.

She set off down the road towards the mill's entrance. She had parked a small distance away from the entrance gate as there had been a few other cars there. Her mind was churning round with thoughts of sausages and pies and the children and Walter. She put her foot down hard on the accelerator.

A large delivery van was pulling out of the gate of Walker's mill, edging out into the middle of the road in order to make a right turn. Bill, the driver, was aware of the car approaching in the near distance. Cars always gave way to let the vans out on to the busy road, or you might be waiting there for ages. But the car did not seem to be stopping. It was coming at a fair speed and Bill put up his hand to signal to the driver to stop. But it was too late. There was a tremendous bang as the car crashed into the side of the van just behind where Bill was sitting. The car that was following was a fair distance behind, or there might have been a pile-up. It drew up with a screech of brakes as Bill leapt from the van and dashed to the damaged car.

The front of the car was completely wrecked and the driver, a blonde woman, was slumped over the steering wheel. There was shattered glass all around her and he could see that her head was bleeding. He looked down at her in shock and horror. Her face was turned to one side and, to his dismay, he recognized her as someone he knew, although it would have been just as bad if she had been a stranger. It was Cissie, the lass who had worked in the mending room, then she'd married Walter, one of the overseers.

The man in the car that was following had dashed to the scene. 'My God, that's a bad do!' he said. 'We'd best get an ambulance quick sharp. She looks as though . . . well, let's hope she pulls through.'

'Aye, right away,' said Bill. 'I'll go back to t'office and ring nine-nine-nine. She drove right in t'side of me; never stopped. There was nowt I could do.'

'No, I know that, mate. I saw it happen.'

The few moments of peace in the office were brought to an end when the door was flung open again.

'I've got to ring for an ambulance right away,' shouted Bill, whom they all knew as one of the van drivers. 'There's been an accident, a bad 'un. It's that lass that used to work here. Cissie, young Walter's missus. She drove right into me. She didn't stand a chance.'

'Cissie!' cried Val. 'Oh no! She's not . . . Please say she's not . . .'

'I hope not,' said Bill. 'But she's in a bad way, that's for sure.'

'Let me phone,' said Susan, taking charge. 'You're all a-tremble, Bill.'

'We'd better let Walter know, hadn't we?' said Val.

'Yes, we must,' agreed Carol as Susan got busy on the phone.

Val dashed off to the weaving shed where she hoped she would find Walter, and she did find him straight away. He was shocked and bewildered to hear the news.

'Cissie? But what on earth was she doing here? And in the car? What about the children?'

'She left them with her mother. It's a long story, Walter, but never mind that now. You need to go to the hospital with her. We've sent for an ambulance . . .'

They found Sam and told him what was happening, and by the time they had all arrived back at the scene the ambulance was arriving with a police car following behind.

Walter stared in horror at his wife. 'Oh, my God! Cissie
. . .' He moved towards her but the ambulance driver stopped
him.

'Hold on a minute, sir. Let's get her out . . . She's still
breathing, there's a pulse there, but we can't waste any time.
You'll come with her to the hospital?'

'Yes, of course. She's my wife!'

Cissie was lifted on to a stretcher and an oxygen mask fitted
to her face. She did not stir and it was impossible to see what
injuries she had sustained.

'Could you let Cissie's mother know, please?' said Walter.
'And what about Paul and Holly? Her mother doesn't mind
having them for a short while but we've never left them with
her for very long. But as it's an emergency . . .'

'Don't worry about anything, Walter,' said Sam, 'except about
Cissie. We'll see to the children. Just let us know how she is
as soon as you can.'

'Yes, we'll be thinking about you and Cissie, and saying
a little prayer.' Val could scarcely speak for the lump in her
throat and she knew that Walter was feeling the same.
Whatever had gone on, she could see that he really cared
about Cissie.

Sam put an arm round Walter's shoulders. 'Yes, we'll hope
and pray that all goes well.'

Walter nodded. 'Oh, God, so do I!'

The ambulance drove away. The policeman was taking
particulars about what had happened from the very worried
van driver, and the man from the other vehicle was explaining
what he had seen. It did seem as though the accident had been
entirely Cissie's fault.

'I don't know what the hell she was doing,' Bill kept repeating.
'She ploughed right into me, well, in t'van.' Fortunately he
had escaped with a few scratches but was suffering from shock.
The van was badly dented and could not be driven, nor was
Bill in a fit state to drive it.

'Go and have a cup of tea,' Sam told him. 'The girls in the
office will make you one, then you take the rest of the day
off. Could you explain to my father what has happened, please?
I shall have to go with Valerie to see Cissie's mother. Someone

else will do the delivery, but that's not your concern. Don't you worry about anything.'

'Thank you, Mr Samuel,' said Bill. 'Aye, it's been a shock all right. I hope the lass'll be OK. She was a real livewire when she worked here, that Cissie.'

Sam and Val went to the small car park where the bosses and the few others who owned cars left their vehicles. It was almost midday now and they assumed that Cissie's mother would be at home. And she was, anxiously waiting for Cissie to arrive.

'What's up?' she said when she opened the door. 'Cissie said she'd be back by dinnertime to see to the kiddies. Where the heck is she?'

'I'm sorry, Mrs Foster,' said Val. 'I'm afraid Cissie has been involved in an accident, a collision with a van. It happened close to the mill and Walter has gone to the hospital with her.'

'We came as soon as we could,' said Sam. 'Walter was concerned about the children but he knew they'd be quite happy with you.'

'Aye, they're OK,' said the woman. 'You'd best come in and tell me. What's happened to our Cissie? Is she badly hurt? I don't like her in that bloomin' car. I never wanted her to drive; she's such a scatterbrain. Not fit to be on t'road.'

Paul looked up from the hearthrug where he was playing with his fire engine. 'Aunty Val, Uncle Sam,' he said, grinning at them.

'Hello, big boy,' said Sam. He looked understandingly at Mrs Foster. 'I'm afraid she's suffered a few injuries. It's hard to tell at the moment but the ambulance was there very quickly and she'll be in good hands now. She's a strong girl . . .'

'Aye, an' a silly girl an' all,' said her mother. Val knew that Cissie and her mother had never been close but Mrs Foster looked very worried now. 'Walter'll let us know, won't he? He's a good lad is Walter. Or should I go t'hospital? No, I can't,' she answered herself. 'I've got to see to these two. Cissie left a bottle for Holly, though she said she'd be back. I've nowt much else, though, for babies. She's gone on to baby foods now, in them little jars, so I could open a tin of chicken soup and give her a bit of that, and Paul can have some an' all with a bit of bread.'

It was clear that she was ready to pull her weight with the children. Paul, although he was a bright little two-year-old, did not seem to have picked up on what they were saying.

'You're going to stay and have some dinner with Gran,' she said to the little boy. 'That'll be nice, won't it? Then Daddy will come for you later. Mummy's . . . not very well just now.'

Paul looked at her and nodded, then went on playing with his cars.

'What the heck was Cissie doing, any road?' she asked. 'She said summat about going in t'mill.'

'Oh, she just wanted to have a chat with me,' said Val. 'I suppose she misses the company of the girls she worked with and she can't really go and disturb them while they're working. Their boss might not like it. But she knows I can spare time for a chat.'

'You being the boss's wife, eh?' said Mrs Foster with a wry smile.

'Maybe . . .' Val smiled at her husband. 'It does have its advantages.'

'We're always pleased to see Cissie,' said Sam. 'She was a good worker when she was at the mill and she's a good mother now. She thinks the world of those two.'

'Aye, so she does. She's surprised me, I can tell you, the way she's settled down to being a mother. I only hope she's going to be all right, the silly lass. I bet she was driving like a mad woman. All the same . . . please, God, let her get better.' She closed her eyes and clasped her hands together as she whispered the words.

'We all hope and pray that things are not too bad,' said Sam. 'Val and I will go to the hospital now and see what's happening. Try not to worry, Mrs Foster, although I know that can't be easy. And Walter will be in contact very soon. Goodbye for now.' He held her hand for a moment and Val kissed the woman's cheek, something she had never done before.

'Goodbye for now, Mrs Foster. Bye, bye, Paul and Holly . . .'

Paul glanced up and smiled at Val. 'Bye,' he said, waving his hand. Holly was sitting in a high chair, playing with a row of coloured beads fastened to the tray. She was ten months old now, a bonny little girl, the image of her mother and with the same blonde hair. She smiled, showing two tiny teeth, and waved a podgy hand at Val, who felt her heart give a jolt. How she longed for Cissie to recover and for her marriage to recover as well. It was clear from their actions and responses that Cissie and Walter still loved each other.

They found Walter in a waiting room near to the ward where Cissie had been taken on arrival. He looked pale and worried.

'Cissie's in the theatre now,' he told them. 'They decided to operate right away. She was still unconscious, of course, and badly cut and bruised. A few broken ribs and possible internal bleeding, they said, but they won't know the extent of her injuries until they operate. All we can do is wait . . . and hope and pray.'

'We've been to see Mrs Foster and the children are fine,' said Val, 'so you don't need to worry about them. But she's anxious to know about Cissie; naturally she's very upset.'

'She'll know as soon as I do,' said Walter. 'I must stay here, though; I can't go anywhere till I know.'

'Have you had anything to eat?' asked Val. It was now almost half past one.

'No . . . I haven't felt like eating.'

'You must have something,' said Sam. 'We've not had anything to eat since breakfast. I'll go to the snack bar and get us some sandwiches and tea. OK?'

Walter nodded. 'I suppose so . . . Er, yes . . . Thanks, Sam.'

'What on earth was Cissie doing at the mill?' asked Walter as Sam walked away. 'She didn't say anything to me about going out this morning. I'd have been worried sick if I'd known she was out in the car. I don't like her driving on her own, even though she's passed her test. She's so erratic. I suppose she seized her opportunity when I said I was cycling to work . . . and look what's happened. The silly girl! What was so important anyway?'

Val was unsure how much to tell Walter, but she decided it would be best to tell him the truth.

'She came into the office,' said Val, not admitting that Cissie had come in like a hell cat. 'I thought she'd come to

see me but she'd come to see Rita. She's got it into her head
that you were . . . well, that you'd got rather too friendly
with Rita.'

'Oh . . . no!' Walter sighed. 'I can just imagine her. Oh,
no, what have I done? It's not Rita, but I suppose somebody's
told her something and she's jumped to the wrong conclusion.
It didn't mean anything; it wasn't really anything much at all
. . . Oh, God, I'll never forgive myself if anything happens to
Cissie.'

Val could see that he was distraught. 'Rita told us afterwards
that it was her sister, Linda, that you'd got friendly with. But
Cissie doesn't know that; she just knows that it's not Rita.' She
was trying not to speak accusingly because she could see how
distressed he was.

'Yes, we have become friendly. Linda's a real lively girl. I
got to know her better when we went on that cycling holiday
in the summer. I've been a bloody fool, haven't I?'

Val didn't answer for a moment. She just looked at him
sadly but with a certain understanding. 'These things happen,
I suppose.'

'It's not gone very far; honestly, it hasn't. Cissie's not the
same as she used to be, although I know that's really no excuse.
She's so wrapped up in the children and it seems that she's
no time for me. She never wants to go anywhere or do
anything, and she used to be such a fun-loving girl. I'd wanted
to marry her for ages, you know, but she kept putting me
off. I was amazed when she changed her mind and said that
it was what she wanted. It was like a miracle.' He smiled
musingly. 'I know that we had to get married, as they say.
And that was another great surprise, that she gave into me,
after all she'd said in the past – all the times she'd told me we
shouldn't. I was so happy, Val, that I'd really convinced her at
last that I loved her. And now . . . I'm so sorry about everything; I just pray she'll be all right.'

Sam returned with the tea and ham sandwiches. He had
heard the end of the conversation.

'I was just telling Val,' said Walter, 'that there's nothing much
going on between me and Linda. I was going to put an end
to it anyway but she clings like a limpet.'

'Try not to beat yourself up about it,' said Sam. 'What's done is done and Cissie overreacted somewhat. Is there anything else Val and I can do to help? What about your parents? They won't know yet, will they?'

'No, I haven't had a chance to tell them. Mum will be only too pleased to help with Paul and Holly, to relieve Cissie's mother. Dad will still be at work, of course, and Cissie's dad.' The two men, who were friends through their work and also because of their membership of the same church, were employed at a different mill at the other side of the town. 'Fortunately Dad's got his car so he'll be able to help with visits to the hospital . . . when Cissie recovers.' The same thought was in all their minds – the hope that the outcome would be favourable.

'Val and I will go back now and relieve Mrs Foster of the children,' said Sam. 'Then we'll go to see your mother and put her in the picture. She'll be at home, will she?'

'I should think so,' said Walter, 'unless it's her day for the Mothers' Union. No, I think that's on a Tuesday; that was yesterday.'

'We'll get off then,' said Sam. 'Phone us, won't you, as soon as there's any news?' He remembered something. 'You've no car now, have you?'

Walter shook his head. 'No, and it looks as though it might be a write-off. But that's the least of my worries. I've got my bike, the use of Dad's car and Shanks's pony! All that matters is that Cissie gets well again.'

Sam gave him a comradely hug and Val kissed his cheek. Walter Clarkson had not been one of her favourite people but he had changed – for the better, she had thought – when he married Cissie, until this recent revelation. She believed him, though, that it was of little importance. But it was serious enough to have sent Cissie off the rails.

Now all Walter could do was wait. Several hours passed as he tried to read the magazines that were on offer, but *Reader's Digest* and *Geographical* magazines failed to hold his attention. Although he was not hungry he ate some more sandwiches at about five o'clock.

It was then that the surgeon came to talk to him. It was hard to tell from the man's expression whether the news was good or bad. Then he gave a fleeting smile.

'We've done all we can, Mr Clarkson, but we are keeping your wife sedated so we can see how she goes on. Her injuries are extensive but nothing too serious: a few cracked ribs and a broken arm, as well as internal bleeding and more superficial cuts and bruises. It could have been a lot worse with a head-on collision like that. However, we see no immediate cause for alarm. You should go home now; there is nothing you can do here and you need your rest. We'll ring you if there is anything you need to know. Come back in the morning. You don't need to wait for visiting hours. Rest assured that we're keeping a close eye on her.'

'Thank you, Mr Jeffreys,' said Walter, feeling rather more hopeful now. He was gratified to know that one of the top surgeons had been in charge of the operation. 'She's a strong girl and that helps, doesn't it? I've hardly ever known her to be ill, and when she is she soon pulls round.'

'Yes, a strong constitution is always a help,' replied the surgeon, seeming unwilling to commit himself too far. 'As I've said, we've done all we can for the moment.'

Walter phoned for a taxi which took him to his parents' house. Holly was already bathed and asleep in the cot that was always ready at his former home. Paul was in his pyjamas and looking at a nursery rhyme book with his granddad. He was delighted to see Walter.

'Daddy!' he cried, holding out his arms.

'Hello, big boy,' said Walter. 'Mummy's not very well just now but you'll be able to see her soon.'

The child nodded, looking a little confused but quite content that his daddy was there along with his doting grandparents.

Walter filled them in with the news.

Mrs Clarkson shook her head. 'She's an impulsive lass, that wife of yours. I know you're not happy about her driving. What was she doing, any road, going to the mill?'

'She went to have a chat with Val,' said Walter. If it was up to him they would not know the full story. 'She misses the girls at work, you know.'

'Aye, I suppose she does,' said his mother, 'but I can't fault her for the way she looks after the kiddies. She's made you a good wife, Walter, lad. Let's just hope there's some good news tomorrow. You must stay here tonight. Your old room's just the same as it always was. I've got plenty of nappies and some of that Cow and Gate milk for the little 'un. They'll come to no harm here, bless 'em, but let's hope their mummy'll be back before long.'

Eighteen

Walter was awake early. He had slept surprisingly well, albeit for only a few hours, tired out mentally and physically by the traumas of the day. He was tempted to dash straight to the hospital but he knew it would be better to bide his time and give Cissie a chance to come round . . . Please God, he added in a silent prayer.

Besides, there were things to be sorted out. His car had been towed away and his bike was still at the mill where he had left it when he had cycled to work yesterday morning. It seemed, now, to be ages ago, not less than twenty-four hours.

'Now, don't you worry about these two,' said his mother. 'We'll look after them for as long as we need to. That's to say I will, while your dad'll be at work. But he'll drive you round to the mill to get your bike, then at least you'll have some form of transport. Eeh, lad, I don't know! What a pickle we're in, aren't we? But nowt much matters so long as your lass gets better.'

Walter was pleased that his mother was not saying that it was all Cissie's own fault, caused by her reckless driving, especially as he knew the reason for it. She had always liked Cissie. The two families, the Clarksons and the Fosters, had been friendly for a long time. And it had long been the idea of the mothers, Millie Clarkson and Hannah Foster, that their son and daughter, their only children, should fall in love and get married.

The two had been courting, after a fashion, for a few years, although it had seemed that Cissie was not at all sure what she wanted. Then, suddenly, it had all changed. The couple had announced that they were engaged and would soon be getting married. What's more, Cissie was expecting a baby. This had cemented the ties between the two families even more.

'Thanks, Mum, you're a star,' said Walter. 'Now, Paul, you be a good boy for Grandma and look after your little sister. Daddy will come and see you in a little while.'

'And Mummy?' asked the child, beginning to notice that she was not there.

'And Mummy as well . . . we hope,' said Walter.

He retrieved his bicycle from the stand where he had left it after first calling in at the mill to say that he would not be coming in that day but would start work again the following morning, all being well.

He cycled to the hospital and made his way to the ward where Cissie was in a side room on her own.

'She's just coming round,' the nurse, who was in charge of her, told him. 'She's still very drowsy and confused. You may see her for a little while but please don't stay too long, Mr Clarkson. We're hoping she will become a little more coherent as the day goes on.'

'She's doing all right though, isn't she?' asked Walter. 'She's going to get better?'

'We're quite satisfied with her progress,' said the nurse, 'considering the multiple injuries she sustained. Fortunately, none of them were too serious, but it's early days, of course.'

Cissie looked pale and almost lifeless, lying motionless between the stark white sheets. Her eyes were closed; her head was bandaged covering what must be a severe cut on her forehead. Her face was badly bruised and her left arm was encased in a plaster cast.

Walter stood and looked at her for a moment, then he spoke quietly. 'Cissie . . . Cissie, love, it's me, Walter.'

She opened her eyes and stared at him, unfocused and with a puzzled expression. 'Walter . . .' she said in a hoarse voice. 'Where am I? I don't know . . . I can't remember . . .'

'You're in hospital, Cissie,' he said gently. 'You had an accident in the car and they brought you here. You're going to be fine but you must stay here and rest until you're feeling better.'

She frowned a little, moving her head back and forth as if trying to remember. 'Paul . . . Holly . . .' she said. 'Where are they?'

'They're with their gran, with my mother. She's looking after them and they're OK. You'll be able to see them soon.'

'Soon . . .' she repeated. 'Yes, I'll see them soon.' Then a look of alarm crossed her face. 'What happened? What did I do? I was cross, very angry, and then . . . I can't remember.' Her voice faltered and she looked at him helplessly.

'Don't worry about it,' said Walter, taking hold of her hand as it lay on the grey blanket. 'It's all right now, love; it's all over . . . I love you, Cissie.'

She smiled weakly at him. 'Love you, Walter . . .'

She closed her eyes again and Walter knew that she was tired and he had stayed long enough. He was satisfied that she had come round and that her injuries, though quite extensive, were not as bad as they could have been.

He cycled back to his parents' house where he made use of their telephone to pass on news of Cissie's progress. He phoned the mill office and spoke to Val, who had been waiting anxiously for news of her friend.

'She's confused about what happened,' he told her, 'but she seems to remember that she got upset about something. She'll remember more in time, I suppose. I told her not to worry about it, that everything was OK. I'm truly sorry for my part in all this, Val. My friendship with Linda, it was nothing . . . Well, something and nothing, compared to what I feel for Cissie. I'll make it up to her. I can't imagine how I'd go on without her.'

'And she feels the same about you,' said Val. 'That's why she acted the way she did; it was the thought of losing you. The girls are really upset about what has happened, even Rita. We're having a collection, from those who know Cissie, to send her some flowers. Do you think I might be able to visit her or is it only relatives?'

'I'm hoping that by the weekend she will be much improved. I'll take the children in if they'll allow it, and our parents will want to see her. But you're just like a family member, Val. You've always meant so much to Cissie. Must go now; Mum keeps a tight rein on her phone bill!'

'Cheerio then, Walter. Give Cissie my love . . .'

'You'd best stay with us while Cissie's in hospital,' said his mother. 'There's no point in you going back home every night. Hannah and me will look after the kiddies between us. I know she likes to hand 'em back when they want their nappies changing but she'll have to pull her weight. Thank goodness little Paul is potty trained. Cissie's done well with him, she has that! And I reckon the best thing you can do, lad, is to go back to work. It'll take your mind off it all.'

He agreed that this was the best idea. He cycled round to the Fosters' home – they were not on the phone, much to Hannah's chagrin, now that her friend, Millie, had got one – to pass on the news about Cissie. Mrs Foster agreed that she would share the workload with the children. After all, it was her daughter, and her only daughter at that.

Walter borrowed his father's car again to visit his wife that evening. He was pleased to see that she appeared much less confused and he guessed that she might be starting to remember what had happened. She was still lying down, however, flat on her back.

He bent to kiss her cheek. 'Hello, darling. How are you feeling?'

'Bloomin' awful!' she replied and laughed, then winced as it was obviously hurting her injured ribs. 'I've broken me arm, haven't I? Thank goodness it's me left one. I'll be able to feed meself when I can sit up, with a spoon, any road. But I can't sit up yet. The nurses have to feed me and help me to drink through a straw. I can't eat much; only enough to keep a bloomin' sparrow alive, but they say I've got to get me strength back.' Her head flopped to one side as she gasped for breath after such a long speech.

'Cissie,' he said, taking hold of her hand, 'don't talk any more just now. It's making you tired. Just listen to me. You're doing fine and everything's all right at home. My mum and yours are looking after the children and I shall bring them in to see you in a day or two.' He was quiet for a few moments, letting Cissie rest, then she opened her eyes and smiled at him, a little worriedly.

'I remember . . . I sort of remember going to the office where Val works. And that girl, Rita. I was angry with her because I thought . . . But it wasn't her, was it? And I was horrible to her . . .' She looked at him fearfully; her lovely blue eyes, though surrounded by purple bruises, were full of concern.

Walter wanted to convince her that she had no need to worry about his love for her and only her. But he had to be truthful, to a degree. 'No, it wasn't Rita,' he replied. 'There's no one, Cissie, love, no one but you. I . . . er . . . I got friendly with a girl called Linda; actually, she's Rita's sister. I saw her a couple of times, usually when the rest of the cycling club were there.'

That was as much as she needed to know. He had never gone very far with Linda – only a few kisses, which he now regretted – but he had been tempted. It was all over now, though. He would tell Linda so, but no doubt the news of Cissie's accident would have reached her ears.

'I'm sorry, Cissie,' he said, kissing her cheek, 'but it's not the same going to places without you. I know you're busy with the children but I miss it being just you and me.'

She tried to nod her head. 'Yes . . . I know. An' I shouldn't drive, should I? I'm a bloomin' awful driver and now I've gone and smashed up your car. I have, haven't I?'

He smiled. 'I'm not sure what the damage is yet. But it doesn't matter. We're insured and they'll sort it out. Nothing matters as long as you get better. And you will. I know you must be feeling pretty awful just now but they're taking good care of you. You'll be able to come home when all those injuries have got a little better.'

Cissie's face crumpled. 'I want to come home now, Walter. I want to see Paul and Holly.'

He could see tears brimming in her eyes. Until that moment she had seemed to be making the best of things.

'I know you do, darling, but you can't, not just yet. I'll bring the children to see you if the nurse says I can, in a day or two. It will soon be weekend and I expect you'll have a lot of visitors then.' Her eyes were closing and Walter knew he must go. At least he had made his peace with her and she seemed content. He kissed her gently on her bruised cheek.

'Bye, Cissie, love. I can see you're tired and there's nothing like rest to get you better again. Night, night, love; sleep tight and I'll see you soon.'

'Night, night, Walter,' she whispered. 'Love to Paul and Holly.'

By weekend she was sitting up, propped against the pillows, but still needed help to get in and out of bed. She was unable to bath or wash herself because of her broken arm and other injuries to the upper part of her body. She had a number of visitors, restricted to two at a time, although Walter was allowed to bring both children in for a little while.

They came on Saturday afternoon, looking puzzled to see Mummy in bed and looking rather different. Paul seemed to understand and was less than his usual boisterous self. He perched on the side of the bed and tentatively touched the plaster cast on her arm.

'You've got a poorly arm, Mummy,' he said, 'and your face looks funny.'

This made Cissie laugh, although it hurt to do so. She winced a little. 'Yes, Paul, I know I look funny but I'll be better soon. You be a good boy for Daddy and your grandmas, and look after Holly. She doesn't know what's going on, does she? Me lying here like a wounded soldier!'

Walter had lifted the little girl on to the bed, holding her on Cissie's outstretched legs, a part of her that had not suffered much damage. Cissie put her right arm around the child who, at first, stared at her uncomprehendingly.

'It's Mummy,' said Walter gently. The child still stared at her unsurely. Then a light of recognition came into her blue eyes and she smiled, reaching out a chubby hand to touch Cissies' face. At ten months of age she was not yet talking, only making sounds like 'baba' and 'dada', which Walter was sure was Daddy. She made a little gurgling sound of delight and Cissie leaned forward as much as she could to kiss her cheek.

'I feel better already,' she said, although Walter knew there was still a long way to go.

They stayed for less than half an hour. Walter's parents were waiting to come in; his father had brought them all in the car. They also did not stay long. Mrs Clarkson had brought some homemade cream buns to tempt Cissie's appetite, knowing that hospital food was not always as palatable as one might wish. Walter had brought her favourite women's magazines and chocolate biscuits. Paul had said they must take some jelly babies for Mummy because she always pinched the black ones out of his packet. Walter had not taken flowers as he knew she would have some the following day when Val visited her.

Many of the girls, and the men, remembered Cissie as a bright and cheerful colleague at Walker's mill and were pleased to contribute to flowers and chocolates for Val to take to the hospital. She chose a bouquet of colourful autumn flowers at a local florist's. Small chrysanthemums rather than the large ones like mop heads, which always reminded her of funerals, in shades of yellow and russet; dahlias in glowing red, orange and purple and a box of Milk Tray chocolates.

To Val's surprise Rita asked if she might accompany her to the hospital.

'But she was so horrible to you,' said Val. 'I know she was sorry afterwards for making a mistake but she didn't half go for you. It's very generous of you to be so forgiving.'

'Well, I feel really sorry,' said Rita. 'I did try to warn our Linda not to encourage Walter. She knows about Cissie's accident and she's gone very quiet and moody. She knows it's over with Walter and, like I said, she was doing most of the running. Anyway, I can't help liking Cissie. I can see she's a good-hearted girl in spite of her quick temper.'

'Well, I'll take you then, if you're sure,' said Val. 'Cissie's parents are going at two o'clock; I believe Walter's dad's taking them. So we'll go at three o'clock for the last part of the visiting time. I'll come and pick you up in the car.' Val still had a feeling of pride when she said that and even Sam admitted that her driving was improving.

Cissie's parents were at her bedside when Val and Rita arrived but quickly left as the nurses were quite strict about the number of visitors.

'She's getting better,' Mrs Foster remarked to Val. 'She'll soon be her old cheeky self again. Trust our Cissie to wreck the car! I don't know, I'm sure.' She shook her head. 'Walter has a lot to put up with but happen she'll realize now that she must leave the driving to him. It's a man's job, any road, is driving.'

'I've driven here,' said Val, smiling – rather smugly – at the woman. 'I passed my test a while ago.'

'Well, let's hope you're better at it than our Cissie,' said Mrs Foster with a disgruntled frown.

'Give over, Hannah,' said her husband. 'Girls do all sorts of things nowadays.' He winked slyly at Val. 'Come on, Archie'll be waiting for us.'

Cissie smiled when they approached the bed, looking a little sheepish at Rita. Val was shocked to see how battered and bruised her friend looked: a bandage around her forehead and her arm in a sling. But her smile was still there, though rather uncertain, as it might well be at seeing Rita.

Val put her arms round her, carefully though, aware of her injuries, and kissed her cheek. 'Hello, Cissie, love,' she said. 'We've been so worried about you but you're still smiling.'

'Just about,' said Cissie. 'It's great to see you . . . and Rita. You're the last person I expected to see.' She looked at the other girl. 'I'm sorry I lost my temper but I thought, I really thought . . .'

'I know,' said Rita. She took hold of Cissie's hand but did not attempt to embrace her. That would be going too far and she did not know her the way that Val did. 'I couldn't tell you then that it was Linda, not me . . . but you know that now, don't you? Your husband has always been very kind to me, helping me to feel at home at the cycling club – I'm quite shy, you see, really. And I met my boyfriend there. I would never dream of . . . well, you know. But our Linda's a terrible flirt.'

'Walter told me about it,' said Cissie. 'He says it's all over and I've got to believe him, haven't I?'

'It is, I can assure you,' said Rita.

'Well, let's hope so. I might not have forgiven him so quickly if I wasn't lying here like this. He's making a real fuss of me now but why shouldn't he? Guilty conscience, I reckon. But I know he really does love me.' She smiled thoughtfully. 'Any road, what's going on in the outside world? I feel shut away in here. Can't wait to get out, I can tell you.'

'You're not missing much apart from a spell of bad weather,' said Val. 'It's done nothing but rain.' The pleasant autumn days had given way to wind and squally showers. Fallen leaves lay in sodden piles in the gardens and on the pavements of tree-lined roads away from the town centre. 'Anyway, we've brought you these to help cheer you up.'

Cissie was delighted with the flowers and chocolates. 'What lovely colours, like a rainbow,' she said. 'It's hot in here, though. I'll ask the nurse to put them on the windowsill where it's cooler.' She was still in a room by herself, which seemed to indicate that she still needed special care. 'And my favourite chocs! I'd best eat 'em before they melt. My appetite's come back, just a bit. I have to manage with one hand; luckily me right hand's OK or else I'd be in a right pickle.'

She sounded cheerful enough but Val could see the strained look on her face and the way her eyes lost their brightness from time to time as she became aware of the recurring pain. Sometimes her voice faltered and it was clear that her medication was taking effect. They knew they must not tire her by staying too long.

'Well, we must love you and leave you,' Val said when she could see Cissie's eyes closing, although she was trying hard to stay awake. 'I'll come and see you again, depending on how long you'll be here.' Val guessed she would be there for quite a while but did not say so. 'Walter will let us know how you're going on.'

'How did you get here?' asked Cissie. 'Did Sam bring you?'

'No, I drove here,' said Val. 'I'm feeling more confident now.'

'Oh, yes, of course. I'd forgotten you'd passed your test an' all. I'm sure you're a bloomin' sight better than I am. Can't see me driving again. Don't suppose Walter'll let me. Any road, we've no car now, have we?'

She looked stricken and Val put an arm round her. 'Now, don't you worry about things like that. It will all be sorted out. You just concentrate on getting better.'

'OK, I'll try.' Cissie gave a weak smile as she raised her hand in farewell. 'Bye, Val; bye, Rita. Thanks for coming.'

'I think Cissie is still in quite a bad way,' Val said to Sam that evening. 'She's trying to be brave but I could see she's still in a lot of pain.'

'She's sure to be,' said Sam. 'It could have been a lot worse. She might have been killed.'

Val shuddered. 'Don't say that! It's so frightening how quickly accidents can happen.'

'Well, the worst didn't happen, did it? She's still here, thank God!'

'And things may turn out better than they may have done in the long run,' said Val. 'I was feeling worried about them. Cissie had become so complacent, so obsessed with the children. And Walter, well, he was beginning to stray, wasn't he? I don't think it had gone very far but it might have done before long.'

'He's learnt his lesson the hard way,' said Sam, 'and certainly poor Cissie has. She's come off worst.'

'I was wondering . . .' Val said thoughtfully. 'Cissie and Walter need to spend some time on their own. Perhaps, when she's well again, do you think we could look after the children for a little while – a weekend, or maybe a bit longer – so that they can have a few days away?'

'You mean that Paul and Holly should stay here?'

'Yes, why not? Paul knows us very well, doesn't he? And Holly's a good baby. Cissie says she's never been much trouble.'

'They have their parents, though, Walter's and Cissie's. How would they feel about someone else taking charge of the children?'

'I'm sure they wouldn't mind. Cissie's mother was never much real help to her until this happened, although it seems to have brought them closer together. And Walter's parents are rushed off their feet, aren't they, now Cissie's in hospital?'

'That's true but it would all depend on what Cissie and Walter think about it. Let's wait and see. Cissie has a long way to go before she's really well again.'

Sam was not unwilling to go along with Val's idea but he was concerned about how it might affect Val to be in such close proximity to the children. He had the feeling that it might make her more anxious than ever to start a family of their own. She did not talk very much about the subject now. The miscarriage had been a great disappointment to both of them but particularly so to Val. There had been a few times before when she had been sure she had conceived, only to have her hopes dashed.

Now, though, she had settled down to her office job again and seemed quite contented. As far as he was concerned, Sam was happy with things as they were, for the time being. They had been married for less than two years and it was a very happy marriage. He would, of course, like a family eventually, but they were young enough to wait a little while. Sam did not want her longing for a child of her own to be intensified by caring for Paul and little Holly.

Nineteen

Val did not waver from her determination to look after Paul and Holly so that their parents could enjoy a short break together. When she told Cissie about her idea some weeks later her friend was delighted at the suggestion.

By the beginning of December Cissie was well on the road to recovery. She had stayed in hospital for ten days and it had been a further two weeks before her broken arm had healed.

Val drove round to see her just after the plaster cast had been removed; it was Val's half day off work. Cissie was on her own in the house as Walter's mother had taken the children out for a short time. Cissie had insisted that she would be able to manage now that she had the use of both her arms again, but her mother-in-law still came round every day to see if she needed any help.

Cissie hugged her friend when she heard of her idea. 'Gosh, that would be wonderful! It's just what we need, Walter and me. We're OK again now, you know. He's been bloomin' marvellous while I've been in hospital and he still is now I'm back home – fussing around me like an old mother hen.' She laughed. 'No, that's not right, is it? An old father cock, maybe! Well, you know what I mean. He can't do enough for me but I've got to start fending for meself and for the kids. Me arm feels all peculiar and me ribs are still sore, but I'm still all in one piece and that's all that matters. He's having to manage without his car – and that's my fault – but it's all being sorted out and he says we might have another one before Christmas. I shan't drive again, though. I've learnt me lesson.'

'You might change your mind; you're sure to feel anxious at first. Anyway, don't bother about all that now. You tell Walter about my idea and see what he thinks. Next weekend we're going over to Harrogate to have a meal at Phil and Janice's place for Sam's birthday. But any time after that would be OK. I know it's getting near Christmas but I'm sure you'd be able to get in somewhere.'

'And I need a bit of time with Paul and Holly before I go dashing off again,' said Cissie. 'I've not been home long but I know they'll be fine with you and Sam. I'll go and make us a cup of tea . . . No, you stay there; I've got to manage by meself.'

Val went with her, though, into the kitchen, watching her carefully as she poured the boiling water from the kettle into the teapot, but not offering to do it for her.

'Choccy biccies,' said Cissie, opening a tin and putting some on a plate. 'Walter kept bringing these when I was in hospital.'

Val did help her by carrying the tray and they settled down near the coal fire in the living room. The guard was always in place in front of the fire and a clothes horse nearby with nappies and baby clothes airing.

'You'll have all this to do for Holly,' Cissie told her friend. 'Are you up for it? We won't stay away too long, though.'

'I wouldn't offer if I didn't mean it,' said Val. 'Anyway, it will be good practise for me. Perhaps, one of these days . . .'

She said no more and Cissie did not comment. The two were such good friends that they were attuned to each other's feelings.

'I wonder where we could go to, me and Walter,' said Cissie. 'It's not really the weather for the seaside, is it? Scarborough'll be bloomin' freezing in the winter. D'you know where I'd really like to go?' She didn't wait for an answer. 'London! I've never been and there's always summat on the telly about the queen and Charles and Anne. Not that we'd see them, of course, but I'd like to see Buckingham Palace and all them other places; the Tower of London and Big Ben and all the posh shops.'

'Well, see what Walter thinks about it.'

'Yes, I will . . . Ey up, here's his mam coming back with the kids. Don't say anything to her, will you, not till I've told Walter?' she added in a whisper.

Val spent another pleasant half hour with the children and their grandmother, a friendly, homely woman, plumpish and smiling, who clearly doted on the children – not at all a typical mother-in-law figure. Val preferred her to Cissie's mother, although she had mellowed somewhat since her grand-children had been born. Val nursed Holly before Cissie put her down for her afternoon nap and played with Paul, zooming his police car around the furniture.

'We'll let you know soon,' Cissie assured her as they said goodbye at the door. 'I'm so excited. I can't wait to hear what Walter says.'

She phoned the following day to say that Walter was very pleased with the suggestion and would the second week in December be convenient? Christmas Day would be on a Thursday and so, provided they could make the necessary arrangements, Cissie and Walter had decided they would have a long weekend away from Friday the twelfth of December, returning on the following Monday. All that remained now was to find a suitable hotel and book the train tickets.

Walter had visited the capital city only once before, with his parents when he was a young boy of eight; that had been before the start of the Second World War. He vaguely remem-bered the excitement of travelling on the underground railway – the tube – and the crowds of people, the big red buses and the black taxis. His father said they had stayed at a small guest house near Bayswater Road, close to Kensington Gardens and not far from the West End. He sent for a travel guide and found a reasonably priced one in that vicinity which could accommodate them for the three nights, bed and breakfast. He booked the train tickets then they were all ready to go, Walter having managed, thanks to Sam, to wangle the Friday and Monday off work.

Val was pleased that they had accepted her offer. Walter's parents were lending them their cot and high chair and she was preparing a bed for Paul in the small spare room. But before the children arrived there was Sam's birthday to celebrate in Harrogate.

They travelled with Jonathan and Thelma in Jonathan's car to the hotel where they would stay for the Saturday night. It faced the Stray, near the town centre, and was only a few minutes' drive from Grundy's. Their meal was booked for seven thirty and they had chosen the three courses in advance to help Phil with the menu planning. The evening bookings were now beginning to become more popular as they became more widely known to the folk of Harrogate and further afield. Phil had decided to start in a small way to see how the idea took on.

There was another small party of four dining at the same time and, fortunately for Phil, they had chosen a similar menu. They had all decided on roast beef and Yorkshire pudding for the main course – it seemed that Yorkshire folk never tired of their traditional fare – although the starters and desserts varied. Sam's small party had all chosen homemade chicken soup then chocolate and walnut gateau – one of Janice's specialities – for their pudding.

As it was already into the season of Advent the restaurant was decorated for the Christmas season in a tasteful fashion. There was a small artificial tree in the window with twinkling lights of green and gold. The same colours were repeated in the tinsel and sprays of flowers which adorned the walls and a large red poinsettia stood on the cash desk.

Phil and Toby, his assistant chef, were busy in the kitchen throughout the meal and did not appear in the restaurant until later, but the guests were served by Janice and one of the usual waitresses.

Coffee and mint chocolates were served at the end of the meal and Janice and Phil then joined the guests at their table.

'You've done us proud,' said Jonathan. 'Congratulations! It was a splendid meal and we're most impressed with your place, aren't we, Thelma?'

His wife agreed that it was all most enjoyable. Jonathan was showing his more agreeable side. He could be affable and charming when it suited him to be so but Sam remembered a time when his supercilious brother had looked down on those he considered were not of his own social standing, including Sam's wife. But that was in the past and the four of them were now on amicable terms.

Phil told them that he and Janice were pleased at the way Grundy's was progressing. They had several evening bookings leading up to Christmas. On the Saturday before the festive season they already had two parties of six booked in, which was quite enough for them to cope with. They were closing down following the afternoon tea session on Christmas Eve and re-opening on the Monday after Christmas. giving them a long weekend in which to recuperate and enjoy their celebrations.

'Will you be going to Blackpool to spend Christmas with your dad and Norma?' asked Val.

'No, it's our first married Christmas,' said Val, 'and we want to spend it in our own home. Dad would have liked us to go but he understands. And it's his first Christmas with Norma, of course. We'll probably pop over for a day and we'll visit Phil's parents as well, maybe on Boxing Day.'

'My dad opens on Christmas Day and Boxing Day,' said Phil. 'Just the bar area, so that people who want to have a drink before their lunch can do so.'

'No doubt it's mainly the men,' said Sam with a laugh, 'leaving their wives to do the cooking.'

'That seems to be the way of it,' agreed Phil. 'Each to his own. My father is far more the genial landlord than I am. I'm usually tucked away in the background. I managed to get a licence to serve drinks in the evening. It's more or less obligatory now to serve drinks with the evening meal.'

'And you've a good choice, too,' said Jonathan. 'We enjoyed the Cabernet Sauvignon. I shall let Thelma drive back; she hasn't indulged as much as I have.'

'And how is your Ian?' said Val to Janice. 'Has he settled down now to life with your dad and Norma?'

'I think he's better,' answered Janice. 'He was disappointed that we're not going for Christmas. He asked if he could come here and help, like he did in the summer, but I told him we were having a break over Christmas.'

'Of course, we're not the only attraction,' said Phil. 'He got himself a girlfriend while he was here. One of our student waitresses; a nice girl called Sophie. She comes to help on Saturdays and I think they're still writing to each other.'

'Gosh, that's incredible!' said Val. 'I still think of him as a little boy, like he was when we stayed at your hotel. He was just about to start at the grammar school and he was mad keen on football.'

'He still is,' said Janice, 'although he has other interests now, of course. I know he took quite a shine to Sophie; he's not had a girlfriend before. But I expect it will just be a passing fancy with them living so far apart. He's fifteen now; he's in the fifth form. Some of them skipped a year because they were in the top form so he'll be taking his O-levels a year earlier. In some ways he's quite grown up but in others he's still young and immature. I think he still misses Mum far more than we realize. He keeps a lot hidden away but I feel that he's still hurting deep inside. When we go to Blackpool after Christmas perhaps he'll come back with us for a few days.'

They went on to talk about Cissie and how she was now recovering from her bad accident. Val told them that she and Sam would be looking after the children while Cissie and Walter had a short break in London.

'How very thoughtful of you,' said Janice. 'You'll need a break yourselves, won't you, after all that?'

'They're good children,' said Val. 'Cissie is bringing them up really well. Paul's at a boisterous age but he does as he's told . . . most of the time. And Holly's a little love.' Val gave a tender smile. 'I'm looking forward to having them.'

It was almost midnight when the four visitors said goodnight and drove back to their hotel.

'A very successful evening,' Phil remarked. 'It was good to

see Val and Sam and to get to know the other two as well. Jonathan was surprisingly affable, I thought.'

'Yes, nothing like as snooty as he used to be, according to Val. Very successful evening, and an enjoyable one as well. I think Grundy's is making a name for itself, thanks to your efforts.'

'And to yours as well, darling,' he replied. 'We're a great team, aren't we?'

Cissie and Walter left Halifax station mid-morning on Friday after leaving the children with Val. They wanted to make the most of their time away so Cissie had made sandwiches to eat on the journey. Walter had bought a tourist guide with maps and a plan of the underground so he had a fair idea about how to get around.

They arrived at King's Cross station in the afternoon, and from then it was a continuous whirl of new sights and impressions, especially for Cissie. Firstly, a drive in a black taxi cab through the busy streets to their small hotel in Bayswater. Their room was on the top floor and over the rooftops they could see the trees of Kensington Gardens. After they had unpacked their few belongings and had a quick wash they went out to explore their surroundings.

They strolled along the path in Kensington Gardens that led to the statue of Peter Pan. Even Cissie, who was not a greet reader, knew about the story by J.M. Barrie.

'Our teacher read it to us when we were in the infants,' she said. 'I remember me and Val jumping off her bed and pretending we could fly. The teacher made Captain Hook sound real scary, and that awful crocodile! I even got it from the library and read it meself.'

'Quite an achievement,' said Walter, grinning at her. 'Come on; let's have a look at the Round Pond.'

They made a circuit of the huge pond where ducks and Canada geese were swimming, then took a look at the outside of the apartments where members of the royal family lived before making their way back to the area near their hotel. There were cafes and restaurants a-plenty, in every price range, in and around the main road, Queensway. They chose a small

Italian one that did not look too pricey and dined on spaghetti Bolognese, which Cissie declared was much nicer than the stuff out of a tin.

They retired early to their comfortable double bed with the brass bedstead. It was not the most salubrious of accommodation but they were satisfied. There was scarcely room to swing a cat, as the saying went. There was a small washbasin and an old-fashioned wardrobe and dressing table. The carpet was faded and worn in places, but to Cissie it was all different and exciting.

Walter had made a plan of sorts for the following day, Saturday. There was so much to see and do and he knew that Cissie tired quite quickly, although she was bravely pretending that all was well. After a substantial breakfast of bacon, eggs and sausages they took the tube from Queensway to Oxford Circus. The crowds of people, with many black or brown faces as well as white swarming around the stations and on the train were a surprise to Cissie. Walter had wisely waited until after the rush hour but, even so, there were more people than Cissie had ever seen in her life.

A tour bus around central London took them near the well-known sights: Marble Arch, Piccadilly Circus, Trafalgar Square, Whitehall and the cenotaph, Downing Street, the Houses of Parliament, Big Ben and, most importantly, Buckingham Palace where the Royal Standard flying from the roof indicated that the queen was in residence.

They alighted there and took a walk round St James's Park where ducks and geese swam or waddled on the pathway waiting for titbits and pelicans resided on their island in the middle of the stream.

It was a good walk to Regent Street and the famous toy shop, Hamley's, that Cissie wanted to visit to buy Christmas presents for the children. They dined at a Lyon's teashop where they managed to find one empty table. A bowl of soup and a sandwich fortified them for their shopping.

Cissie was as thrilled as any child would be by Hamley's. Many children were there with their parents, pointing out the toys that they hoped Father Christmas would bring. There was so much to choose from, on five floors, but eventually they decided on a pink fluffy rabbit wearing a checked dress and some large building blocks in bright colours for Holly, and a big red bus and a box of toy soldiers for Paul, along with various odds and ends for stocking fillers.

Walter good-humouredly agreed to carry the cumbersome bags for the rest of the day. They spent the afternoon mainly window shopping in and around Oxford Street. Cissie bought a silk scarf with London scenes for Val as a thank-you present and Walter bought his wife a pair of dangly earrings that she had admired in a shop window. Fortunately not very expensive but Cissie loved the sparkle of the eye-catching artificial diamonds.

'Let's see if we can get tickets for *The Mousetrap*,' said Walter while they were dining at a Lyon's Corner House on poached eggs on toast. 'It may be fully booked but it's worth a try.'

'Oo, yes, I love Agatha Christie,' said Cissie. She had been encouraged by Val to give the books a try and she had become hooked on the doings of Hercule Poirot and Miss Marple. Another tube train took them to the Apollo theatre where the play was now in its sixth year. Luckily there were a few seats in the upper circle from where they had a good, though distant, view of the play.

'That was flippin' marvellous,' said Cissie as it ended. 'An' I never guessed who it was. We're having a smashing time, aren't we, Walter?'

He agreed that they were. He knew, though, that she was tired, and after their journey back on a tube train that was, at eleven o'clock, still quite crowded, she fell asleep almost at once.

'A leisurely day today,' Walter said after their breakfast on the Sunday morning. 'We did quite enough dashing around yesterday.'

It was cold but bright and sunny, with only a slight breeze, as they boarded a pleasure boat at Westminster pier for a sail along the River Thames. A man with a cockney accent gave a commentary as they passed by more sights that were new to Cissie. London Bridge, Blackfriars, Charing Cross and Tower Bridge, St Paul's Cathedral, the docklands, the Tower of London with Traitor's Gate, the row of cannons on the waterfront and the White Tower visible from far away.

They alighted at Greenwich and strolled around the streets of the old town after viewing the old clipper ship *Cutty Sark*. After a fish and chip lunch they took a boat back to Westminster then strolled along the embankment, sitting for a while to watch the large and small boats on the river. Walter could see that Cissie was tiring again. They had done quite enough walking and she welcomed his suggestion that they should go back to Bayswater and have a nice meal to end the day. Dusk was already falling and by the time they came out of the station at Lancaster Gate the sky was dark but the lights from the hotels and restaurants and the passing traffic made it appear almost like daytime.

'Let's treat ourselves for our last meal,' said Walter. 'What about steak and chips?'

'Ooh, yes, my favourite,' said Cissie. 'That'd be great.'

It was what they ate at home for a special occasion, although most of the time Cissie tried to count the pennies. Here, in London, they'd found that the prices were higher than at home. They had not gone hungry but had dined on snack meals such as sandwiches, soup or eggs on toast. It was time now to indulge themselves.

They found a small place off the main road which looked clean and cheerful with red-checked tablecloths and an appetizing aroma greeted them when they opened the door. It was a substantial meal – sirloin steak and chunky chips with mushrooms and tomatoes – well cooked but with no fancy trimmings to add to the cost. They splashed out on a bottle of the house red wine. Then Cissie declared in her usual forthright way that she was 'ready to burst'.

'We've had a smashing time,' she said again as they climbed into their high bed.

'Yes, so we have,' said Walter, kissing her gently, 'but I hope it hasn't tired you too much.'

'No, I've loved it all,' she said. 'I feel a bit achy . . .' she rubbed at her rib cage, '. . . but I'll be OK in the morning.'

'Goodnight, love,' said Walter, kissing her again. 'Sleep tight.'

They had done very little but kiss and cuddle since Cissie

left hospital but there was time, all the time in the world now that their marriage was back on track.

They caught a morning train so that they could collect the children in the early afternoon. Val was on her own with them as Sam had gone into work.

'Mummy . . . Daddy . . .' shouted Paul excitedly, running to both of them as they entered the room. Holly looked across from where she was sitting on the settee. She looked puzzled for a moment then she smiled and held out her arms. Cissie was sure she was trying to say Mummy. 'Ma . . . ma . . .' she muttered as Cissie rushed to pick her up.

'Hello, darling,' she said. 'Have you been a good girl for Aunty Val?' She turned to Walter. 'Here, you hold her. I forgot about me arm.' She was still limited in her arm movements and the little girl was now quite plump and sturdy. 'Gosh! She weighs a ton. What have you been giving her, Val? Steak and chips?'

Val laughed. 'She's eaten all her meals and they've both been as good as gold, though I'm sure they're glad to see their mummy and daddy again. What about you two? Have you had a good time?'

'Wonderful!' replied Walter. 'We can't thank you enough, Val; you and Sam.'

'We've loved having them,' said Val. 'Now, I'm sure you must be eager to get home. Sam left me the car – he went to work with his father – so that I can drive you home.'

'That's real good of you,' said Cissie. They had taken a taxi from the station and she still felt guilty about Walter's car. 'You're a friend in a million, Val.'

The house felt quiet and empty when Val returned after seeing the Clarkson family safely back home. She had loved looking after the children. She realized now what hard work it was caring for two kids, day and night. But that had not deterred her from wanting a family of her own, although she knew Sam was quite happy to wait a while. And she, too, had tried to settle down following the disappointment of her miscarriage and not get too anxious. She feared now, however, that the longing might start all over again.

Twenty

They finished school early on the Friday afternoon before Christmas. It was 19 December, less than a week to go to the 'big day'. Ian was looking forward to it with mixed feelings. In fact, he thought to himself as he cycled home, he was not really looking forward to it at all. He had been hoping to see Janice and Phil again, taking it for granted that they would be coming to Blackpool for Christmas, but that was not so. They wanted to spend Christmas in their own home, entirely on their own, he presumed, as his sister had not suggested that he might join them. The cafe would be closed over Christmas but he was wondering if he might suggest that he could come to help them in the New Year as he had done in the summer. There would be time to spend a few days there before school started again.

And he would be able to see Sophie again. They had been corresponding during the few months they had been apart. Her letters were friendly and as interesting as she could make them; mainly about school and how she was enjoying sixth form. There had been some references lately, though, to Christmas parties and a get-together with boys from the corresponding sixth form. This had made him envious. There was no such thing going on at his school; anyway, he was not yet in the sixth form.

He had told his mates, of course, that he now had a girl-friend in Yorkshire and his stories lost nothing in the telling. He told them that she was very pretty, and the photo he had asked her to send him – a happy, smiling holiday snapshot – was proof of this. He had also confessed that she was rather more than a year older than himself, already in sixth form, which had invited some nudges and winks. 'Aye, aye! She'll be able to teach you a thing or two.'

But he had just laughed and brushed it off. Ian was, in truth, a very innocent sort of lad, and certainly did not think of Sophie 'like that'. He had a pretty good idea of what went on between men and women when they were married and probably before. He had heard the older lads, even some of his own age group, boasting about their conquests although he did not entirely believe them.

He and Sophie were just good friends – although he had enjoyed the one or two kisses – but he wanted nothing more. He was just pleased that he had a girlfriend and hoped he would be able to see her again soon.

Ian left his bicycle in the shed and went in through the back door. Norma worked only part time at the store since she had married his dad and she was already in the kitchen preparing their evening meal. She greeted him cheerfully, as she always did.

'Hello there, Ian. You're home early.'

'Well, there's not much to do on the last day.'

'Two weeks holiday, eh? It can't be bad.'

'No, s'pose not . . .' He was thinking to himself that there was not very much to do when he was not at school. He was glad of the holiday, of course, but it was wintertime and not ideal weather to play football. Nor did he intend to spend all the holiday studying for 'mock O-levels', the tryout before the big exams in June.

'Would you like a cup of tea?' asked Norma. 'I'm just making one for myself. You must be frozen. I don't know how you manage on that bike in all weathers.'

'I'm a strong lad,' he replied, smiling at her. He was trying his best now to be more friendly. She was always so nice to him. He had resented her at first but things had not been too bad recently . . . until the Christmas preparations had got under way.

'Yes, I'd like some tea; thanks, Norma. I'll take it up to my room; I've some things to sort out.'

He carried a mug of tea and a chocolate biscuit up the stairs to his attic room, the only upper room in the dormer bungalow. He felt happier there than in any other room in the place. There was a little pointed window jutting out under the eaves, giving him a view across the rooftops to the gates and driveway of Stanley Park. This was his own little den, like an eyrie on a mountain top.

He had his football posters on the wall; a photo of the Blackpool team when they won the FA cup in 1953 and photos of the school rugby team. Ian was in the second team but hoped to make it to the first before long.

Most of his surroundings there were football biased; the blanket on his bed, which he had had since he was a little boy, was a design of footballers in action, and the curtains and cushions were in the bright tangerine shade in which his favourite team played. The curtains had been a little too long when they moved house but Norma had now shortened them so they fitted the smaller window.

He was not a great follower of the pop music of the day as some of his pals were but he had a record player – Janice had given him her old Dansette model when she had got married – and he had acquired a few records, although they were quite expensive to buy: Elvis, the catchy songs of Guy Mitchell, the Everly Brothers and Johnnie Ray. He had a crackly radio set and could tune into a few foreign stations like Radio Luxembourg rather than the BBC programmes. It was a bit of background noise when the silence up there became too much, when he started to think gloomy thoughts instead of trying to make the best of things.

He drank his tea and ate his Penguin biscuit, then unpacked his schoolbag, putting his textbooks and exercise books on the shelf, to be ignored for a little while. He kicked off his shoes and lay full length on the bed, staring up at the ceiling. What was he going to do to occupy himself for the next two weeks? He had to do some Christmas shopping. Dad was quite generous with pocket money and he still had some money he had saved from his summer job. Then the presents would have to be wrapped. Just a few, for his dad and Norma and for Janice and Phil. The lads at school didn't bother with all that; they just sent one another jokey cards. He would like to buy something for Sophie, on the off chance that he might see her.

Norma was excitedly preparing for Christmas. She said how much she loved the festive season and Ian's father was good-humouredly going along with her. For years and years, when his mother was there, they had had an artificial tree that came out each Christmas, and every time they took the decorations down from the attic another one or two of the fragile glass baubles would be broken. There was a fairy, too, with a bent wing and bright yellow hair, and lots of coloured tinsel. All the decorations had been brought along when they moved to the bungalow and had been used again last year.

This year, however, Norma had wanted a real Christmas tree with new decorations, and Dad had agreed that the old tree and trimmings had seen better days. He had bought a tree from Moor's market in town and brought it home in the car. It now stood pride of place in the lounge window with a new set of twinkling lights and new baubles that were supposed to be shatterproof. There was gold tinsel and a gold star on the top to replace the tatty fairy. They had also got rid of the paper streamers that used to hang from the ceiling. Now there were sprigs of holly and mistletoe, with just a touch of tinsel, placed here and there around the room. Lots of Christmas cards had arrived from friends, relations and neighbours. Ian remembered how his mum had propped them up all round the room, on the top of the sideboard, bookcase and mantelshelf. They would continually fall down and need to be moved when she dusted and then stood up again. Now the cards were fastened to ribbons which hung neatly from the walls.

'A very good idea,' Alec had said. 'A nice artistic touch, Norma, love.'

Ian had to admit to himself that Norma had a feeling for design and precision but he missed the colour and the childlike chaos of how it used to be when he was a little boy.

He had gathered, by listening with one ear to the conversations between his dad and Norma, that she had ordered a turkey from a local butcher. Ten pounds – in weight, he thought she had said, though goodness knows why they would need such a large one. As far as he knew there would be just the three of them for the traditional Christmas dinner at midday, and he guessed that some of their friends from the club might be joining them for tea. And he thought that his uncle – his mother's brother – and his aunt were coming on

Boxing Day. His dad and Norma, no doubt, would be out and about enjoying the various social gatherings with club members.

Norma had told him he could invite some of his friends round for tea, if he wished to do so, but he had replied, 'No, it's OK but thanks for suggesting it.'

He knew his friends would not be keen on that idea but he would be seeing his mates quite frequently. There were four of them – Gary, Steve, Mike and himself, who were all in the chess club at school. They met at one another's homes to play, or just to chat and play records in their bedrooms. At least that was something to look forward to.

And the four of them were going to a party on Saturday night, arranged by the youth club that they sometimes attended. It was to be held in a church hall not far away and would be closely chaperoned by the adults who ran the club. But it was somewhere to go, and there would be a good spread to tuck into if not much else . . .

'Well. at least the grub's OK,' Steve remarked to the others on the Saturday evening as they tucked into potted meat sand-wiches, sausage rolls and pork pies, then the fruit jelly and ice cream to follow and a choice of fizzy lemonade, Coca-Cola or orange juice.

'I think that little Tracey fancies you,' Gary remarked to Ian. 'She went bright red when she got you in the barn dance. Look, she's watching you now.'

Ian grinned. 'Too young for me,' he answered nonchalantly.

'Oh, yes, you've got your Sophie, haven't you?' said Gary. 'Will you be seeing her over Christmas?'

Ian shrugged. 'I might be. I expect we'll be going over to see my sister and Phil. I've had a card from her – Sophie, I mean – so I'll just have to wait and see.'

Gary said no more. He was the one who was closest to Ian and could pretty well understand the situation. It was true that the girls in the youth club were young, a crowd of giggling thirteen- and fourteen-year-olds. Girls tended to think of the club as childish when they reached fifteen but the boys enjoyed playing table tennis and snooker. That night they had all jigged around on the make-shift dance floor, played a few rowdy games such as musical chairs and pass the parcel, then were sent on their way home at half past ten, an hour later than the club usually finished.

The four friends agreed to meet again on the following Tuesday evening at Gary's home. They all lived within easy walking distance. Gary's father was a solicitor with an office in the town centre and Gary was the one with the biggest bedroom; his mother made cakes that were scrumptious so they all enjoyed going there.

Ian wandered into town on the Monday morning to do his Christmas shopping. A colourful tie for his dad – he had become more of a snazzy dresser since he had married Norma. A box of floral-scented bath cubes for Norma; chocolates with liqueur centres and lace handkerchiefs for Janice; and a handsome-looking diary backed with what looked like leather for Phil. He wondered about a present for Sophie. Should he buy one or not? He looked in the windows of gift shops that sold fairly inexpensive jewelry – he couldn't afford the prices in Beaverbrooks or Samuels, the town's leading jewellers – and noticed a little silver brooch in the shape of a cat. Sophie had a pet cat so he thought she would like it. To his relief it was quite reasonably priced.

'Is it for your girlfriend?' asked the young lady assistant, and Ian, going rather pink, said that it was. She smiled at him as she put it in a little box then wrapped it in Christmas paper with a silver bow.

Time was hanging rather heavy and Ian was looking forward to seeing his mates again on Tuesday evening.

'Norma and I are going to a do at the club,' said his dad. 'I don't know what time we'll be back; it might be a bit late but you've got your key, haven't you, and you can let yourself in?'

'Yes, that's OK,' said Ian. 'Er . . . have a nice time,' he added.

'Oh, I'm sure we will,' said Norma, laughing.

Ian knew they were often quite merry when they returned from an evening at the club. Sometimes they went in a taxi instead of taking the car. Ian knew that his dad drank rather more than he had used to do, although he had not seen either of them the worse for drink, just rather giggly and jolly.

This was something else that was different now. When his mum and dad had gone out – rather infrequently because of the hotel – it was usually to the pictures or to a concert or social evening at the local church, and they would return home quietly, happy in each other's company.

The four lads had a great time at Gary's. Ian played against Gary and Steve against Mike in their first games of chess. Ian was delighted to have beaten Gary for once, as this rarely happened. Then the winners played against one another. It was Mike and Ian who fought it out and Mike was the victor. He was a worthy winner and Ian did not mind at all. He was doing what he enjoyed in the company of his best mates.

Gary's mum had made Christmas cakes: a large one and a smaller one as a taster which she cut up for the boys. They also had a sausage roll, a mince pie and a cup of creamy coffee, and ended the evening feeling very replete.

Mrs Price, Gary's mother, made sure they all left at half past ten, knowing that their parents would consider that quite late enough to be out.

Ian felt contented and at peace with himself as he walked home, saying cheerio to Steve and Mike on the way. As he had anticipated, his dad and Norma had not arrived back. He was tired and feeling very full after his large supper so he went straight up to bed.

But he was unable to sleep. His stomach was full and his mind was full, too, with all sorts of things. Chess pieces and the moves he knew he should have made; thoughts of Christmas which might not be too bad, though he did wish that Janice and Phil were coming; then Sophie . . . He must try to persuade his dad to go over to Harrogate very soon.

He heard his dad and Norma come in, and a glance at his illuminated clock told him that it was twelve thirty. He heard their voices and sounds of laughter, then it seemed to go quiet. But still he couldn't sleep. He tossed and turned; his mind would not switch off and his stomach was tight and uncomfortable. Indigestion, he supposed, although he had always thought that was something that only older people suffered with. He decided he must do something about it or he might lie awake all night. He remembered that Norma had some tablets called Rennies in the kitchen cupboard. He had seen her and his dad taking them occasionally.

He got out of bed and put on his dressing gown and slippers as it had gone quite cold. He crept downstairs, trying not to make any sound as he thought his dad and Norma might be asleep after an evening of merrymaking. But as he tiptoed past their bedroom door on his way to the kitchen he realized they were not asleep. Far from it.

Ian knew that he should hurry past and ignore what was going on but he could not help himself. He stopped and listened, keeping very quiet. He knew, from schoolroom gossip, what went on between men and women but it was something he had not thought about overmuch. He had heard some of the lads telling jokes at school but he had only half-listened. He had not openly distanced himself, not wanting to be considered a wimp. On the other hand, he had never become one of that crowd who liked to talk about such matters and, to his relief, neither had Gary, Steve and Mike. Maybe the four of them, chess fanatics and followers of football, were not as worldly-wise as some of their contemporaries, but Ian had been contented, so far, with his limited knowledge about such things.

He knew, of course, that his parents must have had sex, because he and Janice were proof of that, but it was something that he had never really thought about. It didn't seem right to think of his parents like that. They were just his mum and dad.

But now his dad had another wife and there was no doubt about what was happening in the bedroom. Sounds of heavy breathing and gasping, and the rhythmic thump of the bed springs. Then Norma giggled, a sexy sort of laugh followed by a squeal of delight. He heard his father sigh deeply and mutter, 'God, Norma, I love you. I love you so much. I never knew it could be like this.'

'Me neither,' she answered, then it went quiet.

Ian felt tears welling at the back of his eyes and he turned away. He recalled that he had been on his way to the kitchen to get something for his indigestion but now he just wanted to get back to the safety of his little room, away from the sounds that had distressed him so much. He was sure they had not been aware of him outside the door and he did not want them to know. He crept up the stairs, trying to avoid a stair that creaked, stifling the sobs that were caught in his throat.

Back in his bed, he realized that his stomach was no longer uncomfortable and full but his mind was full of muddled thoughts. He was ashamed of himself for crying. It was childish and something that boys did not do.

What did it mean, though? Had his dad not loved his mum the way he loved Norma? What was so special about her? She was all right but nothing compared to his mum, not in any way.

One thing was certain: he had to get away. He couldn't stay there any longer, feeling the way he did. But he would have to wait until morning. His mind was busy devising a plan, and eventually he fell asleep.

Twenty-One

Ian woke early. The events of the night that had so disturbed him were still filling his mind. He still had to get away. He would go to Harrogate to see Janice and Phil. He knew they would be surprised to see him; they might be annoyed at first. But Janice would understand – he felt sure of that.

He got out of bed and after a quick wash he shoved a few things into his travel bag: socks, underwear, pyjamas, shirts, jumper, toothbrush . . . then, knowing he must act as normally as possible, he went downstairs. His dad and Norma were sitting at the kitchen table eating their breakfast.

'By 'eck! You're up early,' remarked Alec. 'I thought you'd have a lie-in this morning.'

'Er . . . no. I was awake so thought I might as well get up,' said Ian.

'There's some tea in the pot that's still warm,' said Norma, 'and you can make yourself some toast, can't you? Your dad and I will have to be off soon. They want me to work longer hours today as it's Christmas Eve. There are sure to be women wanting a dress at the last minute or changing their mind about the one they've bought.'

'I'll probably finish a bit early,' said Alec. 'There won't be much work today. What about you, Ian? Have you any plans?'

'Er . . . sort of. I said I might go round to Gary's this morning.'

'You were there last night, weren't you?'

'Yes, but we said we'd have another game of chess. I beat him last night and he wants to get his own back.' The lie tripped easily from his tongue although he felt bad, deep down, at his deceit.

'Will you have some lunch there?' asked Norma.

'Dunno . . . perhaps. We didn't talk about it.'

'Well, you can make yourself a sandwich,' said Norma, 'and I'll cook something when I get in from work. I'll wash these pots then we'd better be off, Alec.'

'Leave them . . . I'll do them,' said Ian, feeling a stab of guilt but still determined to carry on with his plan.

'Thank you,' said Norma. 'Are you sure?'

'Yes, 'course I am.'

'By 'eck! That's a first,' said Alec. 'Come on then, Norma, love. See you later, son.'

'Yes . . . see you . . .'

He made two slices of toast, liberally covered with butter and marmalade, then cleared away and washed up, leaving the pots draining as he had seen Norma do. He decided not to leave a note as he didn't know what to say. It was almost half past nine when he boarded the bus to town, dressed in a warm coat – it would be cold in Yorkshire – and carrying his bag filled with clothes and presents. The thought of seeing Sophie again gave him a feeling of happiness for a moment although he was, in truth, a little scared.

Central Station was crowded as he had guessed it might be. He looked at the timetable and worked out that there was a train to Leeds quite soon, and he could change there to get the one to Harrogate. Fortunately he was not short of money. He was quite a thrifty lad and had saved up quite a bit from pocket money and his summer job. He bought a single ticket to Harrogate − he had not thought about the return journey − and joined the crowds of people boarding the train.

He managed to squeeze into a corner seat in a compartment with an elderly couple and a family of four, mother, father and two children − a boy and a girl − wearing Santa Claus hats and talking excitedly. Ian kept himself to himself, reading his *Eagle* comic which he still bought every week; a vestige of his childhood.

The station at Leeds was even more crowded than the Blackpool one had been. It seemed that everyone in Yorkshire was on the move, swarming up and down stairs and escalators with cases, bags and boxes, Christmas trees and bunches of holly. In desperation Ian asked a porter for directions and found the platform where the Harrogate train would leave. He caught it with just a couple of minutes to spare. To his relief it was not quite so crowded as the previous one and he sat collecting his thoughts, trying to decide what to do when he arrived.

It was only a short journey and quite soon he found himself standing in the entrance hall of Harrogate station wondering what to do next. The station was on the perimeter of the town, a fair distance from where Janice and Phil lived. He could get a bus but he was not sure where to find one going in the right direction and he was, by now, feeling rather lost and unsure of himself. He had wanted to be brave and independent but he knew that the best thing to do was to ring his sister to see if he could be picked up at the station.

He found the nearest phone, put in the coins and dialled the number for Grundy's, hoping against hope that someone would answer. To his relief the phone was picked up almost at once. He heard Phil's voice. 'Hello, Grundy's restaurant. How can I help you?'

He wished it had been Janice but at least they were there at home. 'Hello,' he said. 'It's me, Ian . . . I'm at Harrogate station . . .'

'Ian? What on earth . . .? Are Alec and Norma with you? Is something wrong?'

'Er . . . not exactly. I'm on my own. I decided . . . I wanted to come and see you. Can you come and pick me up . . . please, Phil?'

'Yes, of course, but you'll have to tell me what's going on.' The pips sounded, indicating that time was running out. 'I'll be with you as soon as I can. Wait outside, Ian . . .'

Ian knew he would have a lot of explaining to do. He was hungry, too. It had now turned two o'clock and he had not thought about getting anything to eat. And he needed the toilet . . . He bought a Kit-Kat at the kiosk to fortify himself and stood outside on the forecourt to wait for Phil.

He arrived in about ten minutes. He did not say anything at first, just gave Ian a brotherly hug and glanced at his travel bag. 'Looks as though you've come to stay a while?'

'Er . . . I suppose so. I don't know. It's a long story.'

'OK, you can tell us later. Let's get back, eh?'

They set off, driving along the Stray. 'We've more or less finished now,' said Phil. 'There were only a few in this lunch-time and Janice is opening for the afternoon teas. Then we're closed until Monday.' He glanced inquiringly at Ian, but he just nodded.

Then Ian said diffidently, 'I hope I'm not putting you to any trouble. I just had to . . . to get away.'

'Tell us later,' said Phil kindly, aware that his young brother-in-law was quite distressed. 'I told Janice you were here. She was very surprised but she'll be pleased to see you.'

They were back in less than ten minutes. Janice was in the cafe getting ready to open for the tea session. She hugged her brother. 'Now, what's all this about?' Then she noticed his woebegone face and the hint of a tear.

'It's hard to explain . . .' he began.

'Tell us later then. Dad and Norma are OK, aren't they? No one is ill?'

'No, they're fine . . .'

She assumed there had been some sort of a row but it could wait. 'Go up to your usual room, Ian, and get sorted out. Then you can choose some of these sandwiches and cakes. I expect you're hungry?'

Ian nodded, smiling a little. 'Yes, thanks, I am.'

'I shall be busy though we're not expecting a crowd today.

Oh . . . by the way, Sophie's coming in to help. She'll be busy, too, but you'll be able to see her when we've finished.' Ian smiled a little more on hearing that. 'Yes, she's a grand girl,' Janice went on. 'We thought she could do with a little extra money so she's been helping out since school finished. Off you go then, Ian. I'll see you later.'

Ian went upstairs to the room where he had slept during the summer. He unpacked his few belongings and the Christmas presents he had brought. He was relieved to be there – and he would see Sophie again very soon – but he was also feeling rather foolish and embarrassed; guilty too, about what he had done and the explanation he would have to give to Janice and Phil. How could he tell them about what had really made him decide to leave and come to Yorkshire? And what could he say to his dad and Norma? Quite soon they would realize he was not there and he knew that Dad would start to worry. He had given no thought to that in his hurry to get away.

But now his immediate need was his feeling of hunger. He would sample some of the food on offer in the cafe and try to push his worries, temporarily, to the back of his mind. What was done was done and he would have to give an account of his actions.

When he went downstairs the cafe had opened. There were a few ladies sitting at the round tables and his sister and Sophie were waiting on them. Sophie turned round and smiled at him.

'Hello, Ian. What a surprise! Janice told me you had arrived out of the blue.' She looked at him questioningly.

'Well, yes . . . I'll tell you about it later. You're busy now so I'll get out of your way.'

He filled a plate with ham sandwiches, a cheese scone with butter and a slice of Christmas cake which Janice had made.

'Get yourself a mug of tea,' said his sister. 'It'll hold more than these china cups. We'll probably close early unless there's a sudden rush of customers, which I doubt.' She sounded a little harassed and Ian hoped he was not adding to her problems. Phil was busy in the kitchen so Ian quickly crept back upstairs. He made short work of the food then settled down to read a favourite book he had shoved into his bag – a Biggles story, another memory of his early teenage years.

He managed to engross himself in the adventures of the flying ace until there was a knock on his door an hour or so later. He called, 'Come in,' and was surprised to see it was Sophie who entered.

'Janice has decided to close,' she said. 'There's not much trade today. So you'd better go down, hadn't you, and talk to them?' She gave him a quizzical look.

'Yeah . . . I'd better go and get the twenty questions over with, I suppose.' He gave a rueful grin.

'Have you had a row with your dad?' asked Sophie.

'No . . . not exactly. Well, no; not at all. But things were getting a bit out of hand – in my mind, at any rate. I felt sad and all mixed up . . . and I was missing Mum.'

'Yes, I can imagine you would,' said Sophie, as though she understood. 'How long are you staying here?'

'I don't know. A few days, maybe . . . Can I see you sometime?'

'Yes, I'd like to but it might be a bit difficult tomorrow, of course. Mum will want me to be there all Christmas Day. We've some relations coming and it'll all be quite chaotic. I'm not sure what I'll be doing on Boxing Day. I tell you what; I'll ring you that morning. You'll still be here, won't you?'

'Yes, I shall be here for quite a few days; at least, I hope so. Anyway, happy Christmas, Sophie.' He handed her the little gift, wrapped in shiny red paper with a silver bow. Then, very shyly, he leaned forward and kissed her cheek.

'Oh . . . thank you, Ian.' She looked a little embarrassed. 'I haven't . . . I mean . . . I didn't know I'd be seeing you, did I?'

'No, of course you didn't. I came on the spur of the moment. I just hope Janice and Phil are not too cross with me.'

'They won't be. It's Christmas, the season of goodwill and all that. See you soon, Ian.' She kissed his cheek. 'Cheer up! I'm sure you'll have a lovely day tomorrow. Your sister's a very understanding person, you know.' She gave a cheery wave as she left the room.

Ian decided it was time he faced the music. He took a deep breath to steady the churned-up feeling in the pit of his stomach and went downstairs.

'Hi, there,' said Janice in a casual tone. 'Come and make yourself useful while you're here. We're just getting this place ship-shape, then we'll have seen the last of it till next week.'

The three of them set to work in the cafe, stacking the pots in the dishwasher, folding the tablecloths and checking to see if any needed laundering, then putting the remaining scones and cakes into tins for their own use.

'Well, that's that,' said Janice when they had finished. 'We can start to think about our own Christmas now.'

They went upstairs to the family quarters where they had their own private rooms and a kitchen, quite separate from the restaurant.

'I'll make us a cup of tea then you can tell us what this is all about . . . little brother!'

'It's difficult to explain,' Ian began when they were all sitting with mugs of tea in their laps.

'Well, just try,' said Phil encouragingly.

'For a start, do Dad and Norma know that you're here?' asked Janice.

'Er . . . no, they don't. I said I was going to Gary's, then I went to the station and caught a train. They went to work early, Dad and Norma, and left me having my breakfast.' Ian was talking quickly, his words falling over one another. 'I had to get away. It was all so . . . different, and I got upset.'

'Well, the first thing we must do is ring and tell them you're here,' said Janice, sounding a little vexed. 'Didn't you realize they would worry? It's very thoughtless, Ian.'

'Yes, I know, but I suppose I wasn't thinking straight. They won't be worried yet; it's only six o'clock. They'll be getting the tea ready and . . .'

'And they'll be wondering where you are, especially if they think you're out on your bike. I'm going to ring them now to let them know you're safe.'

'What will you say?'

'What can I say?' Janice answered abruptly. 'I suppose I'll say that you felt a bit miserable, missing Mum and all that.

Oh, I don't know, Ian! I'll think of something but I'll say you're all right and they mustn't worry. Actually, Phil and I have decided to go to Blackpool on Sunday so you can go back with us then. OK?'

Ian nodded. 'Yes . . . OK.'

Janice was away for several minutes, talking on the phone. Ian could not hear what she was saying. Phil smiled at him in a friendly way.

'Your sister will calm down. She's rather uptight with being so busy lately. Well, we've both been busy. That's why we planned a nice, quiet Christmas.'

'And now I've come to spoil it . . .'

'No, of course you haven't. We're always pleased to see you. But you must tell us what's going on. OK?'

Ian nodded. 'OK . . .'

'Well, that's all sorted,' said Janice as she came back. 'Dad was quite shocked that you'd come here but very relieved, of course. He'd rung Gary's home and learnt that you hadn't been there at all. Anyway, I tried to make him understand that you were feeling rather sad, and he knows that you miss Mum . . . But I thought you were settling down to the idea of Norma being there? She's very tolerant, from what I see, although I know she's different from Mum.'

Ian shook his head. 'It was all so . . . awful.'

'What was?' asked Phil gently. 'Try to tell us about it. We know there's something bothering you.'

Ian took a deep breath. 'I heard them,' he said, speaking almost in a whisper. 'Late last night. I went downstairs 'cause I couldn't sleep and . . . and they were . . . you know . . . in bed, and I could hear all sorts of things. And he told Norma that he loved her very much, and he didn't know it could be like that . . . And it sounded as though he loved her more than he'd loved Mum, that he wasn't thinking about Mum at all.'

He saw Phil and Janice exchange glances, and possibly a hint of a smile on Phil's lips.

'I do know about it . . . about that!' he retorted. 'Not very much, but I know what happens, sort of. And . . . well, it upset me.'

Janice looked thoughtful but it was Phil who spoke, quite jovially. 'Well, Ian, I hope you won't listen outside our bedroom door!'

Janice gave him a warning glance. 'Phil . . . honestly!'

''Course I won't,' said Ian. 'I didn't want to listen to them but I couldn't help it. It's different with you; you're young, but they're old!'

'Not all that old,' said Phil. 'Not quite in their fifties and they're newly married. Alec is probably still quite . . . well, virile, and Norma's a very lively lady.'

'I can understand how Ian feels,' said Janice. 'It's something you don't think about with your parents, although you know it must take place. I expect Mum and Dad had a mutual understanding as they got older, more about deep friendship than passionate love. They'd been married a long time. But with Norma, well, maybe it's more exciting. But you can be sure, Ian, that he loved our mum very much and he'll never forget her.' Her eyes were starting to fill up with tears. She blinked and tried to smile. 'I understand just how you feel, Ian, but try to put it to the back of your mind. You're very welcome here and I'm glad you felt you could come to us. We'll have a nice Christmas together, the three of us.'

'I don't want to mess up your plans,' said Ian. 'I suppose I wasn't thinking about that.'

'Don't worry. We haven't many plans, have we, Phil? Our own Christmas dinner tomorrow, then we're going to Ilkley on Boxing Day to see Phil's parents, and you're very welcome to come along with us.'

'But they won't be expecting me . . .'

Phil laughed. 'One more won't make any difference to my mum and dad; they're used to catering for large numbers. And they're not serving meals on Christmas Day and Boxing Day, just opening the bar for a while as some of the locals like to get together. Mum said we'd dine mid-afternoon when the rush is over so I'll ring and tell her there'll be one more. You'll be very welcome, I can assure you, and you've met them before, haven't you?'

Ian nodded. 'Yes, thank you for everything. Actually, Sophie said she'd ring on Boxing Day morning. We want to spend some time together. Probably Saturday will be the best day.'

'That's nice,' said Janice. 'She's a lovely girl and sensible, too.'

Ian blushed a little. 'Yes, she is. We're just friends, you know.'

'Of course.' Janice smiled. 'And I'm sure she'll be a very good friend.'

They had a simple evening meal of sausage and mash with onion gravy, prepared by Phil to give Janice a break. Then a quiet evening watching a variety show and a carol service on the television. Ian's eyes started closing by ten thirty, despite his desire to keep awake, and he retired to bed.

'So . . . what do you make of all that?' said Janice. 'He's got himself in a real old pickle, poor lad!'

'He's quite naive,' said Phil, 'but maybe I was the same when I was his age. It's hard to remember.'

'I know I most certainly was,' replied Janice. 'Some of the other girls seemed to know much more than I did. Mum never told me anything about . . . you know . . . the birds and the bees.'

'You mean sex!' said Phil with a grin.

'OK, then; sex! She only told me about periods and the rest I picked up from schoolgirl gossip. And being at an all girls' school didn't help.'

'I suppose it was the same with me,' agreed Phil, 'but being in the RAF opened my eyes quite a bit.'

Janice half grinned and half frowned at him. 'I don't really want to know about that! And then you met me, didn't you?'

'As you say, I met you. And I think we know enough to be going on with, don't we?' He smiled enticingly. 'Come along, darling. Let's call it a day, shall we?'

They had an enjoyable Christmas and Ian was able to put his worries to the back of his mind. They unwrapped presents which had been waiting under the Christmas tree − a real one − in the living room. Ian was delighted with his new football sweater and a stylish bag in which to carry his kit. They dined soon after midday on turkey with all the trimmings and pudding with brandy sauce, then were too full to eat again until late evening, when Janice made turkey sandwiches and cut her special Christmas cake.

Boxing Day at the Coach and Horses followed a similar pattern. Succulent roast pork, as a change from turkey, was the midday meal, followed by sherry trifle. Ian was made very welcome and enjoyed a happy day, especially as he had spoken with Sophie in the morning and was looking forward to seeing her the following day.

They had arranged to meet mid-morning, and at half past ten Sophie arrived at Grundy's. She looked bright and cheerful, dressed in a warm tweed coat with a red bobble hat and matching scarf.

'A present from my aunt who likes knitting!' she replied when Janice remarked how colourful they looked on a wintry day.

Her cheeks were glowing after her walk from home and her eyes shone at the pleasure of seeing Ian again. He was equally delighted and felt a warm glow inside as they smiled at each other.

'Where are you off to, then?' asked Janice. 'It's a nice crisp morning for a long walk.'

'Just what I had in mind,' said Sophie. 'A good chance to walk off some of the extra pounds I've put on over Christmas. OK with you, Ian?'

'Yes, fine,' he replied. 'You lead the way. You know the area better than I do.'

'I thought we could get a bus to Knaresborough and have a walk by the river; maybe have some lunch there. My mum and Graham are seeing some friends today so they're not expecting me back till later in the day.'

'Well, come back and have some tea with us,' said Janice, 'when you've finished your exploring.'

'Thanks, Janice,' said Sophie. 'That would be lovely . . . This is your Christmas present, Ian. Happy Christmas, even if it's a bit late.'

'Gosh, thanks!' he said, colouring a little. He could tell that it was a book. 'I'll open it later when we get back.' He felt embarrassed with Janice and Phil there.

'That's OK,' said Sophie. 'I loved the brooch, Ian. I've had it pinned to my sweater since Christmas.'

'Well, let's get moving,' said Ian. 'Bye, Janice, Phil . . .'

They set off walking along the street to the town centre. 'Have you had a good Christmas?' asked Sophie.

'Yes, it was OK,' said Ian. 'Just the three of us, then we went to see Phil's parents on Boxing Day. What about you?'

'Yes, it was quite nice, I suppose. Too much food, too much sitting around not doing very much. It's nice to get out today . . . Why did you decide to come here so suddenly, Ian? I know you said you were feeling sad and fed up but there's something else, isn't there?'

'I came to see you!' he answered, a trifle too quickly.

She laughed. 'Well, that's very nice but that's not all, is it?'

'Not really. I did want to see you but it was all to do with my dad and Norma. I'll try to explain later.'

They had arrived at the bus station and there was a bus ready to depart for Knaresborough. They sat on the top deck, saying very little as Ian looked out at the passing scenery; mainly rows of houses with stretches of moorland between as the towns were not far apart.

They alighted at the stand which served as the bus station, then Sophie led the way through the narrow cobbled streets to the caste area. They stood and admired the view across to the viaduct, with the River Nidd below and the hills a background to the rooftops of the town.

'Gosh! That's the scene you see on railway posters,' said Ian. 'Smashing view, isn't it?'

'Yes, I remember coming here with my dad when I was little,' said Sophie. 'I haven't been here for ages. You don't often bother to visit your own beauty spots. Come on, let's go down to the river.'

They went down the path, crossing the railway line then taking the steeper path to the river. The trees were bare and lifeless but there was a quiet beauty to the riverside walk. Sophie told him about Mother Shipton and her predictions as they passed by the cavern.

Ian knew that Sophie was curious about what had really happened at home to make him come away so suddenly. He knew she would understand as she had been in a similar position with her mother and stepfather, but how could he explain it to her?

As if aware of his thoughts, she suddenly asked, 'What went wrong, Ian?'

'Nothing really. No rows or anything like that. Dad and Norma . . . they go out partying a lot, something he and Mum never used to do. And Norma's not like Mum. She's jolly and likes a laugh and a joke, and I know they drink quite a lot. I'm not saying that Mum was prudish or miserable. She was a happy person but she was quieter, like, and gentle, and I thought Dad liked her that way. But he's different now, with Norma. I heard them one night – the night before I came away – when they'd come back from the club. I went downstairs because I couldn't sleep, and I could hear them . . . in bed,' he added rather diffidently, looking sideways at Sophie. 'You know what I mean . . . and it upset me. I started thinking about Mum and I felt as though Dad had forgotten her very quickly. I had to get away from them. Do you know what I mean?'

'And they didn't know you were there?'

'No, of course not. I was just passing the room and I couldn't help hearing . . . And the next morning I felt awkward being with them so I got a train and came over here.'

'I suppose I can understand,' said Sophie. 'It will be the same with my mum and Graham, but it's something I've tried not to think about. My parents divorced so I knew things weren't so good between them. But it's different with your mum and dad . . . I'm sure he loved her very much. But time goes on and things change. You'd rather he was happy than looking back and feeling miserable, wouldn't you?'

'Yes, I suppose so, but I'm still sad when I think about Mum.'

'I'm glad you've told me. It helps, doesn't it, to get things out in the open? You didn't let on to them about . . . what you heard?'

'Don't be daft! Janice rang up and told them I was feeling sad, it being Christmas and all that, and missing Mum. I feel a bit rotten about it now and embarrassed, like, but I dare say it will blow over. I'm supposed to be going back tomorrow. Janice and Phil are paying their Christmas visit to Blackpool.'

'Well, you will be going back, won't you? There's no "supposed" about it.'

'Yes, you're right. I'm glad I've been able to see you, Sophie. We can go on being friends, can't we?'

'Yes, of course we can. You'll be coming to help again during the holidays, won't you?'

'Yes, if I can wangle it. The next time would be Easter . . .' He was quiet for a moment, thinking carefully what to say. 'Er . . . you know what I said about Dad and Norma? Well, about you and me . . . I'm not really ready for all that sort of thing yet. I know you're older than me, but I just like being with you and being close to you.' They had been walking hand in hand, and now he hesitantly put an arm around her. 'Do you know what I mean, Sophie?'

'Yes, I know exactly what you mean.' She leaned across and kissed his cheek. 'It's just the same with me. Some girls at school like to boast about what they get up to with their boyfriends. I don't believe half of it, but even if it's true . . . it's not time for any of that, not for me. We're both still at school, then there's sixth form and college or uni. Who knows? Let's just enjoy being together when we can . . . I tell you what; I'm feeling hungry. Let's get back to the town, shall we?'

They went the long way back, following the road that led up from the river then the main road to town. They found a little inexpensive cafe and dined on cheese and pickle sandwiches, sticky cream doughnuts and cups of hot, strong tea.

The shops along the high street were very mundane so there was little else to do there. They took the bus back to Harrogate then walked the couple of miles through the town and along the Stray. Dusk was falling by the time they drew near to Grundy's. They stopped in a secluded spot and Ian put his arms around Sophie. Gently, and a little timidly at first, he kissed her lips. He felt her respond to him, then she pulled away.

'Come along, let's get inside. I don't want your sister worrying about us.'

'Hello, have you had a good day?' Janice greeted them from the upstairs living room, which was a haven of warmth after the chill of the winter's afternoon. They had not realized how cold it was until they were inside.

'Yes, lovely, thanks,' said Sophie. 'We went to Knaresborough and we walked for miles.'

'Oh, how nice. That's become one of my favourite places since Phil first took me there. Come and get warm by the fire and I'll make a pot of tea.'

It was good to see a coal fire although the rooms were centrally heated as well.

'Open your present now,' said Sophie. Janice was busy in the kitchen and Phil was elsewhere.

Ian tore off the holly-patterned wrapping paper to reveal a book. '*Inheritance* by Phyllis Bentley,' he read. 'Thanks, Sophie . . . I'm not sure I've heard of her.'

'Well, you're not a Yorkshire lad, are you? Our English teacher recommended it to us. She gave us a list of books she thought we'd enjoy – not the usual Dickens and Brontë ones, rather more modern. And I really loved this one. It's about the start of the woolen industry in Yorkshire. I thought you might like to know something about us Yorkshire folk and our roots.'

He grinned. 'Yes, I'm sure it'll be great.'

They chatted over a cup of tea, and a little later enjoyed a hearty meal of steak and kidney pie and chips, a change from eating up cold turkey.

Sophie said she must go home quite soon as she had been out all day. Ian walked her back to her house and they said goodbye at the gate.

'Don't worry about going home,' said Sophie. 'I'm sure it will be all right. Try to get along with Norma and don't go listening outside doors!'

He smiled ruefully. 'No, I won't! You'll write to me, won't you, and I'll see you at Easter time, I hope. Bye, Sophie. We've had a smashing time today.'

'Yes, so we have. See you quite soon, Ian.' They kissed, just once, a warm, friendly embrace.

They set off early the next morning on their journey to Blackpool. There was a slight fall of snow on the moorland roads but they made good time and arrived soon after eleven o'clock. Ian was quiet throughout the journey, feeling apprehensive and more than a little regretful about what he had done.

He did not need to have worried. His dad gave him a bear hug and Norma kissed his cheek.

'Good to see you back, son,' said Alec.

'I'm sorry, Dad,' he mumbled. 'I felt sad and sort of . . . all mixed up.'

'If you'd said you wanted to go to Yorkshire for Christmas we would have understood,' said Alec. 'I know you miss your sister.'

'I didn't,' said Ian. 'I mean . . . it was just an impulse . . . sort of . . .'

'Well, let's say no more about it,' said Norma cheerfully. 'It's lovely to see you all. I'm cooking a leg of lamb. A change from turkey! And we'll have a good chat and catch up with all the news.'

Ian tried not to think of times gone by and did his best to join in the joviality: the giving of presents, the eating and drinking and the continual chatter.

Janice and Phil stayed until early evening, hoping that the snow which was threatening would keep off until they were safely home. They phoned at eleven o'clock to say that all was well.

Ian said goodnight and went to bed in a more contented state of mind. He tried to read his new book but after half a page realized he was too tired. He turned out the light and thought about Sophie. She was such a good friend . . .

Twenty-Two

'A happy new year, darling,' said Sam. He kissed Val lovingly as she opened her eyes on the first day of January, 1959.

'Oh, yes, of course . . . A happy new year,' she murmured sleepily. 'Let's hope it's a better year than the one that's just gone.'

'Oh, I don't know. It wasn't such a bad one, was it, all in all? There was our little setback, of course. I know how upset you were about the baby. But you got over it, didn't you? And you've settled back nicely at work again.'

'But I'm hoping I won't be there for very much longer, no matter how much I enjoy the company of the girls,' replied Val. 'Maybe this year will prove to be . . . fruitful. Do you think it might be, Sam?'

'I think it might well be,' he replied warily. 'Let's hope so. And we can have a jolly good try, can't we? What do you say?' He put his arms around her and she snuggled close to him.

'I say yes, that's a very good idea,' she replied.

The months went by, January, February and into March, and there was no sign of their hopes – particularly Val's – being fulfilled. She started to feel worried and frustrated again, although she tried to tell herself that she must not get anxious as she had done before. She recalled that it had led to irritability between her and Sam and a certain constraint.

'I sometimes wonder if there's something wrong,' she suggested to Sam. 'Why I seem unable to conceive a child.'

'But you did,' Sam reminded her. 'You were pregnant for more than six months so we know that everything is OK there.'

'Then maybe I'm just not as fertile as other women,' she said. Or maybe it was Sam, she thought to herself, but did not give voice to her idea. What was it called? A low sperm count. But she would not dream of saying so and she knew that neither of them would like to go through the procedure of having tests to see if there was anything amiss with either of them.

She had even, tentatively, thought about adoption. Seeing Cissie with her children – one-year-old Holly at an adorable age and Paul who was now almost three, a bright and boisterous little boy – did not help. And looking after them before Christmas had increased her longing to be a mother herself. But Sam was adamant that adoption was not the answer.

'You don't really mean it, do you?' he said. 'I don't think the authorities, whoever is in charge, would consider us. We've only been married for two years; that's no time at all, is it? There are couples who have been waiting for much longer, who are unable to have children of their own. I know you're getting anxious again but we must give it time, darling.'

And then in mid-March something happened to change the situation. A tragedy occurred, one that made the headlines and shocked the townsfolk as they read and heard about it. A young couple, not long married and out for the evening in a car that was not really roadworthy, had been killed in a head-on crash with a lorry on a moorland road near the town. They were the parents of a six-month-old boy who had been left at home in the care of young babysitters.

The grandfather of the girl who was killed – the baby's mother – was employed at Walker's mill; a sixty-five-year-old man nearing retirement age. Charlie Pearson had worked there since he had left school at fourteen. He worked in the packing department where Bert Horrocks, Val's father, was also employed, and the two men had known each other for many years.

'Aye, it's a sad business, sure enough,' Charlie remarked to Bert, 'and the wife and me, we can't do owt about the little 'un, not at our age. We never saw much of Shirley, mind you, not since she took up with that good-for-nothing lad. I knew no good 'ud come of it. At least he married her, I'll say that for him. She was four months gone with little Russell when they got wed. And what sort of a name is that, eh? Russell, I ask you! Sounds more like an apple than a little lad. Bonny little bairn he is, though. Aye, it's a sad do.' Charlie's eyes misted over as he told his story.

The management of the mill had been very sympathetic and understanding towards Charlie, giving him time off to make all the necessary arrangements for the funeral of his grand-daughter. It was, as Charlie said, a sad state of affairs. There was a dearth of relatives in his family. Charlie and Alice's only daughter – Shirley's mother – had emigrated to Canada two years ago with her husband and their two younger boys. Shirley, aged eighteen at the time, had dug her heels in and refused to go. She had a good job as a shorthand typist and lots of friends in the area, and was old enough to know her own mind. But it had caused a rift between Shirley and her parents. She had not seen them since they left and they had scarcely bothered to keep in touch. They were informed of her death but were unable to come to the funeral.

'Our Betty never had much time for Shirley, I'm sorry to say,' Charlie confessed to his workmates. It seemed to do him good to talk about the situation. 'She'd wanted a lad; she made no secret of that. Then she got two of 'em – twins – and she spoiled 'em rotten. No wonder Shirley felt as though her nose were pushed out.'

Shirley had shared a flat with two more girls when her family left. Then she had met Jeff Sykes who worked at a local brewery.

'Oh, he was handsome, right enough, and he could talk the hind leg off a donkey. She was taken in by his blarney. I knew no good 'ud come of it. And there's nowt we can do about the little lad . . .'

The child was put in the care of the local authority and then placed in a foster home.

'I just hope he ends up with a nice family,' said Charlie. 'Folks who'll love him like they would their own. And I'd like to think that me and the wife could see him sometimes. But I reckon that's too much to hope for.'

Bert Horrocks listened to all this and felt sorry for Charlie and his wife and the little orphan child. It was ironic. He knew that Val badly wanted to start a family. She had told her mother that she felt very despondent at times and she had lost her baby – a boy – at six months. And there was this little lad who would be adopted and maybe taken to another part of the country. The couple who were caring for him were only willing to foster children with no thought of adoption.

Val had told her mother about her thoughts on adoption but that Sam did not seem very keen on the idea. Sam, of course, knew the sad story of the car crash and the orphaned child, and so did Val. They had been distressed at hearing about the accident and sorry for Charlie, who was a popular member of the workforce.

Sam was not surprised when Val said to him, timidly at first, that the poor little boy would need a good home and there they were, the two of them, badly wanting a child of their own.

'Do you think that we could . . . well . . . that we could have the baby? Adopt him, I mean. You know we'd been talking about it before all this happened.'

Sam shook his head. 'You mean you'd been talking and I'd

been listening, and I wasn't sure about it. I'm still not sure. It's a big step to take someone else's child. But I guessed what would be in your mind as soon as I heard about it. It would be better, though, to go through the correct channels for adoption, rather than taking a child so close to home.'

'But just think how pleased Charlie would be,' Val argued. 'We'd be in the same town and he'd be able to keep in contact.'

'And would that be a good idea?' said Sam. 'Wouldn't it confuse the child?'

'I don't see why it should. Please think about it, Sam. I really feel it would be a great opportunity for us, as though it was meant to be.'

Sam said he would consider it and soon found himself coming round to Val's way of thinking. He knew how badly she wanted a child and month after month they were disappointed. This child was six months old, already into a routine of sleeping and feeding, or so he imagined, but still young enough to get used to a new mother . . . and father, of course.

Having more or less made up his mind, he spoke privately to Charlie to see if the idea would meet with his approval. The tears of pleasure and gratitude that welled up in the man's eyes were enough to convince Sam that they would be doing the right thing. It seemed that Charlie and Alice, in the absence of their daughter, were being regarded as the next of kin. Jeff Sykes and his parents had long been estranged, and so it was agreed that arrangements should go ahead for a private adoption. Only then did Sam and Val break the news to their respective families.

Bert and Sally Horrocks were pleased and not very surprised. Sally had guessed, with a mother's intuition, what might be in her daughter's mind.

Joshua Walker already knew about it. Sam had thought it was only right to tell his father, especially as it concerned one of his employees. But Beatrice Walker, as Sam might have expected, was the one to raise objections and to give voice to her feelings.

'Adoption? Have you any idea what you might be getting into, taking on someone else's child? What bad blood there might be in the child's family? Babies can inherit all kinds of traits, you know, sometimes from way back. I would advise you to think very carefully about it.'

'We already have done, Mother,' said Sam, 'and it's all going ahead. We'll be the official parents of the little boy in a few weeks' time. He's called Russell James. That's the name that's on his birth certificate and we see no reason to change it, do we, darling?' He turned to Val, who nodded her agreement. 'Russell James Walker. It has a nice sound to it, don't you think so?'

'It's a name I've never heard of,' said Beatrice, 'but you could call him James, I suppose, seeing that you're set on the idea.'

'Do try to be pleased for us,' said Val to her mother-in-law. 'It's what we both want, and don't they say that nurture is more important than nature? That the way a child is brought up has more effect on him than anything he might inherit?'

'Well, I only hope you're right, dear. I know that you will be a very good mother.' Beatrice's early misgivings about Sam marrying an employee had long been set aside. She was fond of Valerie and knew that she and Sam were very happy.

'And we know that Charlie Pearson is a decent sort of chap,' said Sam.

'But what about the baby's father?' said Beatrice. 'He was a ne'er-do-well by all accounts, estranged from his parents and the girl was pregnant . . .' She stopped hastily, no doubt realizing that the least said about that the better, considering that the same thing had happened much closer to home.

Sam smiled. 'Whatever his father was like I'm sure our influence will counteract all of that. Anyway, the poor chap's gone, hasn't he, and his wife? Their baby deserves a loving home. Please try to be happy for us, Mother.'

'I only want what is best for you,' said Beatrice. 'And the best thing is to have your own child. But I know you've been disappointed a time or two, and if it's what you want I suppose you must go ahead.' In spite of her words she sniffed disapprovingly. 'I just hope it all turns out well for you.'

'It'll be great, Beatrice, you'll see,' said Joshua. 'A little grandson; how about that? We've already got a girl so we'll have one of each, just to be going on with. I'm sure there'll be more in a year or two.'

Beatrice made no further comment.

'So is it all settled?' asked Joshua. 'When will you be getting the little lad?'

'It's more or less settled,' answered Sam. 'Just a few formalities to go through. We hope he'll be with us around the middle of April.'

'Well, we'll look forward to it,' said Joshua. 'You'll be finishing work, then, Valerie?'

'Of course,' she replied with a smile. 'I shall finish next Thursday, when the mill closes for Easter. You don't mind me not giving a month's notice, do you?'

Joshua could see that her eyes were bright with happiness. 'Not at all, lass. And we both wish you every happiness, don't we, Beatrice?'

His wife gave a half smile and inclined her head in a queenly fashion.

Easter Sunday was on 29 March and the mill would be closed until the following Tuesday.

'Let's make the most of our last weekend of freedom,' said Sam. 'It's all going to be very different with a baby in the house. It'll be great, though,' he added, just in case Val might think he was having second thoughts. 'I'm just as happy as you are about it now I've got used to the idea.'

'That's good,' said Val. 'That's all I wanted to hear. What about a trip over to Harrogate at the weekend? Easter Saturday, maybe. What do you think? Then we can tell Janice and Phil our good news.'

'Good idea,' said Sam. 'Do you want to stay there on Saturday night in a hotel?'

'No, not really. We could go early in the morning, have our lunch there and possibly afternoon tea then come back in the evening. We've a lot to do, you know, before we collect Russell.'

'Yes, I do know, darling, and I'm getting quite excited about it now. I shall make a start on decorating the little room when we've been to Harrogate. Let's go and choose the wallpaper and paint on Thursday afternoon. You can finish a bit earlier, seeing as you're leaving anyway!'

'Oh, I've got your permission, have I? I don't want to take

advantage, you know!' Val smiled happily but she knew she would feel a slight sadness at saying goodbye to her friends in the office.

'Do you ever?' said Sam with a grin. She had managed to talk him round about the adoption and he hoped that it would work out well for all of them.

They drove into town on Thursday afternoon when Val had said her goodbyes. The girls gave her a cot blanket with a design of teddy bears having a jolly time. She shed a few tears, more in joy than sadness and said she would take little Russell in to see them quite soon.

They chose a yellow and white striped wallpaper, a warm shade rather than the more obvious 'blue for a boy' which might look cold in a small room, and the shade called magnolia for the paintwork. Val had never done much decorating but she said she would lend a hand.

'That's enough for today,' said Sam. 'We can go into Harrogate on Saturday and choose some of the other things we need.'

'Yes, curtain material, cot sheets, nappies, baby clothes, bottles . . . goodness knows what else! And a cot, of course, and a pram. Isn't it exciting?'

'That reminds me,' said Sam. 'My parents said they would buy us a pram. I expect it was my father's idea but you can be sure that Mother will choose the grandest one that money can buy!'

'How very kind of them,' said Val. 'I do hope your mother will take to Russell. We will call him that, won't we? Not James, like your mother suggested?'

'She was just being difficult,' said Sam. 'No, Russell is his name and that's what we'll call him. I'm sure babies get used to hearing their names at a very early age. We mustn't confuse the little chap!'

Val phoned Janice to say that they would be coming on Saturday and Janice said she would reserve a table for twelve thirty as they might be busy with it being Eastertime. They set off early and arrived in Harrogate by mid-morning. They found a parking spot then went off to do some shopping before lunch.

'Curtain material first,' said Val as they entered a large department store.

'What sort of design do you want?' asked Sam. 'Nursery rhymes . . . or footballers and racing cars?'

Val laughed. 'Not those; not just yet. I'm not sure, so long as it's not little Noddy!'

'Oh dear! Don't you like little Noddy and Big Ears?'

'I'm afraid not. Very trite and silly, I think. Mind you, I loved Enid Blyton when I was younger. The Faraway Tree, then the Famous Five and the Secret Seven. Anyway, I'm sure we'll find something we like.'

Sam decided that this was Val's domain and that the choice should be hers. There were several designs to choose from but, as it happened, none featuring little Noddy. Eventually, after much deliberation, she chose a fairly abstract design which Sam liked as well. Fluffy white clouds with a golden sun peeping through, rainbows and tiny birds fluttering above against an azure-blue sky.

'It will tone nicely with the yellow walls,' said Val. 'My mum said she'd make the curtains for me. She's got a sewing machine and I haven't. Sewing's never been my strong point but I shall have to make more of an effort now we're starting our family.' She always felt a glow of satisfaction when she made a remark such as that.

Then they bought some sheets and soft blue blankets which could be used for both the cot and the pram.

'Don't forget that you'll get presents as well,' Sam told her. 'People like to buy things for a new baby.'

'Do you think so? Our baby won't be all that new but maybe you're right. We can't take gifts for granted, though, can we? Anyway, it's fun choosing things ourselves.'

'I think we've done quite enough for now,' said Sam. 'Let's get off to Janice and Phil's place.'

Their friends were both busy – Phil in the kitchen and Janice hovering near the cash desk. She was delighted to see them and led them to a table set for two by the window. They were surprised and pleased when Janice's brother, Ian, handed them the menu.

'How nice to see you again,' said Val. 'Helping out during your holiday, are you?'

'Yes, I'll be staying all next week. We're very busy at the moment,' he said with a proprietorial air.

Val did not make a fatuous remark about how grown up he was now. But she noticed how the lad had matured. He was a good-looking boy with glossy brown hair and warm brown eyes, and was much taller than she remembered him. She had heard from Janice that he had a girlfriend here and she guessed it must be the pretty dark-haired girl who was also waiting at the tables.

They chose one of the more substantial snack meals: sausages with chips, tomato and mushrooms. Plain fare but well cooked – plump sizzling sausages and chunky golden chips.

'Come upstairs to our own room,' said Janice when they had finished their meal, 'then we can have a chat. We don't open till mid-afternoon for the teas so I have some time to relax – I'll make sure of that – and Phil will be with us in a little while.'

By the time Janice had made the post-luncheon tea, Phil had arrived.

'Good to see you both,' he said. 'Are you here for the weekend or is it just a flying visit?'

'Just today,' said Val. 'We came to do some shopping and to see you, of course. Actually, we've got some news, haven't we, Sam?'

She smiled at him rather coyly and he nodded and smiled back so intimately that Janice guessed what it might be . . . again. She hoped all would go well for Val this time.

'Do you mean . . . you're pregnant?' she asked.

'Well, not exactly,' replied Val, 'but we're going to have a baby. We're adopting a little boy; he's seven months old.'

'Oh! that's wonderful news.' Janice, in truth, was astounded. 'What a surprise! How did it happen? I mean, what made you decide . . .?'

Between them, Val and Sam told them the full story. 'So he will be officially ours in a couple of weeks,' said Sam. 'Russell James Walker, that's his name.'

Janice and Phil exchanged glances then burst out laughing. 'We'd better tell them our news, hadn't we?' said Phil.

Val guessed at once. 'You mean . . . you as well? You're going to have—?'

'Yes,' Janice interrupted. She took hold of Phil's hand. 'We're starting a family as well, aren't we, Phil?'

'We certainly are,' he replied. 'It was rather a surprise, mind you; rather sooner than we anticipated.'

'Yes, we don't really know how it happened,' said Janice naively.

'In the usual way, I should imagine,' said Sam, winking at Phil.

'Well, yes . . .' said Janice, blushing slightly. 'But it shouldn't have happened – you know what I mean. It wasn't planned.'

'But we're very pleased about it,' said Phil. 'These things happen sometimes and we're very glad it did.'

'So when are you due?' asked Val.

'Mid-September,' said Janice. 'It was Christmas, you see . . .'

'Yes, we see!' Sam laughed. 'Our little lad will be one in September and you'll be just starting out.'

'Yes, isn't it exciting?' said Janice. 'This calls for a celebration drink. Get the sherry, Phil, and we'll have a little toast. I know I have to be careful now but a little glass won't do any harm.'

They toasted each other and their future children with Harvey's Bristol Cream.

'So how is Cissie?' asked Janice. 'She'll be pleased to hear your news, won't she?'

'Yes, so she was,' replied Val. 'She's been saying for ages that she wanted us to push our prams out together. She'll be pleased to hear your news as well. She said it made her feel broody again when she heard about Russell but Walter is adamant that two is their lot, for now at least.'

'And is everything OK now? She's recovered from her injuries and all is well with her and Walter?' Val had told Janice about all the troubles, not in a nasty way but because Janice, over the years since they had met, had become a close friend.

'Yes, all seems to be fine and dandy again,' said Val. 'Maybe we could all meet when we've got little Russell with us. What about you, Janice? You'll be able to carry on working for a while, won't you?'

'Yes, almost till the end, I hope. That's the beauty of working for ourselves and living on the premises. And our staff are very good. We'll see how it works out once the baby is born.'

Val and Sam went back to Harrogate to do some more shopping. Little vests and pants, trousers and jackets to fit a six- to twelve-month-old baby boy.

'Don't buy too many,' said Sam, trying to curb Val's delight at all the brightly coloured little clothes. 'He'll grow out of them in no time and he's sure to get some as presents.'

'But it's all so wonderful,' said Val. 'I can't wait to have him to ourselves.'

They went back to Grundy's for afternoon tea before driving back to Halifax in the early evening, with promises that they would all meet again before long.

Russell James was a beautiful baby. Val knew that all babies must appear so to their parents but he really was – everyone said so – and she was so proud to be his mother.

He had put on a few pounds since they had last seen him. He was a sturdy boy, not fat, but with rounded limbs and a bonny face, brown eyes and mid-brown hair – quite a lot of it – with just a hint of auburn. They learnt from Charlie that Shirley, the child's mother, had had ginger hair and brown eyes as well.

'He might get called Rusty when he's older,' said Sam. 'Don't you think so?'

'He may well,' said Val, 'but I shall always call him Russell. See, he turns his head already when he hears his name!'

Val could not help but be aware that she had missed out on the very early stages of babyhood. He had been bottle fed for quite a while now and it was good that his feeding times were established. He did not wake much in the night, and Val insisted that she should be the one to see to him as Sam was the one going out to work. She soon got into the routine of nappy changing and bath times, and the district nurse visited now and again to make sure that all was well.

He was a happy baby and very soon recognized them when they came near, smiling and gurgling and reaching out his chubby hands.

Both sets of grandparents were delighted with him. Even Beatrice held him, somewhat cagily, and admitted she thought he was a fine-looking boy. And Val and Sam took him to see his great grandparents, Charlie and Alice Pearson, who were thankful that everything had turned out so well and they were not losing the child of their beloved granddaughter.

'What do you think Russell should call Charlie and Alice when he gets older?' said Val. 'They're his real grandparents, well, great ones, so he'll have three lots.'

'Let's cross that bridge when we come to it,' Sam advised her. 'There's plenty of time to think about it.'

They had not made up their minds whether to tell Russell, when he was old enough to understand, that he had been adopted and was a specially chosen little boy . . . or not say anything. Neither of them were sure what would be the best thing to do.

The next event would be the christening. Val and Sam agreed that they wanted a simple service with just the godparents and close relatives present.

Beatrice remarked to Joshua that this was by far the best arrangement. 'After all, it isn't as if he's their own child. It would be different if she'd actually given birth to him.'

'Don't you let Sam and Valerie hear you say anything like that,' he chastised her. 'That little lad is legally theirs. He's got our name. He's a Walker and we're going to welcome him into our family.'

Beatrice sniffed. 'Very well, Joshua. If you say so.'

'I must have Cissie as Russell's godmother,' Val said to Sam. 'I'm godmother to both her children. She would be hurt, I'm sure, if I didn't ask her.'

'Of course you must,' agreed Sam. 'Who else could there be? I know Thelma won't mind. I shall ask Jonathan to be a godfather. The ruling is two godfathers and one godmother for a boy, isn't it? Although I don't suppose it matters too much. The royal family have umpteen, don't they? Jonathan . . . and Walter. I thought we could ask him as we're having Cissie and they're very much a loving couple again, aren't they?'

'Yes, I'm sure they are. They've both learnt something with all the trouble they've had. Though I can't see Cissie ever being meek and mild!'

It was a private baptism in the local church on a Sunday afternoon in late May. The two sets of grandparents were there, as well as Charlie and Alice, Cissie and Walter, Jonathan and Thelma and their children, who all behaved well as if overawed by the proceedings.

Cissie proudly held the baby, wrapped in the fine crochet work shawl that Val's mother had made. Baby Russell did not cry, just smiled at Cissie and at the vicar as though he knew what was going on.

Val had prepared a simple tea and they all went back to their home to drink a toast to the health and happiness of Russell and his parents and to have a slice of the christening cake, again made by Val's mother.

Val had been a teeny bit anxious about having Beatrice and Cissie in such close proximity. The two had only met briefly at Val and Sam's wedding but this was a much more intimate gathering. Beatrice, however, said very little and Cissie was happily engrossed with all the children. The afternoon passed without any discord, most of the guests chatting together happily.

Twenty-Three

'I rather wish that Janice and Phil could have been with us,' said Val soon after the christening, 'but we had decided to keep it small, hadn't we? And if you invite friends you never know where to stop.'

'They would understand, I'm sure,' said Sam. 'Perhaps we could go over to see them before long; you and me, Cissie and Walter and all the children. What do you think?'

'It sounds like a great idea,' said Val, 'but we wouldn't all fit into one car, would we?'

'No, probably not. But Walter's got a larger car now, hasn't he?'

The car that had been in the accident had been a write-off and it had been replaced with a slightly larger Hillman car, by no means new but a good bargain. Cissie had given up all thoughts of driving, at least for the moment.

'I don't know about taking all the children to the cafe, though,' said Val. 'I wonder if Sunday might be best? The cafe's closed on a Sunday. We could take a picnic lunch so Janice and Phil don't need to worry about the food. I'm sure they'd be glad of the rest.'

'Brilliant idea,' said Sam. 'Let's see what the others all think about it.'

They all agreed that it was a terrific idea and they decided on a Sunday in mid-July. You could never rely on the weather, of course; it had been the usual summer mix of sunshine and showers. The week leading up to the proposed day, however, was settled and the Sunday dawned fair and bright with a promise of sunshine.

Paul, now three years old, was very excited and his sister, Holly, now a year and a half, was walking, starting to talk and taking an interest in all that was going on. Russell, at ten months, was now managing to sit up without toppling over and was a source of delight and amusement to the other two children.

Val and Cissie had both prepared picnic baskets, or bags, of assorted sandwiches, sausage rolls, pork pies, packets of crisps, Penguins and Kit-Kats, plus flasks of coffee, bottles of orange juice and Russell's bottles and jars of baby food.

They dispensed with pushchairs and carry-cots, as Phil had suggested they should drive close to a convenient picnic spot and walk just a short distance, taking turns, if needs be, to carry Russell and Holly.

They set off in the two cars at half past nine, the journey taking less than an hour, and were warmly greeted by Janice and Phil. Janice looked radiant and happy in her seventh month of pregnancy.

'I can't believe how well I've been feeling after the first few weeks,' she told them. 'When I go for my check-ups they say that all's well . . . touch wood. I know I look like an elephant, though!'

'You don't at all,' Cissie assured her. 'You look bloomin' marvellous! Anyway, what does it matter? It'll all be worth it in the end.'

Val could not comment. It had gone wrong for her but she now had her lovely baby boy and she had no regrets. Janice was pleased to meet Russell, holding him on her knee and making a fuss of him.

'He's good, isn't he, and so friendly? He doesn't know me but we're getting on fine, aren't we, little chap?' said Janice, giving him a cuddle.

'He's been used to different people looking after him,' said Val. 'He settled down straight away with Sam and me. But I'm sure he'll have his moments as he gets older, as they all do.'

After a cup of tea – always a good start to an outing – they set off in two cars. Instead of using their own car Janice and Phil sat in the back seat of Sam and Val's as they had more room. Phil had suggested they should go to Fountain's Abbey, a local beauty spot. He directed Sam northwards out of Harrogate, with Walter following close behind.

The grounds of the ruined Cistercian abbey were a perfect place for a picnic. They parked their cars in the car park then set off with bags, baskets and rugs to find an ideal spot. Sam carried Russell and Holly toddled along holding Cissie's hand. Paul seemed tireless, running ahead excitedly then stopping to watch the ducks and geese swimming in the stream that ran through the grounds or waddling on the path hoping for titbits of food.

'Gosh! It's a lovely place, isn't it?' said Cissie. 'I've lived in Yorkshire all me life and I've never been here. 'Course, we never had a car. Folks like us didn't have cars when I was a kid; only rich folk, so we didn't get around very much.'

'I came here once when I was little,' said Walter, 'and I've cycled past it lots of times but never stopped. There are some jolly fine views. Has anyone got a camera?'

'I have,' said Sam. 'My parents bought me a new one for Christmas instead of the old box one I had. Nothing too technical, just an instamatic one; it takes colour snaps as well as black and white. You can have them printed as photos or as slides – to show on a screen with a projector. Val and I are thinking of getting some equipment then we can show pictures to everyone, especially now we've got Russell.'

'Gosh! It'll be just like the Odeon,' said Cissie.

Sam laughed. 'Perhaps not quite as good but we'll have a film show when we've got the projector. In the meantime I hope we'll get some good snapshots.'

'I think we've walked far enough,' said Val. 'This bag's getting heavy and I'm sure Russell weighs a ton, doesn't he, Sam?'

'He sure feels like it!' agreed Sam.

'And Holly's getting tired, aren't you, love?' said Cissie. The little girl just realized she was and held out her arms to be picked up.

They managed to find a secluded spot – although there were many visitors there that day with the same idea – on a stretch of grass away from the pathway, with leafy sycamore and beech trees to give shade from the sun, which was now at its midday height.

They spread out the travelling rugs and started to unpack the lunch. Janice was glad to sit down. She had brought a small cushion which she placed to her back as she leaned against a tree trunk.

'And this little lad will need his nappy changing,' said Val. 'No . . . on second thoughts I'll wait till he's had his bottle and some food. It's amazing what paraphernalia you need when you go out for the day. Still, it's all worth it. It's lovely to be all together like this.'

They all tucked in hungrily to the assortment of 'eats' and enjoyed the coffee and orange juice drunk from plastic beakers. They used large paper serviettes instead of plates then deposited the debris in a nearby litter bin. The beakers and plastic containers were stored away in the bags, ten times lighter now, to take home. Baby Russell had his nappy changed and the soiled one stowed away at the bottom of the holdall. His eyes were drooping as he was ready for his afternoon nap.

'Stay awake, little chap, while Daddy takes some photos,' said Sam.

He took several of the grown-ups, the children and a group photo to include everyone . . . except himself. Walter insisted

that he should take one so that Sam could be included. Then
a helpful man from a family who had been picnicking nearby
offered his services. The nine of them crowded together – a
tight squeeze – then they all smiled and obediently said 'cheese'.

'That will be a lasting memory of a very happy day,' said
Sam. 'I'll send you all the photos as soon as they're developed.'

'Russell's ready for his sleep,' said Val. He was already asleep
in her arms.

She put him down in the shade of a tree on one of the rugs
with a towel beneath his head then covered him with the
cardigan she had taken off. The sun was shining in a cloudless
sky; they had certainly been blessed with the weather.

'How about a walk?' suggested Phil. 'I'm sure we need one
after that splendid lunch. Who's up for it?'

Val had to stay behind with Russell and insisted she'd be
OK on her own, but Cissie and Janice opted to stay with her.
Janice admitted she was feeling tired and Cissie was happy for
Walter to take a turn at looking after the children. Holly was
wide awake, although she might have been ready for a nap at
home.

'Studley Park adjoins the abbey grounds,' said Phil. 'There's
a herd of deer that graze there. Let's go and take a look at
them, shall we? It'll be fun for the children . . . and for us,
of course!'

The three young men set off with Holly toddling along
holding Walter's hand while Paul whooped excitedly, just with
the joy of being out of doors on such a lovely day.

'Peace, perfect peace,' said Cissie. She reached for her shoulder
bag and took out a packet of cigarettes. She did not offer them
round as she was the only one who indulged. She lit up and
took a deep drag then sighed contentedly, leaning back against
the trunk of a tree.

'It's lovely to have some time to meself, although I wouldn't
be without 'em, not for all the tea in China. This is a smashing
place, isn't it? What a view, eh? And I never knew it was there.'

The majestic ruins of the abbey, silhouetted against the bright
blue sky, the background of the trees in full bloom and the
silver stream rippling gently through the grounds did, indeed,
make a most idyllic scene.

'The abbey was owned by the Cistercian monks,' said Val, 'and then it was ransacked by Henry the Eighth at the time of the Reformation. But the ruins are well preserved – more so than any in the country, so they say.'

Cissie laughed. 'Never mind yer history lesson and yer bloomin' Henry the Eighth! Mind you, I've heard about him. He had all them wives and had their heads chopped off . . . Like I said, though, it's a smashing view. I'm real glad we came.'

'So am I,' agreed Janice. 'Phil and I haven't been out much recently. We're glad of a rest on a Sunday, although we sometimes go to Ilkley to see his parents.'

'You'll have your hands full soon,' said Val. 'It's amazing the difference a baby makes.'

'Even more so with two of 'em,' said Cissie with feeling.

'You agree with Walter now, do you?' asked Val. 'You're going to stop at two?'

'Oh, I don't know about that. Your Russell made me remember how lovely they are when they're little; they're so dependent on you. And Janice's baby'll be here soon . . . Still, I must be thankful for what I've got.'

She took another drag of her cigarette, inhaling deeply. 'Walter and me are OK again now and that's the main thing. It made me realize how much I loved him when I thought I might lose him.'

'And he felt the same about you,' said Val. 'I suppose every marriage has its ups and downs. Anyway, it's too nice a day to be philosophical . . . Have you thought of any names for your baby, Janice? I won't say do you want a boy or a girl. Silly question, isn't it? As if we have any choice in the matter!'

'I've heard it's the male who determines the sex of the child,' said Janice. 'Something to do with X or Y chromosomes.'

'Flippin heck!' Cissie burst out laughing. 'It's like being back at school with you two. First a history lesson, now we're being blinded with science. Walter and me had a long list of names, both times, then we changed our minds at the last minute.'

'We really haven't thought much about it,' said Janice. 'It's tricky if you want to choose one of your parents' names, and it has to go well with your surname . . .'

The girls chatted idly about this and that until their husbands and children reappeared. Walter was carrying Holly and Paul was running ahead as usual.

'We saw some big deers with trees on their heads!' he shouted.

Walter laughed. 'I told him they're called antlers; sort of horns, like sheep and cattle have; just the male ones, and they use them for fighting.'

'Would you believe it?' said Cissie. 'We're having a nature lesson now!' The girls all laughed but it was too complicated to explain why.

'So you've had a lovely time, have you?' asked Cissie as the children threw themselves down on the rug.

Paul nodded and Holly put her thumb in her mouth, a sign that she was tired.

'Home time soon, I think,' said Sam. 'Are we agreed?'

Janice suggested they should have a cup of tea at their home before they went back but they politely declined. It might delay them too long and the children could become fractious. They gathered together all their belongings and walked back to the car park. They all had an ice cream from the kiosk near the gate, then, with sticky hands and mouths all wiped, they set off back.

They stopped only briefly at Janice and Phil's home, saying goodbye in a flurry of hugs and kisses and waves.

'We'll be dying to hear your news,' said Cissie. 'Only two months now!'

'Let us know right away,' said Val, and Phil promised that they would know as soon as anyone.

All went well and Janice gave birth to a baby girl in the local hospital in the early hours of 25 September. When Phil saw her soon afterwards she was sitting up in bed looking proud and happy, with the baby asleep in a cot at the foot of the bed. Phil kissed her lovingly before taking a peek at the baby.

'She's beautiful, just like you,' he said, although there was little to see except a fair-complexioned face and the merest covering of fluffy down on her head.

'So she is. She hasn't much hair, though,' said Janice.

'It's all the time in the world to grow,' said Phil. 'And she'll be fair, like you.'

'She's seven and a half pounds,' said Janice proudly. 'That's a good weight. And I shall try to feed her myself. That's what they like you to do.'

'I've put a notice up in the cafe,' Phil told her, 'saying that we have a little girl. And Toby and the girls send their love.'

Toby was taking charge in Phil's absence and he assured her that all was going well at Grundy's.

As the baby was born on a Friday there were plenty of visitors at the weekend. Phil's parents came on the Saturday and Alec, Norma and Ian drove over on the Sunday. Alec was thrilled with his first grandchild and Ian seemed astounded at seeing such a tiny baby, the first one he had seen at such a tender age.

'And you are her one and only uncle,' Phil told him.

Ian tentatively touched her cheek. 'What are you going to call her?' he asked.

'We haven't quite made up our minds yet,' said Janice, 'but we have decided on one thing. You are going to be her godfather. Would you like that?'

'Gosh! That's great,' said Ian. He seemed too amazed to say anything more.

Janice said Phil had decided that if they had a girl – or even if it was a boy they could break with tradition – they would ask Val and Cissie to be godmothers. The three young women had become close friends over the years, and although Janice still kept in touch with her old school friends she seldom saw them.

And they had both agreed about asking Ian to be the godfather. It would make him feel even more like one of the family and he was the only sibling they had between the two of them.

'I know he's young,' said Janice, 'but he's sixteen and he's becoming more mature. And now, what about a name for our little one? She must be registered long before she's christened.'

Eventually they decided on Sarah Lilian; Sarah because they both liked the name and it seemed to go well with their surname; and Lilian, of course, for Janice's beloved mum. Alec and Ian were delighted at the choice and Norma agreed that it was very fitting.

'I'll never take her place, nor would I want to,' Norma told Janice. 'I just hope I can be a good wife to your dad and make him happy.'

'There's no doubt that you do that,' Janice assured her.

The christening took place on a Sunday afternoon at the end of November at the local church, where Janice and Phil occasionally attended. They had decided they wanted a simple occasion with just close relatives and friends. Val and Cissie had both been surprised and thrilled to be asked to be godmothers. Their husbands, of course, were invited to the baptism service but the children were left at home in the care of grandparents. The parents agreed that this should be a day just for baby Sarah.

With both lots of grandparents – Norma was touched to be referred to as Nana – the godmothers, their husbands and Ian, there were eleven present at the private baptism. Twelve including Sarah Lilian, the most important one of all.

Val carried her into the church in a hand-knitted shawl made by Phil's mother and Cissie carried her at the end of the service. Back at Grundy's they tucked into an afternoon tea which included many of Janice's specialities from the cafe. She was now working part time, fitting in with Sarah's routine.

Sam took lots of photos, to be the subject of a film show at a later date. It was a happy occasion, ending with a toast to the baby and a slice of the christening cake, made by Janice.

Baby Sarah had stayed awake most of the time but when Janice went to put her down for her sleep, Val crept into the bedroom to join her.

'She's gorgeous,' said Val, holding the child's tiny hand and feeling the tiny fingers close around her own. 'You must be very proud of her . . . I have a secret,' she whispered, smiling confidingly at Janice. 'Well, just one or two people know. It's early days . . .'

Janice looked at her friend's face. Val was smiling joyously but with just a tinge of anxiety.

Janice gasped. 'You mean . . .? Are you . . .?'

'Yes, I'm pregnant again. Would you believe it? But I've heard it quite often happens when you've adopted a baby.

Motherly feelings and all that. So it's fingers crossed, everything crossed. We just hope and pray that all will be well this time.'

'Oh, so do I!' said Janice fervently. 'When will it be?'

'The end of May, we think, we hope . . .'

Janice put her arms around Val and kissed her cheek. 'I'm delighted for you. What a perfect ending to a lovely day.'

Notice in the Halifax evening paper during the first week of June, 1960.

Valerie and Samuel Walker are pleased to announce the safe arrival of their daughter, Lucy Elizabeth, on 1 June. A welcome sister for Russell James. Mother and baby are both doing well. Our sincere thanks to the midwife and doctor.